IN ANOTHER LIFE

CHRONICALLY IN LOVE
BOOK 2

MOLLY MCCARTHY

CONTENT NOTE

This book contains strong language and sexual content. The following topics are mentioned in some capacity: anxiety, including panic attacks (on page); C-PTSD; poverty (in past); parental death (in past); house fire (in past); pyrophobia; unexpected pregnancy (not the MC); allusions to abortion and miscarriage.

For everyone who fights with their own brain each and every day. The world may never realize how brave you are, but I do. Keep up the good fight.

And for the romance readers. You deserve the love you read about in books.

CHAPTER 1
COLE

It's never a bad night at Marty's Tavern. At least, that's what I tell myself to get through these seemingly never-ending shifts. Some weeks it feels like the nights blend into one another with nothing to break up the monotony except our periodic special events or the occasional bar fight.

Slinging drinks may not be my dream job, but it pays the bills, as well as my baby sister, Bailey's, college tuition. The price of an education at Berklee is steep as shit, but Bails is one of the most talented people I know, and she deserves a real shot at making music her career. If Berklee will give her that, I'll do whatever I can to help. Someone in this fucked-up little family has to make something of themself, and it's not like I have.

"Hey, beautiful," I greet a tall redhead who sits down at my bar. She's been here before—with a boyfriend, if I'm remembering correctly. That doesn't stop me from turning on the charm. He's nowhere in sight, and I think I remember her tipping decently.

"Hi, handsome," she shoots back with a smirk that gives me pause. Maybe it wasn't a boyfriend after all. Either way, I'm not interested in *her*, just in securing her gratuity.

I tuck the rag I was using to wipe down the bar into my pocket. "What can I get you?"

She looks at me from beneath long, fake-as-hell lashes. "Gin and tonic."

"You got it," I reply before turning away to prepare the drink, moving around the prep area with ease. I've been bartending at Marty's for about four years now, so I know the back of this bar like the back of my hand.

"Here you go." I slide G&T across the bar.

The redhead receives it with a grin. "Thanks," she says with a bat of her lashes. The longer I look at them, the more they remind me of long, curly, black spiders' legs.

A shiver courses through me. "Let me know if you need anything else," I offer, forcing out a wink before moving along to an older man a few stools down.

Flirting with women, and the occasional man, at the bar has become second nature to me. When I began working here, I quickly realized how lucrative it was to pass out compliments like candy. It's amazing how much someone will pay you to make them feel good, even if it sometimes it makes me feel the opposite.

After preparing an old fashioned for the man, the redhead flags me down again.

"What can I do for you, pretty lady?" I ask, gritting my teeth as she bats those spidery lashes at me once again.

"I was wondering...when you said to let you know if I needed *anything* else...what exactly does that cover?"

Disgust floods my throat. Wait, no, that's just vomit. She's only one drink in, and she's already trying to proposition me? Usually it takes people at *least* three to hit that level of drunken confidence.

"It covers anything I can get you from behind this bar," I answer, keeping my tone as professional as possible. I may not want to take this woman home, but I *do* want as big a tip as I can get. It's been a slow night, and I've already pegged the dude down the bar as a ten-percent Tom.

"I could always come back there and…you know," she says with a suggestive smile. "No one would see my head above the bar."

I cover my mouth and clear my throat to hide a gag. "No can do." I paste on a polite smile. "But, please, let me know if you'd like another drink at any point," I say, turning around to find any busy work that will get me away from her.

Once I've polished all the beer taps, I turn around to see a five-dollar bill sitting on the bar and the redhead nowhere in sight. I grin as I stuff the bill in my pocket.

That's when I see *her* walk in the door.

The raven-haired beauty has been here a couple of times before, usually with another girl and sometimes a guy too. They always sit at a table and have a meal, but today, she's walking straight toward my bar.

I noticed her originally because of her striking complexion— pale porcelain skin against jet-black hair. Today, I notice much more. She's wearing a cherry-red dress with white polka-dots and sheer black stockings running up her long legs. Her dark hair tumbles over her shoulders in a silky waterfall. She looks like a vintage pin-up girl, and I can't look away.

"Hey, gorgeous," I greet her as she settles onto a stool. Her cheeks immediately pinken, and it's endearing as fuck.

This is going to be fun.

"Hi," she replies. "Could I get a vodka soda with lime, please?"

"You can have whatever you want," I reply with a wink as I go to make her order. When I return, she's twiddling her thumbs and glancing around the bar.

"Waiting for someone?" I ask as I deliver her drink.

She bites her full bottom lip. "Yeah."

"A date?" I press.

She takes a small sip of her vodka soda. "A first date."

So she's unattached. *Interesting.* I may have rebuked the woman from earlier, but it's not like I *never* take home customers. Although, as adorable as this one is, she may be a bit too timid for me. Doesn't mean I can't have a little fun with her.

"How'd you meet the lucky guy?"

A smile tugs at her lips. *That's right, gorgeous.* Whoever he is, he's a lucky bastard.

"*Meet Your Match*," she says. "It's an app."

"I think I've heard of it." I've never used dating apps before, but this one made a big splash when it launched. "So, what's he like?"

She shrugs as she squeezes the lime wedge into her drink. "I don't know much about him."

"Come on," I drawl. "You must know *something* about the dude." Secretly, I'm wondering what it takes to make a woman like this agree to go on a date. Is the guy ridiculously good look-ing? Rich? Does he foster three-legged puppies and one-eyed kittens?

"I know he's an accountant, and he grew up locally," she says. "Oh, and he's a huge Patriots fan."

I turn toward the TV behind the bar to confirm my suspicion. "There's a Pats game on tonight. He must really like you if he scheduled a date at the same time."

She glances at the TV, drumming her fingers on the bar. "Huh. Well, that's a good sign, I guess."

From twiddling her thumbs, to playing with the lime wedge, to tapping on the bar, I don't think this woman's fingers have stopped moving the entire time she's been sitting here. Poor thing must be a nervous wreck about this date.

"A very good sign," I agree, hoping to soothe her nerves just a bit. I may not know much about this woman, but I don't see what she's so worried about. She's easy to talk to and drop-dead gorgeous. Any man would be a fool to fuck up a first date with her.

"Rhiannon?" a deep male voice asks. Shit, I didn't even

notice the guy walking over. Normally, I'm hyper-aware of everything that goes on at my bar. No one comes or goes without me clocking it, but this guy snuck right past my notice.

"Gabe?" Rhiannon replies as the guy places a hand on her shoulder and pulls her into a half-hug. He's probably just under six feet, wearing black joggers and a Patriots jersey. Interesting choice for a first date, even if there *is* a game on tonight.

"Nice to meet you," Gabe says as he sits beside her, his gaze trailing over her chest, down her legs, and back up again. Something about his perusal raises my hackles even though I was doing my own—albeit more subtle—once-over not long ago.

"You too," she says.

Gabe turns to me, his brows raising slightly as if he's just now realizing I'm standing here. "Uh, hi. I'll have a Natty Light please."

What is he, an overgrown frat boy? The last guy to order a Natural Light from me was celebrating his twenty-first birthday along with a group of raucous man-children.

"Sure," I reply with a tight smile. Turning away to grab his beer, I keep one ear trained on their conversation. I'm way too invested, but I can't seem to help myself. I'm torn between finding humor in the undeniable mismatch and feeling resentful that this sweet girl has to put up with such a knucklehead.

"How are you today?" I hear Rhiannon ask.

"Pretty good," Gabe replies. "I'll be even better if the Pats get a win tonight."

A pause. Poor girl didn't even know they were playing until I told her, so I'm fairly sure she has no interest in the sport.

"Are they having a good season?" she finally asks.

"Well, they were until..." Gabe launches into a detailed description of the team's season so far. He sounds more like a sports commentator than a man trying to impress a date—unless he thinks having an unhealthy amount of sports knowledge is going to get him laid, in which case he's just a loser.

"Here you go." I cut off Gabe's tangent by placing his beer

down just a bit too forcefully. It sloshes around the glass, but he doesn't seem to notice. His gaze is focused on the TV behind the bar.

Rhiannon takes a long sip of her drink. "So, Gabe, what do you enjoy other than the Patriots?"

Gabe doesn't take his eyes off the TV. "I also enjoy video games." He smirks. "Although, my favorite is Madden NFL, so I guess that's still Patriots-related."

I shake my head, unworried about getting caught since his gaze hasn't faltered from the game.

Rhiannon doesn't miss it, though, and she presses her lips together to smother a grin. We share a small, secret smile before I go off to take care of other customers at the bar.

After about twenty minutes, a rowdy group of men in Patriots jerseys walks in, immediately drawing my attention with their hooting and hollering. They've clearly pre-gamed, which could either mean big, drunken tips or a pain-in-the-ass group that won't leave until the game is over. I'm relieved when they head to a table instead of my bar.

"Gabe! Hey, man," one of them shouts across the room as the group sits at a corner booth with a prime view of another bigger TV.

"Hey, fellas!" Gabe shouts to the group, receiving a few waves in return.

"Friends of yours?" Rhiannon asks as she finishes her vodka soda.

Gabe nods, his head ducking and swiveling as if he's taking attendance. "Yeah, they're some of my buddies that I usually watch the games with."

Rhiannon taps her nails against the side of her empty glass. "You can…join them if you want," she offers.

Gabe's face lights up. "Are you sure you wouldn't mind?"

Rhiannon shakes her head with a tight smile. "No. Go for it. It was nice meeting you."

"You too," Gabe offers over his shoulder, already making a beeline for his friends.

What. A. Loser.

The schmuck couldn't be bothered to dress up even a *little* for this date then basically *ignored* Rhiannon before finally ditching her for some other assholes he could see anytime he wants.

The entire date didn't last longer than half an hour, and it had to be one of the most pathetic sights I've ever witnessed. Feeling terrible for Rhiannon, I begin concocting another vodka soda.

Heavy on the vodka.

CHAPTER 2
RHIANNON

did it. I can't help the giddy smile that stretches over my lips. I went on a first date. It absolutely sucked ass, but I met a guy on an app, agreed to meet him in person, showed up, and did the damn thing.

I know most people consider first dates a necessary evil, and no one really enjoys them, but they're *exceptionally* difficult for me. I was diagnosed with anxiety at the tender age of twelve, and while it's mostly under control after a parade of different therapists and medications, dating remains one of my major triggers. The thought of putting myself on display for a man to scrutinize and potentially pass judgment on makes panic set in faster than a five-hundred-pound grizzly bear cantering toward me would.

I never dated as a teenager. I was anxious, awkward, and, frankly, preferred to spend my time with fictional men. In middle and high school, I was so focused on getting good grades and on my extracurriculars—creative writing club and the school newspaper—that guys were merely a blip in my peripheral.

I was also a huge nerd. I spent my free time reading whatever romance novels I could get my hands on and writing *Twilight* fanfic. No high school boy was ever going to measure up to Edward Cullen. Yes, I was Team Edward—but only in the books. In the movies, it was Jacob all the way.

Once I'd shed most of my bumbling adolescent awkwardness, I finally went on my first date in college with a guy I met in English Lit. He wore tortoise-shell glasses, smelled like patchouli, and I felt very grown up when he asked me out for coffee. Of course, the date didn't come without hours of agonizing over things like what to wear, how to sound smart in front of him, whether or not to tell him it was my first date, and whether or not we would kiss at the end of it.

Spoiler alert: I wore a top with peek-a-boo shoulders (forgive me—it was the twenty-teens), I'm pretty sure I sounded like a nervous wreck, I did *not* admit it was my first date, we *did* kiss, and it was *terrible*—all tongue and no sparks whatsoever, unless you count the ones our teeth probably generated when they rubbed together.

Needless to say, there was no second date, but I remained proud of myself for going on the first one. I'd never been brave enough before, but I went for it because Eric—the glasses and patchouli guy—seemed really great. I'd gotten to know him pretty well in class as we discussed Austen, Dickens, and Shakespeare, and I felt a base level of comfort with him before he ever initiated a romantic interaction.

Problem is, after that experience, there weren't all that many opportunities for me to get to know other men the way I had Eric before going on dates with them. I didn't connect with anyone else in my classes, and I spent most of my free time writing. I didn't go to parties or frequent clubs or bars the way much of my cohort did. It's tough to meet men while sitting in your dorm room typing up fictional worlds.

After graduating, it became even harder to meet guys. I was lucky enough to find success with my writing, and my career as an erotic romance author had taken off, but writing is a solitary activity. While my peers were meeting their significant others through work, my job involved sitting behind a desk alone. Any romance book clubs or writing groups I became a part of were almost always entirely women, and as much as my moms would love for me to settle down with a nice lady, my heart and body just don't swing that way.

Eventually, I turned to dating apps to try to get *some* sort of action. If it wasn't clear by my career choice, I'm a hopeless romantic. I might have intense anxiety about dating, but my most fervent wish for my life is to find a partner with whom to settle down. Dating apps made me nervous, but I liked the idea of getting a chance to chat with a guy for a while first, getting to know him a bit before deciding whether or not to bother meeting.

Turns out dating apps are a *lot* of work. You constantly have to be chatting with your matches, getting to know them while also trying to weed out creeps and douchebags, and simultaneously swiping for new matches and keeping your profile updated. I ended up meeting a couple of guys off apps, but neither one lasted longer than two dates. We just didn't click, and each time, the experience was so stressful for me that I didn't want to repeat it again for a long while.

I can't deny that I was nervous walking in here. Hell, I've been nervous all week, overthinking every little aspect of this date. The more real it got, the more anxious I got. Like, when I agreed via text to meet up in person, I had heart palpitations. By the time I actually arrived at the bar in person, I felt a little dizzy and like I could vomit.

The cute bartender helped, though. He took my mind off my worries with his flirty little comments and smiles. *That* interaction didn't make me anxious, because the bartender is so far out of my league it's laughable. Obviously, nothing romantic would ever happen with him, so my brain didn't even bother worrying about the possibilities.

Standing at least six feet tall with short red hair, striking blue eyes, and a mischievous smile, the bartender seems like the type to get just about any woman he wants. He's smooth, quick with the pick-up lines, and absurdly good looking. I'd love to be with a guy that confident, but I don't think it's in the cards for me.

Maybe in another life.

"For you." The bartender slides another vodka soda across the bar to me. He nods toward Gabe's group, his blue eyes twinkling. "I put it on their tab."

A giggle escapes me as I take the drink. "Thanks."

"I think they owe you at least that." He extends his hand across the bar. "I'm Cole."

I shake his hand, appreciating the masculine feel of it. What is it about a man's hands that can be so attractive? Is it the long, bony fingers? The short-trimmed fingernails? Or the veins popping out on the back? Maybe it's just the thought of what those hands could *do* that turns me on.

"Rhiannon," I reply.

"Cool name," Cole says.

I take a small sip of my drink, noting the stronger burn of vodka in this one. I'll have to take it slow, and I probably won't end up finishing it, but the gesture was really thoughtful. Drinking can help take the edge off my anxiety, but I can't drink *too* much. As soon as I start to feel out of control, I immediately panic.

"My moms are huge Fleetwood Mac fans," I explain. "I think they pictured me being much more mysterious than I actually am."

Cole leans forward, placing his forearms on the bar. Remember when I said men's hands can be sexy? Forearms might be even better. *So. Many. Veins.*

"I, for one, think you're very mysterious," he says. "Like, I'm wondering why you're in such a good mood after that shitty-ass date."

I smile to myself. Little does he know the sheer bravery it took me to be here tonight. I'm in a good mood because I'm proud of myself, but I'm not about to tell him that. Cole oozes confidence, and I don't want him to know how much it took for me to be here.

"Just glad it's over, I guess," I say.

"I don't blame you. That guy is a total loser." Cole glances over as another patron sits down. "I've got to get back to work. Let me know if you need anything, Rhiannon." He sends me one last wink before walking away.

I hope he's here when I come back for another date. I'll have to start swiping on *Meet Your Match* again tonight. As much as I'd love to meet a man out in the wild, twenty-six years have passed without that happening, so it appears I'm beholden to the app gods to find someone.

I hope they take pity on me soon.

"H e *what*?" my best friend, Hannah, screeches after I finish telling her about Gabe and how he ditched me to watch the football game last night.

"Man is just more interested in balls, I guess," I jest.

Hannah massages her temples. "I can't believe he didn't see what a catch you are."

"To be fair"—I look toward her boyfriend, Caleb, who's seated on the couch in the living room while we chat at the kitchen table—"Gabe and I only had a sixty-two percent compatibility rating."

Caleb coded a super-popular dating app called *Meet Your Match* that ranks your matches by percentage of compatibility based on zodiac signs and the results of various personality quizzes. So far, I haven't matched with anyone who has higher than a seventy percent compatibility rating. For reference, Hannah and Caleb had a ninety-six percent rating—one of the highest ever seen on the app.

"I won't be offended if you don't like the app," Caleb says with a wave of his hand.

"It's not the app." I shake my head. "It's the *men* on it."

"Give me your phone." Hannah extends her open palm. I hand over my unlocked phone and watch as she navigates to *Meet Your Match* and begins swiping. "We need to get you back on the horse," she decides. "Time to find your next date."

"Fine." I lay my cheek against the hardwood table with a drawn-out sigh. "My rules are: no pictures holding up fish, no one who overly emphasizes that their love language is physical touch, and no shirtless mirror selfies—unless they're, like, *wicked* hot."

Hannah snorts out a laugh. "I can work with those guidelines."

"Add no one with prompts about pineapple on pizza to your list," Caleb hollers. "I swear, eighty percent of guys have that on their profile. The lack of creativity is astounding."

"Noted," I mutter. The whole dating-app landscape is looking more bleak by the minute. While I wait for Hannah to find me a match, I begin wondering what Cole's dating profile would look like. He's a confident, good-looking guy. Is he the type to post a douchey selfie flexing a bicep? I hope not. Though, I *would* kind of like to see what his biceps look like.

"Aha!" Hannah cries out, followed by a little ding announcing that someone she swiped right on also swiped right on me. "Check him out." She shoves the phone in my face.

I lift my head and allow my eyes to focus on the profile photo. Short, blond hair, greenish-hazel eyes, nice smile. I scroll a little farther down. Bryan is twenty-five, works at a law office, and enjoys hiking and skiing in his free time. Not exactly my jam —I'm more of an indoor cat—but he's definitely first-date material.

"He's cute," I admit.

"Ask him to go out!" Hannah cries, bouncing like an over-sugared toddler.

"I want to vet him a *little* first," I reply, already typing out a "hello" message to Bryan. Before I can hit send, a message comes through from him.

Bryan: Hi, Rhiannon. Nice name. I would stay if you promised me heaven.

The flirtatious message is a bit forward for me, but he gets points for knowing the lyrics to my namesake song, at least.

I love my name. I adore Stevie Nicks. It's a great song. And I love that my moms named me after the witchy woman Stevie sings about in "Rhiannon," but every time my namesake is brought up, I can't help but feel a pang of insecurity. It's like I told Cole the other night: I'm really not that mysterious. I'm not Rhiannon, the ethereal, mystical goddess who can't be tied down. I'm Rhiannon, the anxious romance author who desperately wants a partner but isn't brave enough to find one.

I'm working on changing that, though.

Rhiannon: Ha ha. Props for knowing the song, I reply. *Who is your favorite musician?* I ask, removing myself as the subject of the conversation and hoping to learn a little more about Bryan. A few seconds later, he replies.

Bryan: I'm a big country guy—Zac Brown Band, Luke Combs, and Tim McGraw are my top artists according to Spotify.

Again, country isn't my genre of choice, but I can respect his picks. We talk for a few more minutes, and despite not having all that much in common, I decide he's normal enough to ask on a date.

"Done," I tell Hannah once I've made a plan to meet Bryan at Marty's on Tuesday evening.

At least there won't be a football game on that night. I checked.

Twice.

CHAPTER 3
RHIANNON

Veronica studied him from afar, getting a rare glimpse of Damien when he didn't know she was watching. His usual stony façade had dropped in the minutes he'd been sitting on the garden bench. He appeared to be studying the view of the grassy hills that rolled over her property, a soft smile gracing his sculpted lips.

A deep sigh left Veronica as she prepared to interrupt his peace.

"Damien," she said as she strolled toward her bodyguard. "I need..."

let out a frustrated groan as my mind draws a complete blank. The words should be flowing hours into one of my nightly writing sessions, but tonight, I'm devoid of inspiration. My skull might as well be hollow for how empty my brain feels.

The crickets chirping outside my open window mock me and my writer's block. It's just past midnight, and I'm hunched over my laptop, hair long since tied up in a knot on top of my head.

Instrumental music plays softly in the background as the early autumn breeze whisks in through the window.

I click my nails against the edge of my desk. *Why won't the words come?*

After years of honing my skills, I know that I do my best work after dark. That makes me sound like some kind of superhero, which I decidedly am not. I'm just an erotic romance author. Though, I suppose some may say the two are synonymous.

"Saving relationships and marriages nationwide!" an announcer's voice booms in my head. I can't help but chuckle. Smut may be looked down upon by the general public, but behind closed doors, it's a well-loved life raft for so many.

I turn my gaze out the window, searching the night sky until I set my sights on the moon. It's a waning crescent today, preparing to vanish entirely before gradually building itself back to its full potential. There aren't many stars visible with the light pollution in the city, but I count the ones I can see. I flick off my desk lamp, descending the room into darkness in hopes of catching glimpses of a few more. Sometimes this ritual helps reset my mind, but tonight it's not doing the trick.

All fifteen of my published novels have been written beneath the shroud of darkness, with only the moon and stars as my witnesses. My mind doesn't create the same way when the sun is out. Sometimes I wonder if I use the night as some sort of shield, as if no one can judge me if they're asleep while I write about my deepest, darkest fantasies.

That could also be me overanalyzing everything, per usual.

My therapist says overthinking is a natural response to anxiety. It's your brain's way of trying to predict every possible outcome so it can protect you in any scenario. But considering the fact that ninety-nine percent of the outcomes your brain conjures up will never actually happen, overthinking is a huge waste of emotional energy and brain power.

So, why can't I seem to stop doing it?

Shutting my laptop, I stretch my arms over my head and twist to each side a few times to release the tension in my back. If writing isn't happening tonight, I should probably get to bed. I have an appointment with my therapist, Jodi, early in the morning—earlier than I would prefer, anyway. Nine a.m. is practically sunup for me. Depending on how the words are flowing, I often write until two or three o'clock then sleep in until at least ten, but closer to noon if I'm able. My moms joke that I'm practically nocturnal, but it works for me.

With a yawn, I head to the bathroom to wash my face and brush my teeth then return to my bedroom to get changed. This might sound absurd since I'm painfully single, but I like to wear satin nighties or matching pajama sets to sleep. It makes *me* feel good, even if no one else gets to see them. Tonight, I choose a fire-engine-red nightie with lace borders around the top and bottom. The color makes me feel beautiful, and the satin against my skin feels sensual and exquisite.

I slide under the covers, enjoying the sensation of the smooth satin against my cotton sheets. I have my appointment with Jodi first thing tomorrow and lunch with Hannah after that. Then I'll come home and do administrative work in the afternoon—all the things that don't require so much creative energy—before taking a break in the evening to watch TV, read, and, let's be honest, scroll TikTok.

Running through my schedule helps ease some of my general anxiety. Nothing about my day tomorrow specifically worries me—I've been seeing Jodi for years, Hannah has been my friend since middle school, and I don't have scary emails to send or phone calls to make for work—but simply the thought of existing for another day gives me a baseline level of anxiety.

As long as I have a plan, I feel more in control. Plus, I know that, at the end of the day, I can always dive back into my story worlds where I control everything that happens, and there's always a happy ending.

"How are things?" Jodi asks after I settle into the plush armchair in her office. She sits in an identical one across from me, her loosely crossed legs cradling her clipboard in her lap.

I've seen a bunch of therapists over the years—some more helpful than others—but Jodi is my favorite of them all. Some may have been less successful due to my age—when I began therapy at twelve, with puberty raging in the background, I certainly wasn't the most motivated or compliant patient. Others just didn't jive with my personality.

When Jodi came along in my early twenties, we instantly clicked. She's easy to talk to and totally non-judgmental. I'd put her around fifty-five, and she feels a bit like the cool aunt you talk to about boy problems that you don't want to discuss with your mother—or in my case, mothers. I love Mom and Mimi to death, but they've never understood my anxiety. They're loving and supportive, sure, but they don't get my brain the way Jodi does.

Jodi also wears power suits with funky patterned socks beneath them, and I love that about her. It shows that she's a strong, serious woman, but she also has a whimsical side that makes her approachable. I aspire to be like her when I grow up.

"Things are good," I reply, my gaze catching on the shimmers of light reflecting off the disco ball planter that hangs in the window. Another thing I love about seeing Jodi: her office. There's nothing clinical about it. Everything from the plush green armchairs to the myriad succulent plants on every flat surface radiates warmth and welcome.

"How is your writing going?" she asks, diving right into our session.

"It's...going." I think back to my frustration last night. Like any author, I experience writer's block time and again, but what

I've been experiencing lately feels different. "I feel like I've hit a wall."

"Tell me more," Jodi says.

I bite back a smirk at the cliché turn of phrase. "I've had a hard time finding inspiration lately."

"What do you usually do when that happens?"

I glance up at the ceiling. "Read or watch movies…maybe some porn."

Jodi doesn't so much as flinch. "And have you tried all those things?"

I shrug. "Yeah. Nothing's helping right now."

"Perhaps some real-life romantic experience will offer renewed inspiration," Jodi says, her shrewd eyes no doubt catching the way my fingers curl tighter around my thighs. "You had a date this week, right? How was that?"

"It was…a date," I reply. "I dressed up and arrived early. He showed up in sweatpants and ditched me after half an hour to watch the Pats game. Really inspiring stuff."

"Oof." Jodi gives me a sympathetic grimace.

"Yeah." I shrug. "But I'm proud of myself for showing up."

Jodi nods. "As you should be. I'm sure that wasn't easy for you. It's a big deal that you did it. I want you to keep this momentum up. Do you have another date scheduled for next week?"

My knee begins bouncing. "Hannah found me a guy. Bryan. We're meeting on Tuesday."

"That's excellent, Rhia," Jodi says with a triumphant smile.

I resist the urge to roll my eyes. Jodi has me doing this ridiculous challenge of going on five first dates in the span of five weeks. We've been discussing my fear of first dates for ages, and this is her way of encouraging a form of exposure therapy. She's hoping going on a bunch of dates in a short period of time will reduce my anxiety about it.

"Is it?" I ask. "What if this is all just a huge waste of time and energy? What if I put myself through all this stress and nothing comes of it? What if I never meet someone I really want to be with?"

Jodi uncrosses and recrosses her legs, her pants sliding up her ankles to reveal lime-green and hot-pink striped socks embroidered with flamingos. "Remember," she says, "these dates are for practice, not necessarily to meet a long-term partner. The intention is less to find the perfect match and more to desensitize you to the dating process so you can continue exploring your options."

I chew on my thumbnail, avoiding the flaking black nail polish. "I've got to admit, my options are looking pretty bleak right now."

One side of Jodi's lips curls up. "You've only been on one date so far," she reminds me. "You have to trust the process. You can even frame these dates as writing research if that helps. I seriously think some experience in the dating world could help get your writing mojo back."

Jodi knows the lengths I'll go to to write a good story. I've read books, watched documentaries, traveled to different locations, and much more, all in the name of book research. First, she appealed to my competitive spirit with a challenge, and now she's suggesting that this could help with my writer's block too. I don't have a leg to stand on when it comes to avoiding her plan.

"Fine." I sigh dramatically. "I'll go out with Bryan. But if I get to the end of this thing and I don't get a second date *or* a finished manuscript out of it, I'm firing you."

Jodi just grins at my theatrics. "We'll see about that."

CHAPTER 4
COLE

Using my shoulder to hold my cell phone to my ear, I place the vat of Italian wedding soup I just prepped in the fridge. Tomorrow night, I'm hosting my monthly "family" dinner. On the first Wednesday of each month, I invite my sister, Bailey, a few of my fellow bartenders, and a neighbor to my apartment for dinner. I love to cook, but cooking for one can be a challenge, so I use my monthly dinner as an excuse to make a big meal.

Although Bailey is the only person in the group who's actually blood related to me—and only half of our blood at that—the motley crew is the closest thing to family that I've got. I *do* have my aunt Jen, uncle Tom, and cousins Brett and Steve, but they hardly count. I only see them a few times a year. Holidays. Weddings. Funerals. After four years of working at Marty's and living in this apartment, my coworkers and neighbors have become dear friends who I consider family.

"Hey, Coley," Bailey answers my call after a few rings.

"Hey, Bails." I smile at the sound of my sister's voice. "How were your exams?"

I may not have gone to college, but I'm pretty sure her exams are unlike those at most schools. They consist of a lot of musical performances as well as some traditional tests on things like music theory and history. I know Bailey had a piano performance she was really nervous about, so I'm hoping it went well.

"Pretty good," she replies. She sounds upbeat, so that's good. I fucking hate when she calls me in tears. It's happened a few times since she started college a couple years ago, and it shreds my heart every time. "I'm excited for fam din tomorrow," she adds.

"Good." I shut the fridge. "It's Italian wedding soup. Mac is bringing crusty bread from that little corner store, and Tripp said he would bring dessert, but it's a surprise. So, brace yourself for that. Louisa is making an autumn sangria that you're not allowed near."

Louisa is my elderly next-door neighbor. She has a heavy hand when it comes to pouring alcohol, and although Bailey is nineteen, and I'm under no illusions that she doesn't drink, I'm always on guard about her alcohol intake. Alcoholism runs in my family—specifically my mom's side, which is the genetic lineage that Bailey and I share.

I can practically hear my sister rolling her eyes through the phone. "Sure, Cole."

"You're welcome to bring something less potent for yourself if you'd like," I offer.

"No, thanks," she says in a sugary sweet tone. "I wouldn't want to offend my big brother's delicate sensibilities."

Now it's my turn to roll my eyes. Bailey likes to give me shit for being a protective older brother, but given the childhood we had, that role kind of comes with the territory.

"Great," I reply. "Then you can be the designated driver in case Mac gets hammered like he did last time Louisa supplied the drinks. Remember the great fireball incident of 2024?"

Bailey's throaty laugh rings through the phone. "Yeah, I do. I specifically remember the coffee table Mac broke. He was trying to teach us that viral TikTok dance, and he hopped on top of it to give everyone a better view." Her laughter grows to hysterics.

"Oh, God, the *groaning* sound the wood made. And Mac's *face* when he came crashing down."

I laugh with her, struggling to catch my breath as I replay the scene in my head. "I'll never forget it." I wipe an errant tear from my eye, laughing so hard I'm crying. "Thankfully, that table was a cheap thrifting find," I add once my laughter calms.

"Mac looked like he was going to cry. He felt so bad about breaking it," Bailey recalls once her own hysterics die off.

"He paid for a new one," I assure her.

"He's good like that," she says, her tone a little dreamy. Bailey has had a crush on Mac since the very first time she met him. She's never outright told me this, but it's hard not to notice. She watches him with stars in her eyes at every family dinner, and whenever he comes up in conversation, she talks about him like he's a celebrity or something.

I'm not too worried about it. It's a harmless crush a teenager has on her older brother's best friend. Plus, Mac knows I would strangle him if he did anything to hurt Bailey, and that includes breaking her heart.

"Miss you," Bailey says softly.

"Miss you too, sis," I reply. Bailey and I have always been close despite our five-year age gap. When I moved out of my aunt and uncle's house at eighteen, she took it pretty hard. She was stuck there for another few years, but I visited her a lot, and she came to my place often for sleepovers.

When Bailey started at Berklee a bit over a year ago, I offered for her to come live with me—my apartment being less than twenty minutes away—but she insisted that I needed my own space. As grateful as I am for that, I miss seeing her as often as I used to. She's so busy with classes and friends and God knows what else. It sets me on edge that I'm unable to keep as close of an eye on her as I used to. Bailey is a smart, responsible young woman, but we live in a cruel world. I shudder when I think of all the trouble a college girl could get into in a city like Boston.

"I'll see you tomorrow," I remind her.

"Can't wait," she replies. "I have to head to class now. Love you."

"Love you too," I say before we hang up. With tomorrow night's dinner all prepped, I get dressed, pop a stick of mint gum into my mouth, and head off for my shift at Marty's.

She's back.

I notice her the second she walks through the door. It's as if the air shifts when Rhiannon enters the dimly lit space. This evening, she's wearing dark jeans with an emerald-colored cardigan over a lacy black camisole. The outfit is hot but a bit more casual than the one she wore last week. I wonder if the disastrous date inspired her to put in less effort. I wouldn't blame her if it did.

"Rhiannon," I greet her once she sits down. "Vodka soda with lime?"

She blinks her big brown eyes. "You remember."

I give her a half-smile. "A good bartender never forgets a gorgeous girl's drink order."

She smiles softly, her cheeks gaining a bit of color. "Thank you."

It's been slow tonight, so I continue chatting while I make her drink. "Got another hot date?"

"Mm-hmm," she hums as she twirls a lock of her long black hair with her fingers. "I made sure to schedule it on a night when no sporting events were taking place," she adds, an undertone of sarcasm in her voice. *Attagirl.*

"There's always Wrestlemania on pay-per-view," I joke.

She narrows those dark eyes at me. "You wouldn't dare."

I hand Rhiannon her drink and settle my forearms on the bar, popping my gum in my mouth. "And what if I would? What if I want to sabotage this date so I can have you all to myself?"

Her gaze snaps to mine, and she swallows, but her look of

surprise is quickly replaced by one of displeasure. "Trust me, I'm sure this guy will find a way to sabotage the date all by himself."

"I don't doubt it," I reply with a conspiratorial grin. "Who's today's victim?"

Rhiannon rears her head back in mock insult. "Victim? You say that as if a date with me is some sort of punishment."

"The only one who seems to be getting punished here is you," I point out. I wonder why she bothers going on these dates when they obviously bring her very little pleasure. I'd love to ask her, but it feels like too deep a question for the moment.

Rhiannon sits up straight, holding her glass with both hands. "Tonight's date is Bryan. He's a paralegal who enjoys outdoor activities."

"Ah." I nod. "Stuffy guy cooped up in an office from nine to five all week who walks up big hills on the weekends and calls himself a 'weekend warrior.'"

Her brows draw together slightly. "How did you know he calls himself that?"

I bite back a laugh. "Because that's what all the twenty-something white guys with office jobs say."

Rhiannon purses her lips. "Oh," she mutters.

Her bewilderment makes me feel kind of bad.

"I'm just poking fun," I say. "I think it's great that he's using his spare time to do what he loves. Do you enjoy outdoor activities too?"

I'm relieved when a grin once again touches her pretty pink lips. "Actually, no. I prefer to spend most of my time indoors, unless I'm on a lounge chair by a pool or something—with a yummy drink and good book, of course."

I start to picture Rhiannon lounging by the pool, her bikini-clad body spread out beneath the sunshine, but I cut myself off when the idea gets too enticing. "Sounds nice. You like to read?"

"It's one of my favorite things to do," she replies.

I wonder why she's giving the time of day to this beyond-average dude when he doesn't even share her hobbies. Rhiannon may not think of herself as very mysterious, but she's an enigma to me. I want to learn everything about her. Why is she going on these pathetic dates? Why hasn't someone snatched her up into a long-term relationship yet? Or is she on the rebound from one right now?

"Rhia?" a blond guy asks, placing a hand on Rhiannon's shoulder. I'm immediately miffed that he calls her by a nickname I didn't know she used.

"Hey, Bryan," she responds, her mouth forming into a little O of surprise when the guy pulls her into a hug. I watch his other hand travel dangerously low on her back, and my spine straightens immediately. His fingers linger just above the curve of her ass, and I don't like *that* one bit.

I clear my throat more forcefully than needed. "Can I get you a drink?"

Bryan releases Rhiannon—Rhia. "Sure. I'll have a whiskey on the rocks," he says. At least it's a more respectable drink order than the last guy. My tolerance for him is just starting to grow when he adds, "Whatever's on the top shelf."

Ugh. So he's a snob. A snob with good taste, but a snob nonetheless.

"You got it," I reply with my practiced bartender smile.

"So, Rhia, how are you on this fine Tuesday evening?" I hear him ask as I grab his whiskey. The guy radiates big douchebag energy.

"I'm well," she replies. "How about you? Still sore from this weekend?"

"Not too bad anymore," he says. His hand lands on her thigh as I turn to give him his drink. I don't like how touchy feely he is when they only just met. Judging by the sour look on Rhia's face as she glances down at his hand, she's not a fan either.

"My Theragun has been my best friend these past few days," Bryan adds, totally oblivious to her distaste. He holds his drink up to me in thanks before taking a small sip. "Ahh," he says after swallowing. "That's good stuff."

I go to help some other customers before I have a chance to roll my eyes at his douchebaggery. Bryan seems like the type of guy who thinks he owns the world. I hate that. He was probably born with a silver spoon in his mouth. I bet he went to college on his parents' dime and drives an expensive sports car his daddy bought him. *Not* that I'm judging him.

Okay, fine, I'm hardcore judging him.

Once I've helped the other customers, I round back toward Rhia and Bryan to find him fucking *massaging* her thigh. The sight of his big, meaty paw not only still touching her leg but *kneading* it hardens my jaw to stone. At least she's wearing jeans today and not those thin stockings she had on under her dress last week, so there's a thicker barrier between her and handsy Harry over here.

Still, I'm afraid Bryan is the type of guy to take whatever he wants, and I sense that Rhia isn't interested in giving it.

I catch her eye and tilt my head as if to ask: *You okay?*

Rhia's eyes widen slightly, as if to say: *Help me.*

I nod toward the bathrooms and mimic unzipping my fly, hoping she'll get the message.

She places her hand over Bryan's and forcibly removes it from her body. "I have to use the bathroom," she says, cutting off whatever he was saying. She stands up and hurries toward the bathrooms, which are in a little hallway toward the back of the building. I wait about thirty seconds before following her.

Rhia is leaning against the wall opposite the bathroom doors, her arms crossed over her torso, cardigan tucked tightly around her. She looks even more freaked out now than she did sitting at the bar, and it makes my heart thump wildly. I want to touch her, to ensure that she's okay, but I don't want to freak her out more.

"Hey," I say softly, and her dark eyes dart to mine.

"Hi," she says, her voice a little shaky.

"Are you alright?" I ask.

"I, uh…" She pauses, adjusting her stance against the wall. "I'm fine. Bryan's just…he's a bit too forward for me."

I nod. "I saw him pawing at you. Guy seems like a pig."

Rhia's gaze drops to the floor. "It's not like he touched me anywhere inappropriate," she says. "I don't know why I didn't ask him to stop. I think I just...froze." Her shoulders lift in a shrug.

"Rhia." I wait for her eyes to return to mine before dispensing a bit of wisdom I'd give to any woman. "Touching you anywhere on your body is inappropriate if you don't want to be touched there."

Her shoulders relax, and her arms loosen across her chest, as if I've given her permission to be upset by what just happened. It pisses me off, because she shouldn't need anyone to tell her that. The *world* should be telling her that. Still, I'm glad my words validated her feelings.

"I know." Rhia glances back toward the bar. "I don't want to go back out there."

"I can kick him out for you," I offer. Actually, it would be my pleasure to kick Bryan out of here and tell him to never come back.

Rhia cocks her head to the side, her silky black hair sliding over her sweater. "You would do that for me?"

I give her a reassuring smile. "Wait here."

CHAPTER 5
RHIANNON

Well, at least date number two is officially over. It might have ended with the bartender kicking my date out of the establishment, but I still faced my fear.

Now, I'm waiting for Cole to let me know the coast is clear. It was so sweet of him to help me out when he could have easily left me to handle things myself. Even the fact that he noticed I was uncomfortable lights a little fire in my heart. I'm sure he would do the same thing for any woman in distress sitting at his bar, but the fact that he was paying attention to me makes me feel sort of warm and fuzzy inside.

When Cole returns after a few minutes, there's a swagger in his step that tells me he quite enjoyed kicking Bryan out.

"Mission accomplished." He mimes wiping his hands clean.

Relief washes over me. "Thank you." Lifting to my tiptoes, I spontaneously go in for a hug. Cole's body is stiff as I wrap my arms around his shoulders, but he quickly softens, placing his hands on my back and cradling me.

"It's over," he whispers in my ear, his minty breath traveling to my nostrils.

Thank God.

"Did he give you a hard time?" I ask as I pull away.

"Nothing I couldn't handle," Cole replies vaguely. From the taste I got of Bryan, I imagine he would give someone shit for trying to get him to leave in the middle of a date, especially when he seemed to think I was an easy mark.

"Thank you so much, Cole." I give him a smile that's more genuine than any I gave to Bryan. "You're a lifesaver."

"Don't worry about it." He gestures toward the bar. "Why don't you come back out, and I'll make you a fresh drink. I wouldn't put anything past that dude."

Part of me wants to go straight home and take a shower to wash the creep off, but I might as well salvage this night somehow. "Sure," I agree.

Cole makes me a new vodka soda and helps all the other customers who had to wait while he had his confrontation with Bryan. When he returns to where I'm seated, he leans forward on the bar as if settling in for a long conversation.

"So, where were we?" he asks.

"Hmm?"

"Before Bryan interrupted our conversation, you were telling me that you like to read," he says, as if the conversation we were having before Bryan arrived is the objective of the night, and my date was just some pesky distraction.

"Oh," I say. "Yeah, I'm a big reader."

"Anything I'd have heard of?"

I tilt my head to the side. "Honestly, probably not." I consider whether or not I want to explain further then figure, why the hell not? "I mostly read romance."

"Ahh." Cole throws his head back in understanding. "That explains it."

"Explains what?" I ask, hoping he's not going to make some asshole comment like so many guys do when they find out I read or write romance. If I hear some dumbass line like *that's just porn for women* or *don't you read any real literature?* I swear I'm going to scream.

"It explains why you're giving all these jerks a chance when you're clearly better than them." Cole points at me. "You're a hopeless romantic."

My cheeks heat. "Guilty," I admit. "But that's not exactly why I'm going on these dates."

It seems odd that I'm about to spill my guts to someone I barely know, but I figure it's just friendly conversation with a bartender. That's what they're known for, right?

"Why, then?" Cole asks.

I take a sip of my drink for liquid courage. He made the second one stronger again, so it doesn't take much to loosen me up.

"I have this fear of first dates," I confess. "It's like…really bad. I mean, full body shakes and severe stomach aches when I anticipate them. So, my therapist suggested a form of exposure therapy: going on five first dates in five consecutive weeks."

Cole smirks. "Sounds like something out of one of your romance books."

I can't help but chuckle. "It does, doesn't it?"

If only these *dates* were like something out of a romance novel. Instead, they've been nightmarishly horror-esque.

"Why all the nerves for first dates?" he asks. "It's basically just a conversation getting to know another person."

I fiddle with my glass. "My brain can't see things that simply. It jumps straight to: *I have to decide if I like this person right now. I have to put on my best face and make them like me. I have to know if this is someone I can see myself with forever.* It's a lot of pressure, even though I know it shouldn't be."

Cole nods. "That sounds stressful."

"It is," I agree. "But—like you said—I'm a hopeless romantic, and I really want to find a partner. If going on a bunch of shitty first dates in order to hopefully go on a good one that leads to something is what I have to do, then so be it."

"That's admirable, honestly," he says, pulling a rag out of his back pocket and beginning to wipe down the bar.

"Thanks," I say. "And thank you again for what you did tonight. I really appreciate your help."

"No problem," Cole says easily. "I hate seeing guys be creepy at my bar. I'm always happy to take care of them. Besides, it's what I would want someone to do for my sister."

Of course Cole should do for anyone what he did for me, but I have to admit I sort of liked the idea that he helped me because we have a special little thing going. I come to his bar for first dates, and he soothes my nerves before they begin. I'm also not sure I love the idea of being comparable to his sister in his mind. I know I have no chance with a guy like Cole, but it would be nice to imagine that I might.

"How old is she?" I ask, sipping my drink.

"Nineteen," Cole answers. "She's my best friend and the bane of my existence all rolled into one." The love he has for his sister shines through in the adorable smile he breaks into when talking about her.

"You guys must be close," I reply.

"We are," he says. "We've been looking out for each other our whole lives. Even though she's five years younger than me, we've always been inseparable."

If his sister is nineteen, then that puts Cole at twenty-four, making him two years younger than me. It's funny—I'm typically more attracted to older guys. I've always imagined it's their maturity or wealth of experience that draws me in, but I have an inkling that Cole has both of those qualities even though he's younger than me.

"Do you have any siblings?" he asks.

I shake my head. "Only child. My moms are big on traveling, and I think they realized it would be too difficult with more than one child in tow."

Cole's eyes brighten. "Did you get to go on lots of cool trips as a kid?"

I nod hesitantly. "I did. I went on my first international flight when I was six months old. Barcelona. I had visited four of the seven continents by the time I turned five."

"That's so incredible," he says. "I've never even been out of the country, and you were doing it all the time when you were still a baby."

"I feel very lucky that I had those opportunities," I reply carefully. "And I'm definitely grateful for the experiences, but the constant upheaval and lack of a set routine or schedule was not ideal for a child like me."

Cole's smile falls a bit. "Oh. Sorry." He winces. "Here I am, imagining it must have been a childhood out of a dream, but I can see where that would be difficult."

"It's okay," I assure him. "In some ways, it *was* a dream. I got to meet so many people, experience so many cultures, and learn about lots of important things that school doesn't teach you. But it also placed a level of stress on me that most children don't have to deal with."

Sometimes I wonder if our lifestyle caused my anxiety or if it just brought it to light.

Cole nods silently as he continues wiping the bar. "Sometimes it's good to be reminded that even when the grass looks greener, that doesn't always mean it actually is," he replies. Before I can respond to his cryptic comment, he moves on. "Do your moms still travel a lot?"

I smile fondly as I picture the last photo my moms sent me of them at the top of Mount Kilimanjaro. "All the time," I reply. "Their permanent home is a converted van, but they're constantly hostel hopping as well. I see them sporadically when they're in the States, and we FaceTime a lot. They also send snail mail postcards from all the major cities they visit."

Cole grins. "That's really nice. I'm glad you have good relationships with them even though their lifestyle isn't compatible with yours."

If I *did* have any doubts about Cole's maturity level, this conversation would have erased them. He's attentive, thoughtful, and so easy to talk to—all qualities that make him a good bartender, I guess.

"So, what's the plan for the next date?" he asks as he tosses his rag over his shoulder.

I let out a dramatic groan. "I haven't made one yet. I'll have to get on *Meet Your Match* tonight and start swiping. My friend, Hannah, found Bryan, so I'm definitely not letting her help me again. But whoever I find, I'm sure we'll be back here next week."

"Good," Cole says with a satisfied smile. "I'd miss you too much otherwise."

I know it's just typical bartender flirtation, but it still sets off a little flutter in my belly. I try to hand Cole a ten-dollar bill for my drink, but he pushes it back toward me.

"On the house."

"Consider it a tip, then," I say as I drop it back on the bar.

He slides it across the shiny wood toward me. "Seeing your gorgeous face here each week is tip enough."

"Cole…" I shake my head. He's being too kind to me. Now that I've shared about my anxiety with him and told him how pathetic I am about first dates, he feels bad for me.

I don't want his pity.

Rolling the bill into a tight little wrap, I lean over the bar, tug Cole's t-shirt up slightly, and stuff the wrapped-up bill into his jeans pocket. I have to force myself not to fixate on the small expanse of smooth skin I catch a glimpse of beneath his shirt.

"I insist," I say. "See you next week, Cole."

Then I get up and leave without a second glance.

CHAPTER 6
COLE

I think there's something wrong with me.

Did I hit my head or something? I don't remember hurting myself, but I guess if I was concussed, I might not remember it.

I literally flirt *for* tips, but when Rhiannon tried to tip me last night, I didn't want to accept it. So I guess that means I was just…legitimately flirting with her?

This is the spiral my mind is spinning through when the first knock arrives at my door on Wednesday evening. My soup is simmering on the electric stovetop, and I have Fleetwood Mac's *Rumours* album playing in the background for no particular reason at all.

I open the door to find a grinning Tripp holding a bowl full of an unidentifiable fluffy, pink substance.

"What the fuck is that?" I point to the monstrosity.

"It's Jell-O salad!" he replies, shouldering his way in through the door and placing it on my kitchen table.

"I'm sorry," I say. "I'm gonna need a little more than that."

"It's a popular side dish in the Midwest," he explains. "It's cottage cheese, Cool Whip, crushed pineapple, and a packet of Jell-O mix. I used strawberry flavor."

"That sounds…heinous," I tell him.

"Trust me, it's good," he replies.

"If you say so." I go to close the door to my apartment, but Louisa comes bustling through before I can. Her short, gray hair is sticking up in all directions, and she's wearing two different shoes—one brown loafer and one pull-on Sketchers sneaker.

"Hi, boys," she says as she places a gigantic pitcher of sangria next to Tripp's contribution, huffing out a breath of exertion. "I have to warn you—this stuff is strong. I've already helped myself to a glass or two."

I guess that explains her disheveled look.

"Thanks for the heads up." I give Louisa a quick hug in greeting. She might be a little off her rocker, but she's a good neighbor and a fucking fun person to have around.

Her eyes widen as she recognizes the other dish on the table. "Is that Jell-O salad?"

"Yeah!" Tripp replies. "Have you had it before?"

"My mother used to make it back in the sixties," Louisa replies, and I leave those two to their conversation. I'm all about creative cooking, and I've eaten a lot of strange food combinations in my life, but I think I have to draw the line at mixing cottage cheese and Jell-O.

"Yoohoo," I hear through the still-open door before Bailey enters. Her ginger hair—another thing we share from our mother's genetics—is pulled back into a ponytail, exposing her pink-tipped nose and cheeks. It's a windy fall day, and she probably walked here from the train station. She unwinds her scarf and manages to tug it off before I envelop her in a bear hug.

"Hey, Bails," I say into her hair as I give her a squeeze.

"Hi, Coley," she responds, hugging me back. I never feel more complete than when I have Bailey by my side where I can watch over her.

"Mac's not here yet?" she asks when she pulls away and takes in the rest of the room.

"No, he was going to pick up the bread on his way so it

would still be warm," I explain. "And I think he was bringing someone too, so that might slow him down."

I don't miss the disappointment that flashes on Bailey's face.

"A male someone," I add, though I shouldn't be playing into her crush.

Bailey's face brightens. We both know Mac isn't into guys.

"He's trying to recruit a friend into applying to work at Marty's," I explain. "He thought having him hang out with me and Tripp might help."

Mac, Tripp, and I are the steadiest bartenders at Marty's. Others come and go, but the three of us stay constant.

"That's more likely to scare him away," Bailey says under her breath.

"What was that?" I ask, pulling her into my side and ruffling her hair with my fingers.

"Stop it!" she squeals as Mac walks through the door with his friend, Jesse, in tow. Bailey pushes away from me and hurriedly fixes the hair I mussed.

"Hey, hey!" Mac greets the room. When he arrives, the party really starts. "This is Jesse," he introduces his friend. "Jess, this is Tripp and Cole from Marty's, Cole's sister, Bailey, and his neighbor, Louisa."

Louisa gives the newcomer a onceover and nods approvingly. I think half the reason she hangs out with us is for the opportunity to gawk at a group of handsome young men.

"Nice to meet you." I shake Jesse's hand. He gives me a polite nod but no verbal response. I don't know much about him other than he grew up with Mac and just recently moved to the area. Mac says he could really use a job, but Jesse's not looking like great bartender material so far. You have to be able to connect with customers, and this guy can't even come up with a proper greeting.

"Who wants sangria?" Louisa asks, already armed with two large glasses of the lethal liquid.

"I'll take one, Lou," Mac says, thanking Louisa with a kiss on her forehead that immediately makes a blush rise in her cheeks.

"I—" Bailey starts to say, but I cut her off with a light pinch on her arm. She yelps and begins rubbing at her skin, glaring at me with narrowed eyes.

Jesse happily accepts the other glass before Louisa returns to her conversation with Tripp about classic Midwestern dishes. I tune them out once I hear the words "cheese curds" thrown around.

"Hey, Bails," Mac greets my sister, wrapping her in a half-hug. "How'd the exams go?"

"Good," she replies with a huge smile, clearly pleased that Mac remembered. She spent most of our last family dinner worrying about her piano performance. "I don't have all my grades back yet, but I'm feeling positive about them."

"Way to go, kid," Mac says, dulling Bailey's smile about a thousand degrees with the nickname.

"Thanks," she mutters before sulking over to the table where Tripp and Louisa are, apparently deciding cheese curds are a more pleasant topic of conversation.

"So, Jesse"—I turn toward the newcomer—"I hear you might be interested in joining our team."

"Yep," he replies, sipping his sangria.

I wait a beat before asking, "Do you have any experience bartending?"

"Nope," he says.

Again, I give him a few seconds to elaborate, but he just stands there, sipping away.

"Okay," I reply. "Well, good luck with that."

Mac shoots me an apologetic glance as I head for the stove to check on my soup. I give it a good stir before ladling out a spoonful, blowing on it, and tasting. *Ahhh.* So good. I'd put a little spin on the classic dish by making the meatballs spicy, and my taste test confirmed it was a good call.

"Soup is ready," I call out, grabbing a stack of bowls from the cabinet and placing them on the counter next to the stove. "Help yourselves."

We all ladle out our bowls of soup and sit around the kitchen table. I make sure to move Tripp's Jell-O salad to a counter out of eyeshot so as not to ruin anyone's appetite. I won't knock the taste until I've tried it, but the stuff looks like curdled Pepto Bismol.

Bailey removes her jacket, draping it over the back of her chair. My gaze catches on the tight, low-cut black top that's tucked into her pants. It's sleeveless with black lace scalloping the neckline down into her cleavage—*far* too much of which is showing.

The shirt isn't unlike what Rhiannon was wearing beneath her emerald cardigan last night, but while it looked sexy on her, it makes me seethe to see it on my little sister. I know she's nine-teen-years-old, but in my mind, she's not allowed to have a sexual bone in her body.

"What are you wearing?" I demand.

Bailey's eyes flare. "It's called a bodysuit," she tells me through gritted teeth.

"It looks like underwear."

A rebellious smirk slides over her lips. "If you think that looks like underwear, you should see what I have on underneath it."

Mac muffles a laugh by fake coughing. Louisa licks her finger and presses it to her backside with a *tss* sound. Tripp clears his throat, shifting in his seat. Jesse's mouth remains in a thin line, totally unaffected. I swear, the man is made of marble.

"Bailey," I warn. "Sit down and eat your soup."

"Yes, big brother," she replies, making a show of sitting, crossing her legs primly, and draping a napkin over her lap.

The others are used to our sibling banter, so everyone moves on from the exchange quickly. Dinner conversation consists of more discussion of Bailey's exams, catching up on gossip from the bar, and hearing about Louisa's latest exploits, which include taking up ant farming and trying to perfect her Bloody Mary. Jesse remains nearly silent throughout dinner, only participating with single-word answers when asked questions.

After dinner, I pull Mac aside.

"What the fuck is up with him?" I point toward his pal.

Mac heaves out a sigh. "I know. He's a little rough around the edges."

"Rough around the edges? The man doesn't *speak*."

Mac shrugs. "So, he's a little shy."

"A little shy?" I whisper-yell. "He hasn't formed a full sentence all night."

Mac nods toward the couch. "Looks like he is now."

I look over to the couch to find Jesse sitting there *conversing* with Bailey. Like, talking back and forth, ostensibly using more than one word at a time. I also notice she's leaning toward him in interest, exposing her cleavage even more.

I march over them. "Hey, Bailey, can I grab you for a second?"

She flicks her gaze to mine. "Sure, when I'm done talking to Jesse."

I cross my arms over my chest. "Actually, I need you now."

She stares me down for a moment. Upon seeing that I have no intention of walking away, she stands. "Talk to you later," she says to Jesse, shooting him an apologetic smile. When she turns back to me, there's ice in her expression.

I usher her to the kitchen. "What were you guys talking about?" I ask in a hushed tone.

Bailey taps her foot impatiently. "You tore me away from my conversation to ask me what we were talking about?"

"I tore you away from your conversation because that guy is bad news," I counter. "And you two looked a little too cozy."

"Cole," Bailey snaps. "I know you still like to think of me as a child, but I am a grown-ass woman. I am allowed to wear what I want. I am allowed to talk to who I want. I love you, but you are not in charge of me anymore."

"I just want you to be smart," I say.

Her voice softens. "How could I not be when I was raised by you?"

Oof. She always gets me with the mushy, sentimental stuff. I tug her into a tight hug. "I love you, Bails."

"Love you too," she replies into my chest. My entire body stiffens when I see what's occurring over her shoulder. Jesse has risen from the couch and cracked open a window. He's standing next to it, holding a cigarette in one hand and a lighter in the other. Time stops as I watch him flick the lighter to life, a flame springing from the top of it. My gaze zeroes in on the fire licking at the air. Panic claws at my chest, and it's hard to pull in a breath.

Bailey pulls back, looking up into my hardened face. "Cole?"

Her voice sounds far away, but it's enough to force me into the present.

I stomp over to Jesse, slamming the window shut against the cold autumn air. "There's no smoking in here."

He startles, releasing his thumb off the lighter and holding his hands up. "Sorry, man."

It's the first time I've personally heard him string two words together all night.

"Don't be sorry, just don't do it," I snap. I barely feel Bailey's small hand on my arm, giving it a comforting squeeze.

"My bad." Jesse flicks the lighter on and off a couple of times in a nervous gesture.

"And put the fucking lighter away," I add, equally as furious at Jesse for being a dumbass as I am at myself for my overblown reaction.

Jesse stuffs the lighter into his pocket, tucking the unlit cigarette into the side of his mouth. "I'm out of here," he announces.

"Hold up," Mac says as Jesse storms toward the door. "I'll come with you."

Jesse stalls by the door as Mac apologizes to me.

"I'm sorry about him," Mac says. "I'm trying to help him turn his life around, but clearly it's a slow process."

"It's fine," I reply in a tone that clearly indicates it is anything *but* fine. First, he flirts with my sister, then he tries to light up in my apartment? Oh, *hell* no. But Mac is a good friend to me, and he's clearly trying to be a good friend to Jesse too, so I add, "It's not your fault," in a softer tone.

Mac claps me on the shoulder. "Thanks for dinner. I'll see you at work tomorrow."

I say goodbye to him and then Tripp, who unfortunately never got a chance to serve his Jell-O salad, though he seems delighted to have the whole thing to himself now. He helps get Louisa back to her apartment next door with her mostly empty pitcher. I swear she drank half of that thing all on her own.

"You okay?" Bailey asks once the others have cleared out. I guess my little outburst kind of ruined the mood.

"Fine," I reply as I load bowls into the dishwasher.

"You can be honest with me," she says.

I hang my head. "I know." My sister knows exactly why Jesse's little stunt bothered me. Every time I think maybe I've finally gotten over my shit, something like that happens. "I'm fine, really," I tell her. "Just annoyed at myself for ruining the night."

Bailey shrugs it off. "You didn't ruin anything. Mac seemed understanding, Tripp is thrilled to go home and polish off that pink stuff, and Louisa won't even remember it."

"What about you?" I ask. "I didn't ruin your night by being the macho older brother?"

Bailey rolls her eyes. "I don't know about the macho part, but I can't really blame you for acting like an older brother."

I open my arms for a hug. "So, we're good?"

Bailey sidles over to me, tucking herself against me like she has since she was a baby. "We're good."

CHAPTER 7
RHIANNON

The thin line of Damien's lips tells me he's not going to give me an inch.

"Please?" I ask, batting my lashes for good measure. "I just want to get out of this house for one night."

Damien massages his temples like I'm giving him a headache. I'd hate to break it to him that it's more likely his own hard head-edness doing that.

"It's not safe," he replies.

"But I'll have you with me the whole time," I remind him. "And you wouldn't let anyone hurt me, right?"

The moment I enter Marty's, I can tell things are off. I spot my date, Nate, already seated at the bar. Usually, I arrive about fifteen minutes before a date is set to start so I have time to get comfortable before the other person arrives.

Arriving to everything early is part of my anxiety. Running late stresses me out, and I'm always worried about things that could go wrong on the way, so I consistently arrive ten minutes early. Oftentimes, I just sit in my car, scrolling on my phone or staring into space, but lately I've enjoyed chatting with Cole before my dates. He always hypes me up, and I'm going to miss having that opportunity tonight.

The other thing that's different about tonight is the tall, curly-haired guy setting up a variety of complicated-looking electronics in the corner of the bar. There are a couple of large speakers, a microphone, and all sorts of lights atop a makeshift stage that appears to be comprised of wooden pallets. A banner strung above the stage reads *Karaoke Night!*

Oh. Shit.

I had no idea there was anything special happening at the bar tonight. I doubt Nate did either, since I picked the location. I can only hope we'll be out of here before karaoke begins.

With a deep breath, I walk over to the bar.

"Nate?" I ask when I reach the black-haired guy I recognize from *Meet Your Match.*

He stands, shaking my hand. "Hi, Rhiannon. It's very nice to meet you."

"You too." I sit on the stool beside his. "Sorry, I didn't realize it was karaoke night. Hopefully it doesn't get too rowdy."

Nate frowns, his dark brows sliding together. "You don't like karaoke?"

"Not my thing," I reply.

"Huh. I would have thought with a name like Rhiannon you'd be a music lover."

"I do love music," I reply, "just not making a fool of myself singing in public."

Nate nods half-heartedly, but he seems put off by this. Whatever. If he wants an extrovert, he's not going to find that here.

That's when Cole stalks over to us, giving me a subtle nod before greeting us both. "What can I get you two?"

"Two whiskey sours," Nate says immediately.

Whoa. He didn't even ask me what I wanted, and I hate whiskey.

Cole shoots me a glance, his eyebrows raised as if to ask, *you okay with that?*

Bolstered by his acknowledgement that that was indeed rude, I speak up. "I'd rather a vodka soda, actually."

Nate huffs as if he can't believe I would have a different preference than him. "Fine. One whiskey sour and one vodka soda."

Cole looks between us once before heading off to make our drinks. Oh, how I would love to hear what he's thinking right now.

"So, Nate," I begin, hoping to turn the tide of this date. "Tell me more about your dog. He was so cute in your pictures." Every single picture on his profile, actually. I'm shocked he showed up tonight without the mutt.

Nate smiles at the mention of his furry pal. "Gregory is the best," he says.

Who names their dog Gregory, anyway?

"I rescued him three years ago, and we've been best friends ever since."

Well, that's sweet, I guess.

"Did you grow up with dogs? I've never had a pet," I admit.

The horror on Nate's face almost makes me laugh out loud. "No pets *ever*?" he asks, placing a hand over his heart as if he's about to have some sort of episode.

"Never," I confirm. "My family traveled too much."

"That sucks," he says. "I grew up with dogs, and I always knew I'd get one of my own when I grew up. They're obviously the superior pet."

I'm relieved Cole delivers our drinks before I have a chance to respond. I'd hate to break Nate's heart by telling him I'm more of a cat person.

Cole's long fingers brush against mine as I accept my drink. My gaze lifts to his, and I'm immediately sure from the mischief in his smile that it was intentional. A show of support—some sort of boon to help me get through this night.

"Thank you," I say to him, earning a small nod.

Nate doesn't bother with pleasantries, instead diving right into his drink.

I'm trying to think of what to talk about next when a horrible electronic screech fills the air, followed by a loud, "Sorry, folks!"

I turn to see the guy who's been setting up karaoke equipment tapping on the microphone.

"Just a little feedback loop. Should be all set now."

"Looks like they might be starting soon," Nate notes as the guy finishes his test and hops off the stage.

"It might be fun to hear some of the singers," I say, trying to be positive. Taking the first sip of my drink, I almost start coughing at how strong it is. Looks like Cole took pity on me early tonight. I search the growing crowd around the bar for him. When I catch his eye, he sends me a wink. I shake my head at him, a smile growing on my lips.

"Let's sign up to do a duet," Nate suggests.

I turn back to him and shake my head. "I'd rather not, but I'll watch if you want to sign up for a solo."

Nate scratches at his chin. "I think it would be more fun to do it together. Come on—it won't be so bad."

"No, thank you," I say, leaving no room for objection. There's absolutely no way I'm getting in front of all these people to do *anything*, let alone sing, which is something I guarantee no one wants to hear unless they're looking to shatter their eardrums.

Nate sags a bit in his stool. "Fine," he mutters.

Well, this is going well. There's nothing inherently wrong with Nate. We just don't click. He has very strong opinions, and he's clearly looking for someone who's going to follow his lead.

That someone is not me.

I wonder how soon I can gracefully bow out of this date. Jodi really wants me to stick it out and get the full date experience. I already got out of date number one by telling Gabe to go watch the game with his friends, and date number two was cut short when Cole kicked Bryan out. I should really play this date through until the end just to be able to say that I did.

"Good evening, everyone." The booming voice breaks me out of my thoughts. The karaoke guy is back behind the mic. "I'm Mac, your MC, and welcome to Marty's first monthly karaoke night."

Cheers arise from multiple patrons. In the short time we've been sitting here, the bar has really filled up. They must have advertised this new event, because I can't imagine a Wednesday night would normally be this hopping. *Damnit*, why didn't I research to see if there were any events going on this week?

"We have a sign-up book up front and a binder with a list of the available songs," he explains, holding up a notebook. "We have a few regulars already signed up to get us started. Barry, take it away."

Barry, a middle-aged white man with thinning gray hair jogs up to take the microphone.

"Thanks, Mac," he says. "Can we get some mood lighting up in here?"

Mac shoots him a thumbs-up and returns to his side for a moment to speak into the microphone. "Anyone who has an issue with flashing lights, please be advised that things are about to get funky in here." He scans the crowd for a few moments to see if anyone might have an issue with that, then he flicks a few switches, and suddenly strobe lights are flashing in every color as the instrumentals for "Funkytown" blare through the speakers.

Barry pulls out a pair of sunglasses whose lenses look like disco balls and secures them on his face before diving into the song. Patrons begin rushing to crowd around the stage, singing along and dancing while Barry puts on the performance of his life, shimmying and shaking his little heart out.

Nate grabs me by the arm and hauls me along with him to follow the crowd, once again neglecting to ask what *I* want. In a matter of moments, I find myself amongst a sea of people. It's loud, hot, and the lights feel too bright. Everything about this is overstimulating, and I immediately sense panic setting in.

My heartbeat speeds up, my breathing becomes more shallow, and sweat beads on my neck as my bodily systems rev up to escape whatever enemy has me surrounded. Only, the enemy is a crowd of jubilant karaoke lovers. There's no threat here, and yet my body is acting as if a venomous snake is poised to strike.

I focus on taking deep breaths, hoping to calm my body enough to hang in here for at least this one song. By the time it's finally over, I still haven't been able to catch my breath or stop the sensation that I'm hurtling through a tunnel at lightning speed toward some inevitable but indescribable doom.

"I'm gonna go sign up for a song," Nate shouts over the music, not even giving me a second glance as he heads toward the stage. I use the opportunity to book it for the bathroom. In order to soothe my panic, I need pretty much exactly the opposite of the conditions in the bar right now. I need quiet, cold, and dark. Right now, the best I can do is the ladies' room.

I weave through the crowd, everyone blurring together in my vision, until I finally break free at the edge, bathroom doors in sight. I hurl myself into the small hallway only to come face to face with the only person in this bar that I even remotely want to see right now.

Cole.

He regards me with a lazy grin. "We've got to stop meeting like this."

CHAPTER 8
COLE

My smile instantly drops when I realize that something is *very* wrong.

Rhia is ghostly pale, her already light skin as white as a sheet of paper. Her chest is heaving, and her eyes dart around, searching for something I can't place. When I catch sight of her hands, they're trembling.

"Rhia, what's wrong?" I take a step closer to her.

"I…" she trails off, doubling over and placing her hands on her upper thighs. "Panic…attack," she wheezes.

Shit.

"Come here," I take her arm and pull her into the manager's office, which is conveniently located in the same little hallway as the bathrooms. Leading her to the first surface I see—an old, ratty ottoman with stuffing popping out of various cracks in the leather—I gently guide Rhia down to sit. She remains bent at the waist, fighting for each breath.

Kneeling before her, I manage to catch her gaze. Her eyes are still wild, her pupils dilated to huge, black saucers.

"Did he hurt you?" I demand.

She shakes her head, raking her fingers through her hair. "No. Just…too much…out there." She waves a hand toward the door leading back to the bar, where I can just make out "Respect" by Aretha Franklin now playing.

Someday, I hope we'll laugh about the fact that Barry's rendition of "Funkytown" was so chaotic it actually sent Rhia into full fight-or-flight mode. Right now, though, I'm completely focused on calming her down.

"Hold on," I murmur, reaching over to rummage through the mini fridge we keep back here for employees to store their snacks and drinks. I steal a couple of frozen burritos from the small freezer at the top, hoping no one will miss them.

Perching myself behind Rhiannon on the ottoman, I hand one of the burritos to her. "Put this against your forehead," I instruct while I hold the other one on the back of her neck. She follows my command, leaning into the comforting chill. Shivers continue to wrack her body, but now I don't know if they're from anxiety or from the cold.

Desperate to end her suffering, I wrap the arm that isn't holding the burrito to her neck around her from behind, exerting deep pressure to try and calm her nervous system.

"Just breathe, Rhia," I whisper softly next to her ear. "In through your nose, slow and steady."

She nods, drawing in a deep breath.

"Good job. I've got you," I add, continuing to hold tightly onto her waist as she breathes. I inhale and exhale in time with her, hoping maybe she can feel the synchronicity against her back as it presses into my chest.

After a couple of minutes that feel like hours, Rhia removes the burrito from her forehead with a steady hand and places it on the ground beside us. I take that as my cue to release her and remove the other one from her neck. Gathering them both, I toss them into a nearby trash can.

"Well, fuck." Rhia rubs at her temples. After the five minutes she just spent in fight-or-flight mode, she probably feels like she ran a marathon. She seems to have stopped shaking, and she's regained some of her color, but she looks absolutely wrecked.

"What can I get you?" I ask.

Rhia clears her throat. "Some water would be great."

I open the mini fridge again to find a bottle of water, opening it and handing it to her.

"Thank you," she says softly before taking a few gulps.

I pretend to read a poster on the wall while giving Rhia a few minutes to gather herself. During the glances I steal every few moments, I see her combing her fingers through her slightly tangled hair and rubbing beneath her eyes. Despite her dishevelment, she still looks gorgeous to me.

"Want me to let your man know you won't be coming back?" I offer once she seems to have pulled it together.

A bitter laugh flies out of her. "First of all, he is *so* not my man. Second, he seemed to care more about karaoke than me, so I'm not too worried that he'll miss me."

Fucking asshole. Seriously, how is she having such bad luck with these dates?

"Thank you, Cole, for…"—she gestures between the ottoman and the trash can that now has two half-frozen burritos sitting at the top—"that," she finishes.

"It's no problem." I stuff my hands into my pockets. "Are you…feeling better?"

Rhia nods. "Much." She picks at one of the rips in the leather, pulling out a small tuft of stuffing. "How did you know what to do?" she asks, staring down at her fingers.

I sink into the ratty armchair beside the ottoman. "My sister used to have panic attacks. That's what I would do for her." Bailey always thought she was dying, and I would hold her until it passed. She was too young when it happened to remember a time when her life actually was in danger, but her body clearly did, and it liked to remind her. I crack a smile to lighten the mood. "I usually used ice packs, not frozen burritos, but anything in a pinch, am I right?"

Rhia's lips tilt slightly upward. "Right," she replies, finally giving me a glimpse of those gorgeous brown eyes.

"Does that…happen to you often?" I ask, hating the idea that she experiences that sort of pain regularly.

Rhia places her palms flat behind her, relaxing a bit. "No, thank goodness," she answers. "It used to when I was younger, but it's only once in a while now. Thank God for medication."

"Good." I nod, glad she's found relief over the years. "Do you know what…set it off?" I try to choose my words carefully, not wanting to be rude or disrespectful, but I'm honestly curious.

Rhia sighs. "Anxiety about the date compounded with the overstimulation of the crowd, noise, and lights. Sometimes my brain gets overwhelmed when there's too much input, and it sends me into fight-or-flight."

My brows shoot up. "That was a quick and suspiciously sophisticated answer."

Rhia smirks. "I've had a lot of therapy and a lot of time and experience to help me understand my anxiety."

"I hate that for you," I admit.

She shrugs. "It is what it is. It was harder when I was a kid and didn't really understand what was going on."

"Were your parents helpful?" I have no concept of what it's like to have parental support of any kind, but my understanding from popular media is that parents are supposed to help their kids with issues like this.

"My moms…they were compassionate, but they never really got it, you know?" Rhia shrugs and tucks her hands beneath her thighs. "They supported me when I panicked, but they were quick to say stuff like *just relax* or *don't worry*. Things that are the opposite of helpful. They slowed down on the traveling when they realized it was making things worse for me, but ultimately, I think they expected me to grow out of it. I didn't, obviously."

"That's tough."

"How is your sister doing now?" Rhia asks. "Does she still have panic attacks?"

"Not so much," I reply, honestly forgetting the last time

Bailey had one. "Although we haven't lived together in years, so I suppose she could be having them and not telling me."

"Do you think she would hide that from you?"

I tilt my head to one side. "It's possible. I can be a little… overprotective," I confess. "I wouldn't put it past her to hide things in order to keep me from worrying about her. She's always trying to get me to lighten up when it comes to her, but I can't seem to. She means too much to me."

Rhia smiles at that. "You seem like a really good brother."

The praise lights up my heart. "Thank you." For some reason, that means a lot coming from her. "I wish you could meet Bailey. She was supposed to come to karaoke tonight, but she ended up having too much homework to do."

"I would love to meet her," Rhia replies, but then her smile falls a bit. "I mean, if we ever happen to be here at the same time," she adds. Right. There's no real reason for her to meet my sister. I'm just her bartender, and she's just a customer.

But it feels like so much more.

Most bartenders don't end up in the back room holding their customers from behind while they breathe together. Most bartenders don't watch their patrons go on first dates and spend the entire time waiting for them to end so they can spend time with them again.

But I do. And only for Rhia.

I don't know *what* to call what we have. I don't know if we're quite friends—I don't know what she does for work, where she lives, or even her last name, for God's sake—but we're something more than acquaintances. That much I know for sure.

"I should get going." Rhia rises from the ottoman. Her coloring is much better, and everything else seems back to normal too, but I still worry.

"Let me take you home," I offer.

She runs her palms down her thighs, flattening out the wrinkles in her pants. "Aren't you in the middle of a shift? I already took you away for too long."

"It's fine," I reply, even though I have no idea if it actually is. It could be chaos outside this door, but I've been too focused on Rhia to notice. Either way, Mac's here, and he can handle the worst of it.

Rhia chews lightly on her lip. "If you're sure…"

I head for the door. "I am." Holding it open, I gesture toward the kitchen. "We can head out the back." I lead her through the kitchen and out the back door toward the employee parking spots. "This one's mine," I tell her, pointing to my beater of a car then opening the passenger side door for her.

I stop to shoot a quick text to Mac, letting him know he's in charge before heading around to the driver's side. Suddenly, I feel a little nervous myself. This will be my first time with Rhia outside of the bar. That feels momentous in some way.

"Okay," I say as I settle into my seat. "Where are we off to?"

"What if I told you I lived in Worcester?" Rhia fires back, naming a city that would take me at least an hour to get to.

I smirk as I turn the car on. "I would say that you must really love my bar to drive all that way just to go to it every week."

She scoffs. "Don't give yourself so much credit. I live a couple blocks over. Cherry Street."

I back out of my space, following Rhia's directions to her apartment building.

"So, you're three for three on shitty dates," I point out as we sit at a red light.

"Don't remind me," she says with a groan. "At least I'm more than halfway there."

"How did your therapist come up with five?" I ask. "Seems like an arbitrary number."

"It is," Rhia replies. "I think it's small enough that it doesn't feel too overwhelming while also offering enough practice to hopefully get me in the groove of dating. I think Jodi also hoped I would click with one of the guys and want to continue seeing him. Statistically speaking, I should want to go on a second date with at least one out of five people, but so far that hasn't been the case."

I hit the gas when the light turns green. "There are still two more dates to go," I remind her, unsure what to make of the unease that fills my gut when I say that. "You never know what will happen."

I can feel her studying my profile as she responds, "No, I guess I don't."

CHAPTER 9
RHIANNON

"You haven't had a panic attack in a long time," Jodi points out at my next weekly appointment. She's nestled into her armchair, and I can see her outer space socks complete with planets, stars, and rocket ships poking out from beneath the hem of her trousers.

I just finished telling her about the panic attack I had on my date with Nate and about how Cole took care of me. This conversation is the first time I've brought him up in our sessions. I didn't *intentionally* leave out details about Cole from my other dates; I just chose to share about the actual dates instead. That's what Jodi is interested in, after all. Why would she care about my interactions with the bartender?

"I know," I reply, crossing my legs. "I think the chaos of karaoke night compounded with the anxiety I already had about the date just sent me over the edge."

"That's a good hypothesis." Jodi nods. "Do you feel like your anxiety is decreasing with each date? Or is it staying at about the same level?"

I have to think about that one for a moment. I *do* feel like the dates have gotten a bit easier as they go. I have to spend less time talking myself into going on them, and I'm not quite as miserable leading up to them. Though, truthfully, I don't know if my anxiety about the dates is decreasing or if my excitement to see Cole each time is just increasing, canceling out some of the nerves.

If I said that to Jodi, I'm sure she would remind me that anxiety and excitement are very similar emotions, and I should try to reframe my nerves as being excited, and *blah blah blah*. I've heard the spiel before.

"I think it's decreasing, but some of that might also be that I'm becoming more comfortable at the bar. The bartender is really good at getting me in the right headspace. It's like he calms me down and hypes me up at the same time. I don't know how to explain it."

"And that's Cole?" Jodi confirms.

"Right. He must work there most weeknights, because he's been at the bar for every date I've had."

A slight smile touches Jodi's lips. "That predictability must give you some comfort."

"I guess so." I hadn't thought of it that way, but she's probably right. Cole's steady presence gives me something to count on even when my dates go awry, which seems to be becoming a terrible pattern. "It's nice to know I have a sort of ally, you know? Cole is so easy to talk to, and he's always looking out for me."

Jodi arches a brow—one of her signature moves that means *Rhia, be honest with yourself.* "You seem more interested in Cole than any of your dates."

"Oh." My cheeks flame, and I desperately wish I could do something to cover my face without Jodi psychoanalyzing the movement. "He's just...a friend?" I say, but it comes out like a question.

Jodi's lips twitch. "It sounds to me like you want to be more than friends."

"Cole's not my type," I reply. "He's super confident, and he flirts with every woman who walks into the bar. He would never go for someone like me."

Jodi shifts in her chair, steepling her fingers together by her stomach. "Is it really that Cole isn't your type, or is it that you think that *you're* not *his*?"

Goddammit, Jodi. I might pay her the big bucks to tell me these types of things, but that doesn't make them any easier to hear.

"I guess I feel like he's out of my league," I admit. "He's clearly the type of guy who has experience, and, as you know, I don't. He seems confident and carefree, and I'm not. He had to remind me how to freaking breathe, for God's sake."

Jodi waits until I meet her gaze to respond. "Or, maybe, he saw your strength through that experience. He watched you fight against your own brain and win. And I know you've heard the phrase *opposites attract*. Just because he might have more romantic experience than you doesn't mean he won't like you. In fact, he might find it refreshing."

I sit and stew in her words for a moment. "Do you really think a guy like him could like me?" I ask, feeling like a fifteen-year-old girl again, wondering if any of the guys at school think I'm pretty.

Jodi uncrosses her legs and sits forward, drawing my attention. "Rhiannon, I want you to really hear me when I say this. You are a beautiful young woman with an incredible talent that you've turned into a successful career all on your own. You are smart, savvy, and you have an incredibly kind heart. You deserve a lot more than you think you do. Please don't sell yourself short."

My eyes well up with tears. I've always viewed Jodi as this badass boss bitch, so hearing her say those things about me means a lot.

"Thanks, Jodi," I reply, swiping at an errant tear.

She glances over at the clock she keeps prominently displayed on her desk. "Our time is up for today. Good luck on your next date, and think about what I said. You deserve the love you've always wanted, and you never know what package that's going to come in."

I try to keep those words in mind as I head into date number four.

"So, what do you do for work?" Tyler asks.

This night already sucks. Tyler was fifteen minutes late, so I had to sit here for that entire time *plus* the normal fifteen minutes early that I typically arrive. And Cole's not even here to chat with. I really should figure out what his schedule is.

I take a small sip of my drink as I consider my answer to Tyler's questions. I love talking about what I do, but I never know how new people will react. Might as well tell him the truth and find out.

"I'm a writer."

"Really? What do you write?"

I take his genuine interest as a good sign. "Romance novels," I reply.

"Huh." Tyler takes a swig of his Jack and Coke. "That must be some nice, easy money."

I freeze. Easy money? Not only does this career require writing books—which includes coming up with original plots and characters, writing thousands upon thousands of words, and editing those words—but it also requires you to be a businesswoman. Once the book is written, you need to market it, which involves learning and keeping up with all the social media platforms, making content, maintaining a website, having a newsletter, and researching promotions and giveaways that you might want to be a part of. You need to hire all the professionals you work with, from editors to cover designers, and you need to manage all the finances that go into publishing. It's a lot of work, and nothing about it is easy.

I grit my teeth. "Excuse me?"

"You know." He shrugs. "Write a book with a predictable plot, throw it up on the internet, and let the cash flow in."

Ugh. As if this night couldn't get any worse, Tyler is one of *those* people. The ones who think romance novels are a joke, not taking into account that it's the highest-selling genre. The ones who think the predictability of the couple living happily ever after takes away from the validity of the growth they go through individually and as a couple throughout the story.

"Actually, it's a difficult and time-consuming job," I reply. "I'm incredibly lucky to have found the success I have. It's taken years of practice, research, and keeping up with trends to get to a place where I'm able to make a living at it."

Tyler sips his drink with a blank expression. "Do your books have, like, sex in them?" he asks.

"Yes," I reply through gritted teeth. While I have no problem admitting that my books contain erotic scenes, I know when a meathead like Tyler hears that, he's picturing whatever questionable porn he views each night while he jacks himself off because he can't get a woman to sleep with him, *not* the emotional, meaningful, *important* stories I craft.

Tyler lets out a little laugh. "Cool."

I take a swig of my vodka soda, grateful he's leaving it at that.

"So, like, is the sex kinky?" he asks, and I shoot him a glare. *Spoke too soon.*

Again, I'll readily discuss the kink that I do, in fact, incorporate into my scenes with someone who I think will view the topic in a mature and healthy way. There's something so beautiful about people exploring their mutual desires—particularly those that may not be readily accepted by society at large. But I'm not going to tell Tyler any of that. Not only did we just meet, but I have a funny feeling his mindset about the topic is wildly different from mine.

I'm winding up to tell him how inappropriate his line of

questioning is when Cole appears behind the bar like my knight in shining armor. Except, instead of armor, he's wearing his usual work uniform of a black t-shirt and dark jeans. His ginger hair is damp, as if he just finished a shower, and his eyes are shooting daggers at my date.

"Refill, Rhia?" Cole asks me, his gaze gentling when it meets mine.

I look down at my glass, surprised to find it empty. I must have been chugging it while planning my response to Tyler.

I grin at Cole. "I'd love one."

Tyler throws back the rest of his drink. "Same," he says before sliding his empty glass across the bar.

Cole looks at me and lifts a brow. Before he can steal my thunder by bitching Tyler out, which I'm sure he's dying to do, I turn to my date.

"Look, Tyler, you seem…" I pause, searching for a complimentary adjective for him and coming up blank. "Well, anyway, I don't think things are going to work out between us. If you don't respect my career and you don't have the social awareness not to ask me if I write kinky sex scenes on a first date, then I have no interest in pursuing any sort of relationship with you. I hope you find what you're looking for, but you're not going to find it here. So, no, Cole's not going to refill your drink, and I'd appreciate it if you would leave so I can hang out with my friend."

Tyler looks to Cole with indignation, perhaps expecting a fellow male to back him up, but Cole just snaps his gum between his teeth as if in punctuation to my monologue.

With a huff, Tyler rises from his stool and storms off toward the door.

Cole reaches out his fist, and I bump it with my own.

"That was badass," he drawls.

"How much of that horrible conversation did you hear?" I ask as Cole turns to make me a new drink.

He chuckles softly. "Enough to know that Tyler is a complete douche canoe and to spark my interest about your job. I had no idea you were a writer."

"I don't usually tell people right off the bat unless they ask, for obvious reasons," I reply. "People's questions can be quite invasive."

"So, *is* the sex kinky?" Cole asks as he hands me my drink.

I pin him with an icy glare, and he chuckles. "Just kidding."

I take a sip, confirming my suspicion that he's made me a Cole special—an extra-strong vodka soda—and bat my eyelashes at him. "To answer your question: yes. Yes, it is."

CHAPTER 10
COLE

nearly choke on my own saliva. *This fucking girl.* She never ceases to surprise me. I'm so glad Mac texted me when she came in. I wasn't supposed to work tonight, but when he alerted me that Rhia was here, I took the quickest shower known to man and hauled ass to get over here.

Rhia smiles, a sly little tilt of her lips. "Surprised?"

"I mean…a little," I admit.

Her grin grows. "Why, because I practically have panic attacks over dates, but I write about kinky shit?"

"Well…yeah," I reply, my mind still reeling. Rhiannon is a total mystery to me. One minute, she's a nervous woman sitting at my bar, dreading a first date, and the next she's telling me she writes romance novels with kink. She's going to give me whiplash if she keeps this up.

Rhia takes a long, slow sip of her drink. "I'm different when I'm comfortable with people. More open, more…myself. I write under a pen name, so I feel comfortable with my readers. They don't know me in real life, and they only know the version of myself I give to them."

Interesting. I have to admit, the fact that Rhia sharing more about her writing means she's comfortable with me makes pride kick in my chest.

"A pen name, huh?"

"Yes," she replies. "And, no, I'm not going to tell you what it is."

I put on my best puppy dog pout. "Why not?"

"Because then you'd look up my books, and you'd learn far too much about me."

"What if I *want* to get to know more about you?"

Rhia's big brown eyes go wide, as if she's shocked I would want to get to know her. How can she not see how fascinating she is? She told me once that she's not mysterious, but I think she's an absolute puzzle—one I desperately want to piece together.

Rhia still looks like a doe in the headlights when a new customer sits down a few seats away.

"Be right back," I promise before turning away to prepare a Long Island iced tea for the customer. If I had a job as cool as Rhia, I'd be shouting it from the rooftops. All I know how to do is mix drinks. I understand why she wants to keep the more taboo parts of her writing private, but it bums me out that she isn't loud and proud about her career.

"So, why do you have to hide behind a pen name?" I ask when I return to Rhia's corner of the bar. "I think your career is super interesting, and a lot of people would be jealous that you get to live out a dream like being an author.

Rhia spins her glass in her hands. "It's not exactly hiding, more just showing the world only what I want them to see. People make a lot of assumptions when they find out I write romance, and sometimes I get sick of defending myself."

"What kinds of assumptions?" I ask, though in many ways Tyler already answered that question for me.

Rhia's lips pull into a sneer. "Oh, that romance novels are unrealistic mommy porn that serve no purpose other than to give women false expectations of what relationships should be like. People see romance as fluff—or worse, trash—instead of the meaningful, empowering, *important* genre that it really is. Romance is the best-selling fiction genre for a reason." She takes a gulp of her vodka soda before continuing her tirade. "Romance novels give people hope that love is real and that it can be found anytime, anywhere, even when you least expect it. They typically show women being uplifted, and the patriarchy can't stand that. The so-called 'unrealistic expectations' are often just women being treated well. Our society has set the bar so low that a fictional hero putting in any effort whatsoever is seen as a threat to all the real-life men who think women should live to serve their every whim."

Rhia stops to take what is seemingly her first breath in minutes. This is clearly a topic she's passionate about.

"I have to admit that I've never read a romance novel before," I reply. "But you've sparked my interest. It sounds like I could probably learn a thing or two from them."

"I'd be happy to give you some beginner recommendations," Rhia says. "But the guys who *really* need to take a lesson from romance novels are the duds I've been going on these dates with." She slings back the rest of her drink and slams the empty glass down on the bar.

I nod toward it. "Another?"

Rhia follows my gaze. "Oh." Her brows lift as if she's surprised to find her drink is gone. "Uh...sure, why not. I'll need it if I'm going to start swiping for my next date," she says as she pulls out her phone.

I do a lap of the bar, making sure all the other customers are settled before making Rhia another vodka soda. When I bring it over to her, she sets her phone on the bar and mimes slamming her face against it.

"That bad?" I ask. Her screen is open to a dating app. There's a photo of a dude flexing his bicep in a mirror front and center. He has no facial hair other than a bushy mustache that eclipses his upper lip. I'm guessing he's going for a Travis Kelce look, but the guy just can't pull it off the way a two-time-Superbowl-winning tight end can.

"Worse." Rhia accepts her drink with greedy hands, bringing the glass right to her lips for a swig. I study her mouth as she sips, her pillowy lips closing around the glass. They look so soft and delicate, and I errantly wonder how they'd feel against mine.

"Thanks," Rhia says as she sets her drink down.

Her voice snaps me out of my wayward thoughts. "No problem. I wish I could be of more help."

"It's fine." She sighs. "Just one more first date, and I can tell my therapist I completed the challenge."

After the four awful dates Rhia has already endured, she doesn't deserve to go on another one where she'll be ignored, disrespected, or otherwise mistreated. She's never going to get over her anxieties about dating if she keeps going out with jackasses. She needs to go on a date with a gentleman. Someone who will show her a good time and nothing else. Someone whose sole mission it is to give her an ideal first date.

Someone like me.

"I have an idea," I say.

Rhia's weary eyes lift to meet mine.

"Go on a date with me."

Her mouth drops open slightly. "What?"

"Go out with me," I say.

Her brows draw together. "I'm sorry. I know I've had a bit more than usual to drink tonight, but it sounds like you just asked me out."

"I did." Someday, I'll tell her how much it bothers me that she's surprised when I show an ounce of interest in her. Why doesn't she believe she's worth it? Tonight, I just want to get her to agree to this plan. "You have to go on one more date, and I happen to be great at them. Let me show you what a first date should be like."

Rhia stares at me as if gauging whether or not I'm serious. "Where would we go? What would we do?"

"I haven't thought that far ahead yet," I reply. Ideas swarm my brain, but I want to take my time to really plan out the perfect date.

She nurses her drink, and I just know her mind is whirling. "I don't exactly love surprises," she says with a cute little scowl.

I lean forward on my elbows. "I can give you the exact details later on. Times, places, everything. But first you've got to commit. I don't want to waste my time planning a date if you're not going to go through with it," I say, half joking. I'm less worried about wasting my time than I am her turning me down and finding some other dipshit to go on a date with while I'm stuck watching from behind the bar again.

Rhia swirls her glass around in her hand, the small amount of liquid left in it sloshing against the sides. "It *would* be nice not to have to torture myself with another poorly matched guy from a dating app."

"Exactly," I say. "You already know me, so there's no need to stress. Just sit back, relax, and get excited for the best date of your life."

Her dark brows lift. "The best, huh?"

"Oh yeah. You're not going to know what hit you."

"Fine," she agrees before downing the rest of her drink. "Let's do this."

CHAPTER 11
COLE

t's not until a few minutes later, when Rhia can't stop giggling at a silly cat commercial playing on the TV, that I realize she's tipsy. I should have known back when she admitted to writing kinky sex scenes, and if not then, I *really* should have realized when she agreed to go on a date with me, but I was too wrapped up to think about the cause of her rapidly lowering inhibitions.

Rhia hides it well, but now that I'm paying more attention to the signs, I realize that her cheeks are rosy, and her eyes have turned glassy. She just finished her third drink, and I don't think I've ever seen her finish a second before.

Turning away from the TV, she meets my gaze with a lazy smile.

"You're drunk," I accuse with a grin, amused at this new side of her.

Rhia's eyebrows scrunch together in the most adorable grimace. "Am not." She crosses her arms, the movement causing her to lose her balance on the stool. Her arms uncross and fly forward to steady herself on the bar. She lets out a giggle. "Okay, maybe I am a little."

I fill a cup to the brim with water and slide it over to her.

"Drink up."

She takes a gulp of the water then shakes her head. "I blame Tyler. He was such a—what did you call him, a douche canoe?—that I felt the need to inebriate myself."

"Inebriate?" I repeat the overly formal word with a chuckle.

"I'm a writer," Rhia retorts with a flip of her glossy black hair. "I know big words."

Damn. Drunk Rhia is funny. And cute as shit. Hell, who am I kidding? She's always cute as shit.

"I have no doubt," I reply. I'd love to read some of those words, but Rhia won't give up her pen name. Maybe I'll work on weaseling it out of her on our date—if she doesn't cancel it once she comes to her senses, that is. I'm dying to know more about these sex scenes. Maybe that makes me as much of a pervert as Tyler, but, frankly, I don't really care. I want to know all about Rhiannon, including her kinky side—*especially* her kinky side.

Rhia stretches her arms over her head. "No more drinks for me," she says. "I should get going."

"How are you getting home?" I ask.

"I'll walk."

"I'll drive you," I offer immediately. No way am I letting her walk home alone in the dark, not necessarily wasted but most definitely not sober. Has she been walking home alone after all these dates? The thought makes my stomach sink.

"You don't have to," she says as she slides off her stool. "You already ended your last shift early because of me."

She's not wrong about that, but tonight I wasn't even supposed to be working. Mac headed to the back office to get some work done when I arrived, but he can take back his place behind the bar for the rest of the night.

"It's no problem," I press. "Let me grab someone to cover the bar." I speed to the back office, hoping like hell Rhia won't disappear on me in the next thirty seconds. "You're up," I tell Mac as I grab my jacket and shrug it on.

"Huh?" He glances up at me, clearly not picking up on the fact that I'm in a rush.

I slam the laptop in front of him shut. "You're back behind the bar. I'm taking Rhia home."

"Oh." Mac breaks out a goofy grin, raising his eyebrows up and down a few times.

"She's drunk," I reply, deadpan. "And she was planning to walk home alone, so I'm driving her."

"What a gentleman," he says with a snort, still making no move to get up.

"Mac, please," I plead, and he finally takes mercy on me, rising from his chair and following me back to the bar.

"Good luck," he whispers to me with a wink before snapping back into bartender mode.

Though I'm not sure what I'd need it for as my only goal tonight is to get Rhia home safely, I'll take all the luck I can get when it comes to her.

"Ready?" I ask, pleased to find that Rhia is still hovering by her vacant stool. She nods, and I walk her out the door and around the building to my car. I open the passenger side door for her, and she slides into the seat. It's the second time Rhia has ridden in my car, and the sight of her nestled into my passenger seat looks like the most natural thing in the world.

She's unusually quiet as I start up the car. I glance briefly toward her as she picks up the packet of mint gum I keep in my center console, giving it a shake.

"Help yourself," I offer.

"No, thanks," she says softly, placing it back down.

"You doing alright?" I ask, wondering where my giggly, unusually confident Rhia went.

"Yep," she replies with a yawn. "Just starting to get sleepy." She pats her stomach. "And *hungry*."

Ah, the drunk munchies. I've been there more times than I can count.

"If you let me up, I'll make you something," I say. It's not even a ploy to get her to let me in. It's just an honest reaction to her hunger—cooking for others is my love language—but I wouldn't hate the opportunity to spend more time with her tonight.

"You would make me food?" Rhia asks. When I glance over, she's picking at a hole in her jeans, a frown marring her brow.

"I would love to make you food," I reply.

"I don't have much in my fridge," she warns, but I'm confident I can make something work. It's kind of my specialty.

"Leave it up to me," I say as Rhia points out where I should park. I hold on to her elbow as we walk up to her apartment. The alcohol has definitely taken effect, making her unsteady on her feet.

"I'm getting a little dizzy," she says as she stumbles through her doorway.

"Let's get you sitting down," I suggest, tugging her toward the small kitchen. She heads for one of two chairs at a small, circular dining table and plunks heavily into the seat.

"Shit, Cole, I *am* drunk," Rhia whines, burying her face in her hands.

I chuckle. "I know. Just relax and let me see what I'm working with," I say as I open various cabinets to find where she keeps ingredients.

"I hate being drunk," Rhia complains, her words muffled by her palms. "My head is spinning, and I think I might be getting nauseated. What if I have to puke? What if I puke in my sleep? What if I *die*? Oh my God, Cole. This is so bad." She groans, rubbing her hands over her face.

I toss a loaf of bread onto the counter as Rhia begins spiraling. Stepping behind her, I place my hands firmly on her shoulders and dig my thumbs into her upper back, massaging away the tension there.

"Rhiannon," I begin in the strictest tone I can manage, "you are okay. You had a bit too much to drink, and you need to get some food in your system. I'm going to help you, and then you'll feel a lot better." I continue massaging firmly, giving her some of the deep pressure that seemed to help when she had a panic attack at the bar.

"Okay," she whispers, her shoulders softening. I wonder if it's the physical touch or my assured tone that's relaxing her. Either way, something's helping.

"Let me get you another glass of water." I step away to grab it. When I return, Rhia has lifted her head up. Her makeup is smudged from her hands, leaving black rims around her eyes, but she still looks absolutely beautiful. I'm so glad I came inside with her. I'd feel awful if she was experiencing this anxiety alone. Though, I suspect that's how it goes most of the time.

"Thank you," Rhia says quietly, taking a large sip of water.

"That's it," I say. "Keep drinking, and I'm going to whip you up something good."

She takes dutiful sips as I rifle through the fridge. She really *doesn't* have much in here, but I manage to find a bottle of Dijon mustard, some unopened cheddar cheese, and butter. I know exactly what I'm going to make.

"What are you gonna do with those?" Rhia asks as I butter two slices of bread.

"Grilled cheese," I answer as I squeeze a thin layer of mustard onto one piece of bread.

"With *mustard*?" She narrows her eyes, seeming slightly appalled.

I chuckle under my breath. "Trust me, it's delicious."

Rhia is quiet as I assemble the sandwich in a pan on the stove, setting the heat to medium low. "You've tried this before?" she asks when I step to the side and lean against the counter to wait for the bread to brown.

"Yep," I reply. "Ate it all the time growing up. Though, we often didn't have cheese, so it would just be grilled mustard."

Her nose scrunches up adorably in disgust. "Just mustard on bread?"

I pull at the back of my neck. "Yeah. My mom had some

trouble keeping food on the table growing up. Cheese is expensive and goes bad. Mustard is shelf stable."

Rhia's disgust vanishes, her scrunched nose replaced by wide eyes as some small bit of understanding of my childhood dawns. Yep, while her moms were carting her all over the world on grand adventures, mine was drinking, fucking anything with a dick, and only occasionally managing to keep a job.

"Oh," Rhia says. Her tipsy, giggly attitude is gone, the sad reality of my childhood sobering her right up. "I'm sorry, Cole."

"It was a long time ago," I reply, pushing off the counter to check on the sandwich. "My mom spent most of her money on alcohol," I explain with my back to her as I slide the sandwich around the pan, soaking in all the melted butter. "She was usually either too broke or too drunk to go shopping. When groceries were scarce, I would come up with creative recipes to cook for my sister and myself. Trust me, grilled mustard was a delicacy when there was no other food in the house."

When I turn back to face Rhia, her big, brown eyes are brimming with tears. The sight tugs at a loose string in my chest. "There's no need for that," I insist, stepping toward her and cupping her cheek in my palm, my thumb poised to wipe away any tears that may fall. "It's all in the past."

Rhia sniffles. "But it's still sad. I had no idea you grew up that way."

"There's a lot you don't know about me," I reply, pulling my hand away from her face. "That's why you have to go out with me." I go back to the stove to flip the grilled cheese, pleased to find the bottom side is a perfect, crispy brown.

"I already agreed to go out with you," Rhia says.

"Yeah, I know. I just like hearing you say it."

"You are too much," she mutters.

"Or maybe I'm just the right amount," I counter as I transfer the grilled cheese to a plate, adding a squiggle of mustard to one side to make it more aesthetically appealing. I wish I had some parsley or something to really top it off, but this will have to do.

"This looks professional," Rhia says when I present her with the plate. She actually sounds impressed, which shouldn't make me as proud as it does.

"Try it," I encourage her, eager for more praise.

She sinks her teeth into the crispy bread and the gooey cheese beneath it, taking a big first bite. The orgasmic moan she lets out as she chews threatens to give me a half chub.

"Good?" I ask.

"*Great,*" Rhia replies before taking another bite. "I wasn't so sure about the mustard, but *damn,* it really adds something."

"Right?" I reply. "It elevates a simple grilled cheese to something totally different."

She nods as she swallows. "It's excellent, Cole."

I preen at her words. I love cooking for people, and I wish I got to do it more often. Bailey comes to my place to eat sometimes, and I have family dinner once a month, but cooking for Rhiannon feels especially satisfying for some reason.

"Let me see your phone." I put my hand out with my palm up.

Rhia's eyes narrow over the top of her grilled cheese. "Why?"

"I'm going to put my number in it. A real first date would involve a talking stage leading up to it. We need each others' numbers so we can text this week."

Rhia sets her sandwich down and digs into her pocket before pulling out a phone in a sleek black case. She holds it up between us but doesn't hand it to me right away.

"There have to be rules," she says, her expression serious.

"Okay," I reply. "Like what?"

"*No* dick pics," she implores in a way that makes me think this has been a big issue for her in the past.

"Rhiannon." I hang my head with a sigh. "I would have thought you'd realize by now that I'm not the type to send unsolicited photos of my penis. Solicited ones…that's another story. But, yes, I agree to that rule."

Rhia studies me for a moment. "Is that something women have asked you for before?"

I grin widely at her. Rhia has this air of naivety that doesn't jive with her chosen career, and the juxtaposition is downright charming. "A few times," I respond honestly.

Her lips part in surprise. "Oh. Well, you won't be getting that request from me."

I nod, though I'm not totally confident she won't eventually change her mind on that one. "Noted. Any other rules I should know about?"

Rhia chews on her lip. "That's all I can think of for now."

"Great," I reply. "Then I'll text you in the morning."

"Are you leaving?" she asks, a hint of disappointment in her voice.

"Do you need anything else?" I ask. She seems a lot less tipsy than she was when we arrived at her apartment, so I'm not worried about her getting herself to bed. And I'm afraid if I stay here too much longer, I'll be tempted to make a move that Rhia isn't ready for. If I did something foolish, like try to kiss her, she could get spooked and call off our date, and that's the last thing I want.

"No," Rhia says. "You've done so much for me tonight—and these past few weeks. Thank you, Cole."

Her genuine gratitude spreads warmth in my chest. I walk around the table, planning to give Rhia a casual little side hug while she's in her seat, but she stands and wraps her arms around me instead. I stand frozen for a beat before hugging her back, tucking my nose into her hair to smell its floral scent.

"You're welcome, Rhia," I reply. "I'll talk to you tomorrow," I add as I pull away and head for the door, a secret smile stretching across my face.

CHAPTER 12
RHIANNON

Cole: Good morning. How are you feeling?

Rhia: Pretty good, actually. I think the water and grilled cheese staved off the hangover I may have gotten otherwise.

Cole: Good to hear. I've been thinking about our date.

Rhia: Yeah? Want to clue me in?

Cole: How do you feel about mini golf?

Rhia: I feel like I suck at it.

Cole: That's ok, I can teach you ;)

Rhia: Fine. I guess it's better than some other alternatives. When do you want to go?

Cole: I'm off tomorrow…

Rhia: Works for me.

Cole: I'll pick you up around five?

Rhia: See you then.

'm lounging on the couch the next afternoon, still in the pale-pink silk pajama set I wore to bed, when there's a knock on my door. I look out the peephole to find Hannah standing there, holding a bag from the gas station nearby.

I open the door, and she looks me up and down, taking in my pajamas and messy bedhead. I was up late writing—or trying to write—so I slept in. When I got up at noon, I made myself some food then sat on the couch and got sucked into social media. Not only is it something I enjoy, but social media is a vital part of my marketing strategy for my books, so it's important that I stay up to date on trends.

"*Why* aren't you getting ready for your date?" Hannah asks as she barges past me, tossing her bag onto my kitchen table and spilling out a few cans of seltzer and a variety of candy, including my favorite sour gummy worms, which I spot right away.

"It's not like it's a *real* date," I reply as I snatch a bag of gummy worms, tearing it open and fishing out a blue one.

"But you're supposed to be treating it like one," Hannah says.

I sink my teeth into the fat, soft worm, promptly beheading it. "I guess so." I shrug. "I'm not worried about impressing Cole, though."

Hannah's brow cinches. "Don't you think he's hot?" she asks, knowing damn well that I do. I've expressed that fact to her on multiple occasions, and I may have drunk texted her the other night about how excited I was that Cole asked me out.

"Of course," I reply. "But this is just a practice date to fulfill a promise I made to Jodi." I stare Hannah down with what I hope is a menacing gaze. "And nothing else."

She pops a lemon candy into her mouth. "Huh. You're usually the one romanticizing everyone else's relationships, but now that it's *you*, you can't even see it."

"What are you talking about?" I ask.

"He likes you," Hannah replies as if it's obvious. "Yes, he's trying to help you out, but he asked you out because he *likes* you."

"Why would he like me?" I ask, biting hard into another gummy worm and severing it in half. "He's a hot, confident, flirtatious bartender, and I'm an anxious, inexperienced, reclusive romance author. In no world would he be interested in someone like me."

Hannah's eyes narrow. "I think you forgot to add some of your positive qualities in there. You're also a talented, thoughtful, sexy goddess who any man would be lucky to have by his side."

I can't help but smile at my best friend. She sounds like Jodi now. The two of them insist on boosting my ego, but I really don't want to dive into a deep conversation about my insecurities right now.

"You know, I really do have to get ready for this date," I say. "I might not feel the need to look my absolute best, but I definitely can't go out looking like this." I gesture down at my pajamas.

"Let's go, then," Hannah says, getting up to lead the way to my bedroom, her red ponytail swishing behind her.

"You going to style me?" I ask as I follow behind her.

Hannah huffs out a laugh as she sits on my bed. "You're the beauty guru. I'm just here for moral support."

"I was thinking about this." I pull an army-green dress from my closet and drape it over my bed. It will show off my legs but not enough that I'll flash Cole while bending down to pick up a golf ball. "Paired with this." I layer the dress with a dark denim jacket that should be enough to ward off the chill of this early fall evening.

"Cute." Hannah nods her approval. "What about shoes?"

I dig through the bottom of my closet until I find the trendy white sneakers I was thinking of pairing with the outfit. "We're golfing, so I want to be comfortable," I explain.

"I like it." Hannah lies back on her side, propping her head on her hand as she watches me continue to put together my outfit.

I sift through my lingerie drawer for a matching pair. I haven't done laundry in a bit, but there's a gorgeous navy-blue set I know I haven't worn in a while that must be somewhere in here. Finally, I pull out the lacy bra and barely there panties I was looking for.

"A little racy for just a practice date, hmm?" Hannah murmurs. When I glance over at her, she's wearing a shit-eating grin. *Good Lord.* Now I know why she was always annoyed when I poked at her about her crush on Caleb.

"You know I always wear lingerie like this," I chide. "In fact, I've worn it plenty of times when we've hung out, and I've never made a move on *you*, have I?"

Hannah chuckles. "Touché. You're gonna look hot."

I snatch up each article of clothing and whisk it off to the bathroom to get ready. "I know."

Hannah sits on the closed toilet while I blow out my hair after getting dressed. We're mostly silent, since it's difficult to be heard over the blow dryer. Afterward, she hugs me goodbye and wishes me luck before heading out. All that's left to do is put on makeup and jewelry, but without Hannah to keep me on task, I get distracted by my phone. The black hole of scrolling social media gets me every time.

By the time I remember I'm supposed to be getting ready, it's four-thirty, and I still don't have any makeup or jewelry on. I rush through a no-makeup makeup look (oh, the joys of being a woman) that consists of foundation, a little blush and high-lighter, mascara, and lip gloss. I'm clasping the back of a silver hoop earring when I hear a knock at my door.

"Coming!" I shout as I hastily shove the second earring in.

I'm clasping it with one hand as I pull open the door with the other. "Hi," I breathe as I'm greeted by the sight of Cole in a dark-blue flannel shirt, holding a bouquet of a dozen red roses in his fist.

"Hey, gorgeous," Cole says, his gaze raking over me. I'd say that heat flares in his eyes momentarily if I didn't know better. He presses the bouquet of flowers to my chest, prompting me to take it.

"What are these?" I ask as I accept the bouquet.

"A million dollars," he replies sarcastically as he enters the apartment.

"No one's ever given me flowers before," I say without thinking.

Cole looks at me, a slight frown tugging at his lips. "That's a damn shame, but I will say I'm honored to be the first."

I just stand there, holding the flowers, my brain trying to compute this moment. A dozen roses feels very romantic. And expensive. Why bother wasting that kind of gesture on me? Although, he *is* supposedly trying to show me what a first date is supposed to be like, so maybe he's simply pulling out all the stops.

"Typically, people put flowers in water so they don't die," Cole says when I still don't move.

"Sorry, yeah," I say with a shake of my head. I carry the bouquet to the kitchen and fill a large glass with water, transferring the flowers into it. I set it on my kitchen counter and admire it for a moment.

"They're beautiful," I tell Cole. "Thank you."

"You're welcome," he replies. "Are you ready to get going?"

"Sure." I grab my bag and allow Cole to lead me out to his car. The mini golf place he picked is only about ten minutes away, and we catch up on the way over. He tells me how he had lunch with his sister today and how he feels like she's been cagey lately. He wonders if she might be dating someone and hiding it from him.

"I'm sure she'll talk to you about it when she's ready," I tell him, remembering how he admitted to being very protective of his sister. She probably just wants to date in private for a bit before unleashing her big, bad older brother on the poor guy.

"I guess." Cole's hands tighten on the steering wheel. "I just don't want her to get hurt."

"That's sweet," I say. As much as it must annoy his sister that he's overprotective, I have to admit that it's an attractive quality.

"Anyway, how was your day?" he asks.

"Oh, fine," I reply, unwilling to tell him I spent most of it getting ready for this date. "I'm ready to kick your ass at mini golf."

"Yeah?" he asks with a chuckle. "Bold words coming from someone who said they suck at it."

"I'm a quick study," I reply as we pull into the parking lot.

"We'll see about that," Cole says in a tone that makes me think he's confident he'll win. He probably will, but it's fun to tease him while I still have a chance. Once he wallops me, the teasing privileges will be all his.

Cole parks and walks around the car to open my door for me, even going as far as to help me out of the car with a hand on my arm. Then, he slips his hand down to clasp with mine, beginning to lead me toward the building where we'll pick up our clubs and balls.

"What are you doing?" I ask, trying to tug my hand out of his. He doesn't let go.

"Holding your hand." He doesn't add a *duh*, but it's implied.

"It's a little soon for hand holding," I point out. "Isn't that, like, at least a second-date thing?"

Cole squeezes my hand in his. "Not when you're on a date with *me*."

I would complain further, but honestly, I like the feeling of his hand encapsulating mine. The pressure brings a sense of calm. It feels like he's *got* me. So, I let him guide me into the shop by the hand. Cole picks the blue ball, and I choose orange. I bite back the joke I want to make about "blue balls" because it's not very ladylike, and I'm *trying* to practice making a good impression.

We head to the first hole, and Cole tees up first, placing his ball on the starting dot. He looks toward the hole, back down at his ball, then toward the hole again before raising his club back in the air. With one smooth stroke, his ball sails toward the hole and plunks right in, circling around a few times before stilling. This must be the golf equivalent of nothing but net.

My jaw drops. I'd expected him to be good, but I thought he'd at least need some warm-up time or something.

Cole chuckles as he takes in my expression. "Still think you're gonna kick my ass?"

"I'm sure as hell going to try." I march up to the starting dot and place my ball on it, getting into position with my club. I stick my ass out a little and lean forward like I've seen most golfers do when they prepare for a shot. Out of the corner of my eye, I catch Cole shift, and I wonder if he likes what he sees. Maybe that would be the key to winning—distracting him with my feminine charms.

My hopes of ever winning are dashed when I take my shot and the ball flies right past the hole, hitting the small wooden barrier and bouncing out of the course. With a huff, I chase it until it stops in a small bush, snatching it up before rejoining Cole. He's holding the back of his hand to his mouth, but I don't miss the amused grin behind it.

"Don't even start," I warn him.

Cole takes a moment to compose himself before speaking. "I was just going to suggest going a little softer next time."

I shoot him a glare. "Obviously." I put my ball back on the starting dot and reset myself, rolling out my shoulders and mentally judging the distance to the hole. After a deep breath, I take my shot.

"Why choose mini golf for a date anyway?" I whine when the ball rolls halfway to the hole then slides down a slope to the left into a pit that it'll be a bitch to get it out of. At least it stayed inside the course this time, I guess.

"You really want to know?" Cole asks, one brow cocked and a twinkle in his eye.

Based on that reaction, now I *really* want to know.

CHAPTER 13
COLE

Rhia nods eagerly in response to my question.

I point to her ball, which is hopelessly entrenched in a small valley. "Keep going and I'll tell you."

She frowns fiercely but walks over to her ball and begins using small strokes to coax it back onto flat ground.

"Mini golf is the perfect first date because it has a solid start and end time," I explain. "If things are going well, you can always extend the date with another activity, but if they *aren't* going well, then you know you just have to make it to the last hole."

"That makes sense. Smart," Rhia says. She's finally gotten her ball within a few feet of the hole, and she's concentrating so hard that she's sticking her tongue out. It's fucking adorable. Before I can get to my next point, she takes the shot that finally sinks her ball into the hole. At this point, I've lost count of how many strokes she's taken.

Rhia lets out a squeal. "Oh my God!" she exclaims, literally jumping for joy at the sight of her ball in the hole.

"Nicely done," I say with a laugh. "Only seventeen more holes to go."

Rhia must still be running on the ecstasy of completing the

first hole, because she doesn't sass me as she retrieves her ball, and we head to the next one.

"Mini golf is also a good date because it gives you a natural subject to discuss," I say as I set up my shot. "Sometimes it's hard to come up with stuff to talk about, especially at the beginning of a date. Once you get past the boring stuff like your job and where you grew up, you need something to break the ice. If you're doing an activity like mini golf, you can talk about how much or little you've played it in your life. Maybe you always used to do it on family vacations, and you have a funny story to share about it. It gives you something to talk about that will organically lead to conversations about other topics like what sports you've played or your family and childhood." It takes me two strokes this time, but I maneuver my ball into the hole easily once again.

"How did you become such a dating guru?" Rhia asks as she sets her ball at the starting dot.

"Lots of practice," I reply.

She nods, and it almost looks like a sad movement. "Right," she says, and I wonder if she's lamenting her lack of dating experience. It's nothing to be ashamed of, but I think she feels insecure about it. If I can do one thing tonight, it's to show her a great first date. She needs something to look back on to bolster her confidence.

Rhia's initial shot isn't horrendous, but it's clearly going to take her quite a few strokes again.

I follow her to where her ball sits off to the right of the hole.

"You want to know the last reason?" I ask.

"Please." Rhia begins positioning herself behind the ball but freezes as I come up behind her, resting one hand atop hers on the club.

"May I?" I ask.

"Uh…sure," she says, her body tense as I wrap my other arm around her, covering both of her hands with mine on the club. Her soft backside presses into the front seam of my jeans.

I'm not sure if either of us is breathing as I notch my head beside hers, my mouth resting right by her ear. "Mini golf offers the perfect opportunity to touch your date," I say in a low voice, "while simultaneously teaching them."

"Oh," Rhia breathes as I guide the club back and gently swing it with the perfect amount of force to nudge the ball right into the hole. We stand there for a moment, our hands still joined on the club, as it sinks in that this hole is over, and it's time to move on.

I release Rhia, breaking the magic, and scoop her ball out of the hole, handing it to her.

"The old touch and teach, huh?" she jokes once she's come out of her stupor.

Rhia accepts her ball back, and I flash her my most charming grin. "Works every time."

Holes three through five go about the same as their predecessors—painfully slowly if Rhia is left to her own devices, achingly tortuous if I press my body close to hers to help her with her swing. Rhia's hair smells like the roses I gave her earlier this evening, and her body feels like it was made to fit with mine. She's so soft where I'm working overtime *not* to get hard.

On hole six, Rhia gets overzealous again, shooting her ball with an overabundance of force. We both watch in horror as it pings off a metal pole and soars through the air, right into the rushing water that winds throughout the course.

"Shit," I mutter, knowing that if someone doesn't grab it quickly, her ball will be washed away for good. I hurry after it, navigating around small shrubs, rocks, and even a couple of toddlers to get to the ball. Luckily, its journey gets stalled by a strategically placed windmill. I end up face down on the ground, my arm stretched across the expanse of water, barely able to grasp the ball with the tips of my fingers. I finally fish it toward myself and retrieve it, tucking it into my chest like an infant.

"My hero," Rhia gushes sarcastically as I jog up to her, presenting her with the ball as she claps at my heroics.

"Do you think we should call it?" I ask, glancing around at the eleven holes we have left to play. Given how things have gone so far, it's going to be a long night if we finish out this whole course.

"After everything you just went through to get this back?" Rhia holds her orange ball in the air. "And what about what you said about mini golf having a solid end time? Are you giving up on me early?"

"I'm not trying to end the date," I assure her. "Just both of our suffering."

She thwacks my upper arm with the back of her hand.

"Why don't we return our clubs and balls and get some food?" I suggest.

Rhia's plump lips pull into a pout, but I think she's secretly relieved, because she gives in easily. "I think I saw that they have ice cream here."

"They do." I tuck my club into my elbow and grab her hand. "Let's go."

We return the golf equipment and venture over to the ice cream counter, where Rhia's eyes widen like a little kid's.

"What's your favorite flavor?" I ask.

She scans the extensive menu. "I usually just stick with chocolate chip."

"I'm thinking about trying something new," I reply. This place is known for its fantastical flavors, like banana cream pie, cinnamon raisin crunch, or the exotic but intriguing ghost pepper peach. In the end, I settle on "birthday bear"—a birthday cake base filled with rainbow gummy bears. Was it probably created for three-year-olds? Sure. Will I absolutely devour it despite that? You bet.

We order our ice cream, which I insist on paying for, and find a bench in a quiet corner beneath some trees. It's not too busy since it's a weeknight in the fall, but there are some families here having ice cream. Luckily, they've gravitated toward a cluster of picnic tables a distance away.

"How is it?" Rhia asks after I take my first bite.

"Wicked good," I reply, licking a bit off my upper lip. "Want a taste?"

Rhia blinks at me, her gaze on the spot where my tongue just was. She nods. "Sure."

I hold my cone out to her and watch as she licks up some ice cream, using her tongue to dig out a blue gummy bear. Her gaze meets mine just as she's closing her lips, and I swallow hard.

Rhia pulls back, letting out a moan as she tastes the ice cream.

"Good, right?" I ask.

"*Really* good," she replies, looking down at her chocolate chip cone with disappointment.

"Want to trade?" She clearly regrets her safe choice, and this date is supposed to be her perfect night.

Rhia's nose scrunches in confusion. "But I thought you liked it?"

"I do. But I want you to have it if you'd prefer it over what you got."

Her confusion deepens, her brow crinkling. "Why?"

"Because I want to make you happy."

Her eyes soften. "I *am* happy, Cole. I'm having a really good time tonight."

"Good." I gently take the chocolate chip cone from her hand and replace it with the birthday bear one. "Then this will only make it better."

She stares at me for a moment. It looks like she's debating arguing with me, but in the end, she accepts the ice cream, digging in with a vengeance.

I smile in satisfaction as she devours her treat. I'm perfectly happy eating chocolate chip, and watching Rhia enjoy something she was too hesitant to ask for but clearly enjoys tickles something within me.

It's long past dark by the time we finish our ice cream and I lead Rhia back to my car. I don't really want to take her home, even though this is the natural end to our date. Our casual conversation revealed so much I didn't know about her, like the fact that she loves gummy candy, she's a cat person, and she unironically believes in astrology. I find Rhia fascinating, and I want to keep getting to know her, but I'm not sure what that looks like after tonight, when her challenge is complete.

I park outside of Rhia's building and immediately exit my car, cutting off any expectation that we'll say goodbye right here. I need more time. I walk Rhia to her door, where she turns to face me.

"Thank you for tonight." She grins as she gazes up at me. "I had a lot of fun."

"Me too," I reply, taking in her content expression and relaxed body language. It took her a while to get to this point, where she feels this comfortable on a date, and *I'm* the one who got her there. That makes pride flare in my chest, but it's quickly overtaken by apprehension. Is this it? My one shot at a date with Rhiannon? After this, we go back to occasionally chatting when she comes into my bar? I'm not sure if I can live with that.

I use a finger to tuck one side of Rhia's hair behind her ear. "Can I ask you something?"

A little shiver moves through her at my touch. "Sure."

I let my hand fall to her shoulder, kneading it like I know she likes. "Do you ever kiss on the first date?" I ask, my voice hoarser than I intend it to be.

Rhia's eyes widen a bit. "Um…not usually."

I feel tension trying to creep into her shoulders, so I lift my other hand to her other one and continue massaging gently.

"You don't have to," I say, "but I really want to kiss you right now."

In a matter of moments, my touch has her eyes lowered to half mast, looking drugged with lust. Yeah, she wants this, even if she won't admit it to herself.

"You do?" she asks.

I move one of my hands to the back of her neck. "I really, really do."

"Okay." She tips her head back even more as I move in closer to her. I look into her deep brown eyes, making sure I see nothing but desire in them, before lowering my mouth to hers. Her lips are soft and hesitant beneath mine at first, but there's an undercurrent of need pulsing through our kiss. It vibrates beneath my skin every time she's near me, but now that we're actually connected, that need burns brighter than ever before.

Rhia's hands land on my back, pulling my body flush to hers as any hint of timidity quickly vanishes. I massage the back of her neck with that same pressure I used on her shoulders, pulling a moan from deep within her throat. The sound is so sexy I want to die.

I trace my tongue across Rhia's lips, and she parts them, inviting me in. I accept her invitation with enthusiasm, plunging my tongue into her mouth and tangling it with hers. For someone who I'd guess doesn't have a lot of experience with kissing, Rhia is excellent at it. I may be leading, but she follows beautifully. I swallow another moan from her as my tongue slides against hers.

When we eventually part for more than a stolen breath here or there, I drop my forehead against Rhia's. My breath comes out in pants, but I've never been more satisfied. At the beginning of the night, I never would have guessed that Rhia would let me kiss her, but I'm goddamn grateful that she did.

"So." I try to sound casual. "Does that earn me a second date?"

I can feel Rhia's brows wrinkle beneath mine. "Do you *want* a second date?"

"Hell yeah," I reply, pulling back to catch her gaze. Her pupils are wide, her eyes slightly glazed.

"But...why?" she asks, her lashes fluttering in confusion.

I smooth a hand over her hair. "Because I had fun tonight.

And you deserve to know what a good second date is like just as much as you deserved a good first one."

Rhia blinks, clearly surprised by my proposition.

"This weekend?" I suggest, desperately hoping to nail down a time to see her again.

"Okay," she replies slowly, as if still computing the idea.

"Great." I drop a kiss on her forehead before she can take back her acceptance. "I'll text you the plans." I take one last look at her wide eyes and messy hair, loving her state of dishevelment. "Goodnight, Rhiannon," I rasp before turning to walk away, already looking forward to the next time I'll see her.

CHAPTER 14
RHIANNON

Veronica shuddered as Damien grew nearer and nearer, his hulking back blocking her view of the worst of it. Despite Damien's bodily blockade, Veronica could still hear their nasty shouts. The paparazzi had been hounding her for weeks, all of them vying for the flashiest shot of the disgraced heiress. In the wake of her tell-all book announcement, it seemed like everyone wanted a piece of her—except the one person she wished would.

Damien.

Her faithful bodyguard was frustratingly distant, his proverbial shields seemingly impenetrable. While Damien was always close by in proximity, he kept just enough distance emotionally to have her questioning his true feelings.

Veronica raised her arm almost straight up to tap Damien on his shoulder. "I think I'd like to go home now," she announced.

Damien grunted in response. "Working on it," he added as an afterthought.

Veronica stretched up on her tiptoes so he could hear her whisper, "Take me home, Damien."

Her bodyguard spun abruptly to face her, his face expressionless, save for the flicker in his ice-blue eyes.

"As you wish."

Cole: Thoughts on rented shoes?

> Rhia: Good morning to you too.

Cole: LOL. Good morning, gorgeous.

Cole: So, rented shoes? Yay or nay?

> Rhia: I guess it depends on why I'd be renting shoes…

Cole: Was thinking bowling or roller skating for our next date.

> Rhia: I see. I'll be terrible at either, but I'm cool with rented shoes.

Cole: Don't worry, gorgeous. I'll teach you.

> Rhia: Yeah, because that went so well with the mini golf. I'm pretty sure I left a permanent ding on the windmill at hole #4.

Cole: It adds character.

> Rhia: I'm afraid of what I could do with a bowling ball.

Cole: Skating it is.

"So," Hannah drawls around a sip of her iced caramel latte. "How did the big date go?"

We're sitting at Waffee—her favorite coffee shop where every single food item is put through a waffle press—having lunch. I went for a green tea since coffee isn't always my friend. Anxiety and caffeine don't tend to play nicely together, and anything more than a single shot of espresso gives me the jitters.

"Can you please stop calling it that? It was *not* a big deal," I insist, stabbing a waffle-shaped crouton with my fork. Yes, even the croutons in Waffee's salads come in the shape of tiny little waffles.

One of Hannah's brows arches. "Then why are you acting so weird about it?"

I wash down the crouton with a sip of tea. "I'm not acting weird."

"Rhiannon, you haven't asked about Caleb's and my sex life once since we sat down fifteen minutes ago. That's got to be some type of record for you."

I almost choke on my drink as a laugh spills out of me. She's not wrong. Ever since Hannah started seeing Caleb, I've grilled her about their relationship almost every time we're together. I suppose some would say I've been living vicariously through her love life. I've always been fascinated by relationships, sex, and love.

I think that fascination is what led to my love of story. Stories provide a glimpse into others' realities, giving us the opportunity to experience a million different lives. And when you're not necessarily living the story you'd like to be, that opportunity is invaluable.

"How *is* your sex life?" I ask in a feeble attempt to shift the conversation. "Still getting that good dick?"

Hannah's gaze quickly scans our periphery to make sure no one overheard then narrows on me. "I am, in fact," she replies in a hushed tone. "But I'm more interested in hearing about you and Cole. How was mini golf? Did you guys hang out for long? Did he score a hole in one?" she asks, wiggling her brows.

I shrug nonchalantly. "Golf was…fine. I sucked at it, and Cole was great. We got ice cream after and chatted. Then he took me home and…he kissed me goodnight."

Hannah's eyes widen comically. "He kissed you?"

My cheeks warm, and I can't help the shy grin that stretches over my lips. "Yeah. I wasn't expecting it at all. But it was…

fantastic." I recall the feeling of Cole's lips on mine while his big, strong hands kneaded the back of my neck. The hold felt possessive, though it could have just been to give him better leverage. I wonder what it would have felt like for his hand to travel to the front, circling my throat...

"Rhia, this is huge," Hannah says. "Cole is the first guy you've kissed in years, right?"

I nod. Hannah is well aware of how rare it is for me to be comfortable enough to let someone kiss me. She saw me through my boy crazy high school years, when I collected crushes like trading cards but never had the courage to do anything about them. She witnessed my foray into the dating world in college, my incredibly brief fling with Eric, and most recently, my epic failure with online dating. She knows this is a big deal for me.

"I usually spend so much of real dates nervous about whether or not he'll try to kiss me," I tell her. "If we'll be compatible, if I'll be good at it... With Cole, I wasn't expecting anything, so there wasn't time to be anxious about it, and then... it just happened, and it was really, really good, Hannah," I gush.

I haven't had much practice kissing, but I think our kiss was pretty damn great. Given the hardness I briefly felt against my stomach toward the end of it, I'd say Cole thought so too.

Hannah beams at me, genuine happiness radiating from her expression. "I'm so thrilled for you, Rhia. Are you guys going to hang out again?"

"He wants to go roller skating this weekend," I reply. "He said I deserve to know what a good second date is like too."

Hannah's smile is contagious. "He sounds really sweet."

I grin as I think back to the gentle way Cole soothed me during my panic attack, how he switched ice cream flavors with me, and his general kindness during every interaction we've had.

"He is," I agree. "I just wish... I wish it was all real, you know? He's so kind, and thoughtful, and generous, but it feels like he's doing everything out of pity for me. He sees me as this poor little loveless woman that he wants to help for whatever reason, and I'm afraid I could fall for his charm so easily. What if I never find a real prospect as good as him once he decides to stop humoring me? I just have to live with having had a few incredible dates with a wonderful guy and then never finding anything that measures up ever again? Maybe I should stop this before I get in too deep."

"Rhia." Hannah waits for me to meet her gaze, and I find disapproval in her eyes.

"I'm spiraling, aren't I?" I ask sheepishly.

Hannah holds up her hand, her thumb and index finger hovering about an inch apart. "Little bit. Look, I know it's hard for you not to jump to a million conclusions in your head, but I really think you should just enjoy whatever this thing is with Cole. You clearly really like him, and you're having fun with whatever this is, so why not just enjoy it while it lasts? And I know you're having trouble believing this, but I think there's more to his actions than pity."

My heart perks up a little at the thought. "You really think so?"

Hannah nods. "He crossed over from 'just a good guy' territory to 'good guy who has a crush on you' when he asked you out. I can see him protecting you from creepy dates and helping you through a panic attack out of the goodness of his heart, but no one agrees to show someone what a good date is like, flirts with them the entire time, and then kisses them at the end unless they feel something for them."

She has a point. I place my elbow on the table and rest my chin on my fist. "I haven't let myself have a real crush in so long."

Sure, I dream about being in a relationship all the time, but I haven't allowed myself to really focus my attention on one person since I was delusional enough to believe my feelings might actually be reciprocated, and that ended many years ago after a lifetime of disappointment.

"You deserve to let yourself have one," Hannah says. "Crushes are fun. Don't think too far ahead—no doodling your first name with his last one or picking out your wedding dress—just try to live in the moment and enjoy it."

Easier said than done when your brain constantly barrages you with potential problems and "what ifs," but I respond with an earnest, "I'll try."

there's a little skip in my step when I leave Waffee, entirely fueled by the idea that a man like Cole could *actually* like me. Hannah's right—no one would go to all the trouble Cole has for some random stranger they don't care about.

Marty's is only a few blocks away from here, so I decide to pop in and see if Cole is working just because I want to see his face, hear his voice. We have our date scheduled for Saturday, but waiting that long to lay eyes on him now seems like an impossible burden.

I don't spot Cole right away when I enter, so I sit down and order a sparkling water from Mac, the karaoke MC, who's currently working the bar. He's wearing a face-splitting grin for reasons I can't quite figure out, and he's studying me a little too intensely.

"Is, uh…is Cole working today?" I ask, partially because I want to know and partially to get this guy to stop looking at me like he is.

"I thought you'd never ask," Mac murmurs before sidestepping to the edge of the bar. "Cole, your girl is here," he calls out toward the back office.

My heart flips at his words.

Cole saunters out a few moments later. "Hey, gorgeous," he greets me with a wide grin. That smile alone could probably get him any girl he wants.

"I'm heading to the bathroom. You're on," Mac tells Cole with a pat on his back.

Cole nods and leans on the bar by me. "What are you doing here?" he asks, still wearing that panty-melting smile.

"I was in the area," I say. "Hannah loves that place, Waffee, down the street."

Cole sticks his bottom lip out. "So you didn't make a special trip just to see me?"

I take a sip of my water to suppress a giggle. "You're not *that* special."

Cole sticks his lip out farther and bats his eyelashes, which are much too long and pretty to be wasted on a guy.

A laugh bubbles out of me. "Okay, fine, scratch what I said. I totally came out today just to see you."

Cole breaks into a grin. "Much better."

I cross my legs beneath the bar. "So, are we still on for Saturday?"

"Hell yeah. Wouldn't miss it," Cole replies as two women sit down at the other end of the bar. "Hold tight," he tells me as he steps over to help them.

"Hey, beautiful," Cole greets one of the women with the same huge smile he just gave me, and the happy little bubble I floated in here on instantly pops, shattering into a million shards of disappointment.

I don't know what made me think Cole would stop flirting with other customers. That very first night I met him, he was calling all his female customers by pet names. It's part of his charm, but with the way my feelings for him have grown lately, it stings to hear him use a term of endearment with another woman.

It also cements my understanding that none of this is real for him. Cole isn't harboring some sort of secret crush on me, as I'm starting to realize I am for him. He's simply a fun guy who's trying to show a pitiful woman a good time. End of story.

My conversation with Hannah gave me a seed of hope that

Cole might actually be interested in me, but hope is a dangerous thing. Because once you have hope that something will happen, it makes it that much worse when it doesn't.

I toy with the idea of leaving right then. I could go home and bury my sorrows in a tub of ice cream with the two men who will never let me down—Ben and Jerry. I could cancel my upcoming date with Cole and pretend like this weird little relationship never happened. Eventually, it would become a blip on my radar, a time period I look back on with amusement.

But another thing that Hannah said comes to mind. She told me to enjoy whatever this is with Cole, regardless of what it may or may not turn into. And I *deserve* to enjoy this, goddamnit. The truth is I'm having more fun with Cole than I've had with any guy in a long time. I can continue having fun with him. I just need to cool it with all the mushy feelings.

Cole hands the two women their drinks and heads back toward me. I grasp for something to talk about that's nowhere remotely near my thoughts. There's a poster sitting on the bar top by me.

"An open mic night?" I ask, reading the headline.

"Yeah." Cole whips a rag out of his back pocket and polishes a spot on the bar. "Next Thursday. You should come. My sister is going to be performing. She's pretty amazing."

"I'd love to hear her," I reply honestly, though my tone sounds doubtful as thoughts of the last event I attended at the bar flood my brain.

"It won't be as chaotic as karaoke night," Cole promises. "We realized we need to tone down the events a bit after Barry tried to crowd surf later that night and got dropped. He hurt his arm pretty badly. Luckily, it wasn't broken or anything, but it could have been way worse. He's a chill guy, so he didn't try to sue us or anything, but yeah. No more rowdy crowds." Cole flashes me his most charming smile. "And you have an open invitation to the back office if things *do* get out of hand."

It takes me a moment to process since the visual of the

middle-aged man with gray hair and a beer belly crowd surfing is so potent. Cole wants me to meet his sister and offered me a place to retreat in case of a panic attack, yet just moments ago, he was flirting with a woman a few feet away. The mixed messages I'm receiving are making me dizzy.

"I'll think about it," I say. I need to get out of here before my brain explodes with confusion. "I'm going to get going, but I'll see you this weekend?" My words come out as a question, as if I need to confirm yet again that he does actually want to see me. I instantly loathe the undercurrent of insecurity in my voice.

"Totally," Cole replies. "I'm glad you stopped by. You made my day."

"Really?"

"Yeah." He reaches for my hand, brushing his thumb over mine. "I'm always happy to see you."

His words seem so genuine, but now I wonder if this is just another line.

"I'm always happy to see you too." I get off my stool, not allowing myself to get sucked into his charm. "I'll see you Saturday."

"Can't wait."

I walk away from Cole more confused than ever, and despite his blatant flirting with other women right in front of me, I'm afraid that seed of hope that Hannah planted still hasn't died.

CHAPTER 15
COLE

When I pick dates, I do it with purpose. As I explained to Rhia when we went golfing, I like dates where we're *doing* something. Sitting silently together at a movie doesn't give you the opportunity to learn more about a person, and honestly, I just find it plain boring.

Although, come to think of it, I can't imagine anything being boring with Rhia by my side. I'd probably enjoy all those mundane dates—like movies or dinner—if they were with *her*.

Regardless, I'm hoping skating will be a hit.

Rhia's wearing tight jeans and a sweater that keeps falling off of one shoulder, making me want to tug it back into place so no one else gets to see her looking a little messy. I only restrain myself because I like the peek of pale skin it gives me. We've just grabbed our skates from the rental window, and we're sitting on a bench to try them on. My feet slide right into the twelves I asked for, but I watch as Rhia tries to stuff one foot into her sevens.

"Too small?" I ask when she winces.

"I don't think so." She's staring down at her skates like they're adversaries.

"Why don't you ask to try on a half size up?"

"I don't want to bother them. These will be fine." She starts to tie up the skate, but I place my hand over hers.

"If they're too tight, you're going to get gnarly blisters. And you wouldn't be bothering them. They're literally getting paid to do this."

Rhia seems to shrink on the bench, and it's clear to me that she's not going to ask for help.

"I'll exchange them for you," I offer.

Her eyes find mine, and I soak up the gratitude in them. "You will?"

"Sure."

Before she can refute, I gently pick up one of Rhia's feet and work the skate off of it slowly so I don't hurt her. She watches as I do the same to her other foot.

"Be right back." I head over to the rental counter and wait in the short line until I reach the front and exchange Rhia's skates for a seven-and-a-half. The whole process takes under three minutes. When I return, Rhia's wearing a sheepish grin and pink-tinged cheeks.

"Thank you," she says softly, reaching for the new pair of skates.

"Uh-uh," I tell her, dropping to my knees in front of her. "I'm putting these on you so I can see if they fit properly. And if they don't, I'm bringing them back and exchanging them again."

I'm afraid if I don't do this, she'll wind up skating in the wrong size and hurting herself. While I wouldn't be opposed to treating her to a foot massage later, the idea of Rhia being in pain is unbearable to me. I'm pretty sure I'd do just about anything to avoid it.

Rhia is patient enough as I slide the first one on, but then she starts fidgeting, shifting her weight around impatiently.

I place a hand on her thigh to halt her jiggling leg. My touch instantly freezes her entire body. "Almost done," I assure her as I slide the second skate on. When I'm finished tying the laces, I glance up at her. Her cheeks are stained with the prettiest blush, her plush lips pressed tightly together.

"There." I give Rhia's thigh a pat before standing and offering her my hand to help her up. She takes it, her grip tightening as she slowly rises from the bench. I begin leading her toward the rink, but the second she starts to move, she also starts to fall. She lets out a surprised squeak, grabbing for me with her other hand. It catches a handful of my t-shirt, and now she's holding on to me for dear life.

"You okay?" I steady her with a hand on her hip.

"I...I think so." She releases my shirt and shuffles her feet a few times, testing out her balance.

"Have you ever skated before?"

"I've ice skated," Rhia huffs. "This can't be that different."

Taking both of her hands in mine, I tug her toward the entrance to the rink. All she has to do is hang on for the ride.

"That's more similar to roller blading, when the wheels are all in one line," I explain. "Having the wheels side by side takes a bit of getting used to. You'll get it."

Rhia glances around the rink, where people of all ages are zooming around on their skates like it's second nature.

"If you say so," she mutters as we cross the threshold into the rink. She lets go of me as soon as she's able to grab onto the wall. I mourn the loss of her touch as she begins taking tentative glides forward.

"Good job," I tell her as she picks up a bit of speed. And by speed, I mean a pace faster than an elderly turtle with a broken leg, but it's an improvement nonetheless.

Rhia watches as I skate effortlessly around her while she continues her slow journey. "How did you learn to skate so well?" she asks.

I scratch a spot behind my ear. "My mom couldn't afford a car when I was a kid, and there wasn't always money for the train. One day, I found a really cheap pair of skates at Goodwill, and I figured they would get me places faster than walking could, so I taught myself."

Rhia eyes me thoughtfully. "That was resourceful."

"I would have done just about anything to get away from my house back then," I admit.

She slows to a stop, anchoring herself with an iron grip on the wall. "That sucks, Cole."

"Yep," I reply, not really wanting to get further into it. I reach both of my hands out to her. "Why don't you try letting go of the wall?"

Rhia's brows knit together. "Are you sure? If I fall, I could take you down with me."

"If you fall, I'm going to catch you." I wave my hands, beckoning her toward me.

One hand at a time, Rhia releases her death grip on the wall and transfers it to me. Having her hands in mine eases a bit of the tension trickling down my spine.

"There you go," I encourage Rhia as she starts to glide forward.

"This is so unfair," she whines as I guide her at a slow but steady pace. "You know how to skate backward?"

"Once you master skating forward and you learn how to stop, I'll teach you that too."

Rhia's eyes spring wide, as if a thought just occurred to her. "Oh, God." She groans. "Is stopping hard?"

I chuff out a laugh. "Don't worry about that. You're not going fast enough to really need to know how to stop yet. There are different ways to do it, and we'll find what works for you."

Rhia nods, and I notice her shoulders soften slightly. I love that I have the ability to relieve her worries with my words.

"Want to take off the training wheels?" I ask, flexing my hands to test her grip. Rhia seems to have found her stride.

"Okay," she says, less panicked than I expected. She lets go of one of my hands, pauses to make sure she's balanced, and then releases the other. I hold my breath as she takes her first few strides all on her own. Pride grips my chest as I watch her light up.

"I'm doing it!" Rhia squeals, beaming at me. "This is amazing!" she adds as she picks up a bit of speed.

I'm about to warn her to slow down when one of her feet slips, and her leg shoots out from under her. I watch in horror as she flails like a baby giraffe that just discovered its legs, ultimately crumbling into a heap as she falls straight down onto her magnificent ass.

"Shit," I mutter as I kneel down beside her. "Are you alright?"

For a few grueling heartbeats, Rhia sits still on the ground, her veil of black hair covering her face so I can't see whether her features are twisted in pain or not. She lets out a breathy sound that I'm terrified is a sob until she whips her hair back with her hands, revealing an expression that's bursting with delight.

"What a rush!" she says.

I'm still inspecting her body for open wounds. "Did you hurt anything?" I ask. "Break anything?"

"I'm fine," Rhia replies, her eyes softening as she takes in my concerned expression. "My ego is a little wounded, but I'll recover."

"Maybe we should have sprung for the knee and elbow pads," I muse as I help her up.

"I don't think that's necessary." She secures my hand in hers. "Maybe I'll just keep holding on to you, if that's okay?"

I give her hand a squeeze. "More than okay."

We do a few laps around the rink at a mild pace, chuckling when an elementary-schooler laps us. I don't care at what speed we go. I'm just happy to be here with Rhia, talking and laughing and enjoying our evening. She's so easy to be with. It feels like I've known her a lot longer than I have, and she already knows me better than any woman other than my sister does.

I don't like to talk about growing up in poverty, living with food scarcity, or my mom's alcoholism, but I've told Rhia about all those things. There's still something that I *haven't* told her, but to be fair, I've never discussed *that* with anyone but Bailey.

A booming voice comes over the loudspeaker, announcing that it's time for the couples' skate. Children and their parents begin making their ways off the rink, making space for the couples present to have the spotlight. Rhia tugs at my hand as if trying to pull me toward the exit.

"What are you doing?" I demand.

"It's the couples' skate. We're not a couple."

"We're on a date," I remind her.

"Sure, but we're not…" she trails off, as if she's not sure how to end that sentence.

I fasten my fingers with hers. "No one here knows what we are," I say. *And I'm not so sure either*, I add silently to myself.

Rhia's brow furrows, but she continues skating along without further complaint. The opening beats of "Crazy in Love" by Beyoncé start bumping over the loudspeaker as we glide around the rink hand in hand. I observe some of the other couples, ranging from two teenagers that stop every few feet to make out obnoxiously to an older couple with graying hair and laugh lines that skates at a leisurely pace, her head resting on his shoulder as they skate in perfect sync. I feel like a total imposter among this crowd of people who are so clearly in love, but I also feel a seed of hope that I could be part of this group one day.

I've never really wanted that before—love, that is. I've spent so long looking out for myself and Bailey that having another person to worry about always seemed like a burden. But I've noticed that I worry about Rhiannon near constantly—wanting to make sure she's comfortable, that she's not panicky—and it doesn't feel burdensome at all. It's second nature to think of her needs, and I don't fully understand why that is. But it makes me think maybe I *could* love someone someday, and I could do it half decently.

It won't be Rhia. She deserves someone far better than me, and hopefully once I finish showing her what it's like to enjoy dating, she'll be able to go out there and find him. Maybe then I'll be able to find someone too. I just hope there's a woman out there who can hold a candle to Rhiannon James, because right now it seems highly unlikely that there is.

The song comes to a close just as we're passing the exit to the rink. Rhia grabs onto the wall, stopping us.

"Want to take a break?" I ask.

She nods. "I think I'm all skated out for today."

We head back to the bench to remove our skates, and I'm shocked to look at my watch and find that an hour has passed. I completely lost track of time while we were skating. And although this was probably the appropriate length for a second date, I'm not ready for our night to end.

That must be why relief floods me when Rhia asks, "Want to come back to my place and hang out for a bit?"

CHAPTER 16
RHIANNON

The one and only other time Cole was in my apartment, I was drunk enough that I couldn't have cared less what he thought of the place. Now, insecurity lances through me as he scrutinizes the bookshelves lining my living room wall. As my book collection has grown, so has my storage system. I now have five full bookshelves side-by-side, and even at that number, they're bursting at the seams.

I keep my books organized by genre and then author. I tried organizing the spines by color once, putting them in rainbow order, but that was much too chaotic. It made it impossible to find specific books when I wanted to reach for them. I have *way* too many books to remember what color the spine of each one is.

Even when I read e-books, I always end up buying physical copies of the ones I love. I tell myself it's because I might want to reread them someday, but really I just like to look at them. They're like trophies. Some might call it wasteful, but I love having physical copies of the stories I adore. So sue me.

As Cole inspects the hundreds of books lining my shelves, it hits me that they're the perfect showcase of how little a life I have. After all, who has time to read all those books if they're busy being social? Cole probably thinks I'm a total loser.

He brushes a long finger across a row of books on the far left shelf. "You've read all of these?" he asks.

I cross my arms self-consciously. "Well, that's my TBR shelf. I've read all the ones on the other four."

"TBR?"

"'To be read,'" I explain. "Those are all the books I want to read but haven't started yet."

Cole's brows lift. "These are all books you've bought and never read?"

A nervous laugh slips from my lips. "I know, it's silly."

"Not silly at all." He moves over to the shelves of books that I've read, trailing his finger over one of my all-time favorite series. "Everyone has hobbies." His finger stops on a spine I recognize. "What's this?"

Cole pulls the book from the paranormal section of the shelf. That's probably the last place I would've liked him to go snooping. The genre has some of the more niche tropes that many would consider strange, but I eat them up. When you've been reading romance as long as I have, you need to spice things up a bit sometimes.

"That," I begin as I step beside him, taking the book from his hands and gently sliding it back onto the shelf, "is a shifter romance. Not for romance beginners."

Cole looks dumbfounded. "Shifter?"

I roll my bottom lip between my teeth. "Uh, yeah. The main characters can shift into wolves." I shrink a bit, feeling like a teenager explaining the plot of *Twilight*. If Cole didn't think I was a freak before, he definitely will now.

"That's cool," Cole says before heading to the next shelf, which houses contemporary rom-coms.

A wave of relief settles over me. Not only is Cole not making fun of me for my literary tastes, he actually seems to think they're kind of fascinating.

"I know it sounds a little weird, but it actually *is* cool." I take a seat on my couch, curling up beside one of my chicken nugget-shaped throw pillows. "Every subgenre has its own rules and expectations, and it's fun to switch things up sometimes."

After glancing over the final shelf of books, Cole joins me on the couch. He sits on the opposite end from me, a full cushion between us. Part of me loves that he's so respectful of my space and comfort, but another part wishes he would snuggle in closer.

"I never knew how many sub-genres there were," Cole says. "Romance is a lot broader than I realized."

I lean toward the coffee table to light my candle of the week: a light, fresh lilac scent with hints of citrus. It's a reflex to light it as soon as I sit on the couch. I constantly have candles burning while I'm writing, eating, and watching TV—doing pretty much anything, really. Mostly I just enjoy having a pleasant scent in the background, but I also buy candles from an aromatherapy company that are meant to help with anxiety.

"There's a lot of variety within romance," I reply as I settle back into the couch, hoping I'm subtle about the way I nudge myself slightly more toward the middle of the couch. "The genre only has two rules: the growth of a romantic relationship must be a main plotline in the story, and the story must end with a happily ever after or, at the very least, a 'happy for now.' Other than that, anything is fair game."

Cole's gaze lingers on the lit candle, and it takes him a moment to answer. "Sounds a little like fairy tales."

A smirk lifts my lips. "The Disney ones, maybe. Grimm's originals weren't overly optimistic. But the happily ever after is my favorite thing about the genre. It gives me a sense of security while reading that, no matter what happens in the story, no matter what trials and tribulations the main characters face, there's going to be a happy ending for them. It keeps my anxiety at bay."

Cole finally lifts his gaze, but his eyes hold a faraway look, as if his mind is in another place. "That makes sense."

"Do you read at all?" I ask.

His fingers sift through his ginger hair. "Not really."

Cole has never seemed to have trouble with his conversational skills before, but right now he's flailing. He suddenly seems distracted, and I wonder what caused the change. Am I talking too much about my borderline nerdy love of romance novels? Or did he notice I was trying to get closer to him, and that made him uncomfortable?

I feel like I've been waiting for the other shoe to drop with Cole, and it just did, with a reverberating thud.

I give him a moment to see if he'll continue the conversion, but Cole just sits stoically, his gaze occasionally flicking to the candle on my coffee table.

"You know what," I say, finally breaking the silence. "I really should be getting to bed soon. I have to be up early to write." It's a total lie—I never write in the mornings—but Cole doesn't need to know that.

"Oh." He rubs his hands over his thighs. "Okay."

The fact that he doesn't even put up a fight, doesn't try to charm me into chatting for a few more minutes, cements the fact that something has changed for Cole. Something about me has turned him off like I always knew it would.

I stand, hoping to shuffle him out the door quicker. I just want to be alone so I can lick my wounds in peace.

"Thanks for today. It was fun learning how to skate."

Cole stands too, shoving his hands into his pockets. "Yeah, it was."

Now he's proven that he isn't even really listening to me, because he did *not* learn how to skate today.

I walk Cole to the door, where he lingers in the open frame for a moment, scrubbing his hand over his face. When he pulls it away, he's wearing a smile that looks forced.

"So, have you ever had a good third date?" he asks, but his tone lacks its usual luster.

"Cole." I breathe out a sigh. "You don't have to keep going on these pity dates with me."

His brows pinch together. "They're not pity dates."

"No? Because you didn't seem that into it just now. I thought we had a good time together today, but then you just seemed to shut down."

Cole's face pales slightly as he tugs at the back of his neck. "I…" His voice cracks on the single syllable. "I can explain."

I lean back against the wall, arms crossed over my chest, waiting expectantly.

Cole's gaze flickers somewhere behind me then lands back on my face. "Can we go for a walk?"

"A walk?" I ask, confused. It's getting dark, and the fall air is cooling down. It's not freezing, but it's not exactly nice walking weather.

"Yes," he replies. "Please, I… I need some fresh air, but I want to talk."

"Okay." I'm so thrown off I forget to grab my coat.

I begin to shut the door behind us, but Cole stops it with a strong hand.

"Make sure to put out your candle first."

"Right," I say, irritated that he's still being so thoughtful. I spin on my heel, stomping over to the coffee table and blowing out the candle. "Let's go," I tell him as we head out the door. We're both silent as we exit the building, and he sets a hand on my lower back to guide me to the left, dropping it once our steps are in sync.

It takes almost a full block for him to begin talking.

"My mom died in a fire when I was eight," Cole announces as he stares straight ahead.

My heart plummets into my gut. I stumble over my steps, and he catches me by my arm. I steady myself, and we continue walking. Cole still doesn't look at me, but he fastens our hands together. I hold on tightly, silently begging for him to go on.

Eventually, he does.

"We were living in an apartment in the projects after hopping between shelters for months. Bailey and I had gone to bed, and my mom was out in the living room, smoking. She was drunk, like she was most nights, and she passed out before putting out the cigarette. It lit a magazine on fire, and things progressed from there." Cole pauses, and I squeeze his hand so he knows I'm listening and that I'll wait as long as he needs to continue.

"I woke up to my bedroom filled with smoke," he goes on. "It was so thick I felt like I was suffocating. Bailey was still asleep, but luckily, we shared a room, so I was able to wake her up quickly. I got her out the window of our room. I tried to go back in for my mom, but a neighbor physically held me back. He probably saved my life, but at that moment, I hated him with every fiber of my being." Another pause, and this time Cole takes a deep breath. "The fire may have been my mom's fault, but she didn't deserve to die in it. I had to watch my home burn with her inside it, and I couldn't do a damn thing about it." His voice is haunted, ugly memories of the past infiltrating what would otherwise be a nice night.

My stomach sinks, and my mind reels as I consider how the long-reaching implications of that night must still affect him to this day. And my heart is shattered for the little red-haired boy who watched his life literally go up in flames while he stood by, helpless.

We've reached a small park a couple of blocks from my apartment, and I tug Cole toward a bench to sit down. I need to look him in the eyes. Touch him. Bring him back to this moment with me.

Sitting beside him, I reach out a hand to cup his jaw, running my thumb over his cheek until he meets my gaze.

"Cole, I...I'm so sorry you had to go through that," I say. "Thank you for sharing it with me."

"Thanks for listening," he replies. "I don't tell many people about that night."

"It means a lot that you trust me enough to tell me." I stroke his cheek one more time before dropping my hand. For the first time, I realize that Cole must feel as safe with me as I do with him. I know it takes me a while to feel comfortable with someone, but I never considered that it might be the same for him. He comes across so confident and self-assured, but deep down, he has demons he keeps hidden from the world.

"Back at your apartment…the candle you lit threw me off," Cole admits. "The therapist I saw as a kid says I'm hypervigilant around fire because of what happened. I get really nervous, and it makes it impossible to focus on anything else." He plants a palm on my thigh. "Even a really beautiful woman who's sitting right next to me."

My cheeks heat as his finger sneaks beneath the hem of a rip in my jeans, sliding over bare skin.

"I'm sorry if I seemed distant earlier," he says, his finger drawing patterns on my skin. "I promise it had nothing to do with you."

"It's alright," I reply, feeling bad about the attitude I gave him now that I know what I took as disinterest was actually fear.

"It's not," he insists. "I don't want you to think I pity you, Rhia. It's not like that."

"What's it like, then?" I ask.

"I like you," he says, still stroking my skin. "A lot."

"I like you too, Cole." I place my palm over his hand, stilling it. "A lot," I add, catching his eye so he knows I'm serious.

Cole's boyish grin lights up his face, and it dawns on me that he might crave affection just as much as I do. I think we're a lot more alike than I ever realized.

His grin softens, his eyes turning hazy as his head lowers slightly toward mine. He pauses as if he's waiting for me to meet him halfway, which I eagerly do, craning my neck up so I can reach his lips.

The kiss is soft. Sweet. A recognition that we're both still a little unsure about this, but we want to try. Cole tastes like the minty gum he's always chewing, and I savor the taste as his tongue caresses mine.

I've never had a kiss feel easy the way this one does. Past

kisses have always been shackled by expectations and worries, rendering me incapable of enjoying them. Kissing Cole feels as natural as breathing.

After a minute, we break apart, lips lingering inches from each other as we both drag in air. I can feel Cole's breath on my cheek, minty fresh and cool on my heated skin. A shiver dances its way down my spine.

"You're cold." Cole tugs off his hoodie. "Take this." He drapes it over my shoulders, helping me weave my arms through the sleeves. He gazes around at the darkness that has descended. "We should probably head back to your place."

I take him by the hand and guide us to standing. "Let's go."

CHAPTER 17
RHIANNON

Everything feels different as we enter my apartment for the second time tonight. Knowing more of Cole's back-story puts his earlier reaction into perspective. It also explains why he's so protective over Bailey. He's literally saved her life once already. And confirming that Cole actually likes me and isn't just hanging out with me because he feels bad for me changes…everything. I think it would crush me to give him any more of myself just to find out he only saw me as a pet project.

I lead Cole to my couch, and he collapses onto it like he's just run a marathon. Emotionally, I suppose he did.

"Stay here. I'll be right back." I head for my bedroom and root around in my closet until I find what I'm looking for. I bring it out to the living room and place it on the coffee table, fussing with the cord until it's untangled enough to plug into an outlet.

"What's that thing?" Cole watches as I place my coffee table candle beneath the light bulb of the warmer.

"It's a candle warming lamp," I explain, flicking the switch to "on" and turning up the brightness. "It has a light bulb that gets hot enough to melt the candle wax, so you get the scent without any fire involved."

Cole is silent for a moment as he stares at the contraption.

"Thank you," he says softly as I sit beside him, our legs brushing.

"You're welcome," I reply, my hand finding his thigh. "You've become such a…safe person for me, Cole," I tell him. "I want to be safe for you too."

Cole's gaze flicks over my face before settling on my eyes. His blue irises burn with an emotion I can't name, but it looks a lot like hunger. "I feel safer with you than I ever have with anyone," he says. One of his hands settles on the back of my neck. "I'm so glad you came into my bar."

I squeeze his thigh with a smile. "Me too."

We're so close together now that our foreheads are practically touching. I don't know how much of it is me leaning into Cole and how much is him pulling me in, but in a heartbeat, our lips are pressed together, picking right up where we left off at the park. This time, though, there's no cold air or threats of gawkers to hold us back.

My arms circle around Cole as he cradles my head in his hands, tilting it to his preferred angle. His tongue slides against mine as I arch even closer, pressing my body against his. I'm nowhere near cold anymore. Indoors, still wearing Cole's hoodie, with my body plastered to his, I'm burning with desire.

A small moan slips from my throat as Cole's hand slides slightly forward from the back of my neck to the side, his thumb grazing my jugular. The noise turns into a full-on groan when he gives my throat just the slightest of squeezes, speaking to so many of the fantasies I've held in the recesses of my mind for so long, afraid to speak them out loud to anyone, but somehow Cole just intuitively knows.

"Fuck, gorgeous," Cole rasps, drawing in a breath as he rests his forehead on mine. The nickname is like a bucket of cold water being splashed over my head.

I tear my face away from his. "Don't call me that."

His face freezes on an expression of pure shock. "What? Why?"

I start to pull my body away, but he grabs my hands gently in his. "Rhia? What did I do?"

I shrink a bit, feeling silly now. This type of insecurity is exactly why I assumed Cole would never want me.

"I don't want to be just another woman you call a pretty name," I confess.

Cole exhales sharply. "I'm sorry, I…I don't get it." He shakes his head, brows drawn in concern.

"At the bar, you flirt with every woman you serve," I say. "And I get it—that's part of the job. But I don't want to be just another woman you call gorgeous. It makes me feel…cheap. Like I'm just another conquest or something."

Cole's brow crinkles further. "Rhia, you're the furthest thing from that. And I've never called anyone else gorgeous."

I give him a *get real* look.

"I haven't," he insists. "Pretty, beautiful—sure. Lots of women are beautiful. I'm sorry you had to hear me say that to another woman—I didn't mean to, but it must have slipped out —but I never called anyone gorgeous until you came along."

I blink, trying to think back to every time I've seen Cole flirt with a customer. I guess I can't *exactly* pinpoint any times he used that particular nickname.

"That word never fit anyone until I laid eyes on you." Cole twists a lock of my hair around his finger. "This dark hair. I was always certain it was full of secrets." A smile tugs at the corner of his mouth as he drags his thumb across my lips. "These lips. Fuck. I wondered how they would taste for ages. You're gorgeous. I want to *gorge* myself on you. Never come up for air. If I could do nothing but kiss these lips until my last breath, I would."

My heart pounds at his heady words. My panties are soaked, and I've never felt more sure that I want something than that I want Cole. He started out as a fantasy I only imagined living out in another life. But now, he's real, he's here, and he's hard, which

I discover when I climb into his lap, straddling his thighs and sinking down onto him.

With a slight moan at this discovery, I fit my lips to his, winding my fingers into his short hair as I kiss him. Cole responds eagerly, lapping up the soft sound as it escapes the back of my throat. His arms circle around me, hands settling on my lower back. His fingers dig into the fabric of the hoodie as if he might reach my skin if they burrow far enough. After a long taste of him, I pull away so I can tug the piece of clothing off.

I fumble with the zipper for a moment, and Cole takes advantage of my distraction by finding those holes in my jeans again, tucking his fingers beneath the denim and kneading my bare flesh.

"Cole!" I say with a giggle as his thumb brushes over a ticklish spot on my inner thigh. I toss the hoodie to the other side of the couch and dive back to his lips, yanking his hands out of my pants and swatting them back toward where they were. This time, though, Cole's hands run lower, gliding over my ass where he tucks one into my back pocket. The other slips up beneath my thin cotton shirt, cool against my heated skin.

A shiver dances down my spine as his fingers skate over my back. I gasp when the hand in my back pocket gives my ass a slight squeeze. I feel Cole's smile as he releases my lips, his own moving to my jaw, where he peppers kisses down to my neck, soft sips of my skin that leave goosebumps in their wake.

My head tips to the side to give him better access, begging for more. Cole obliges, his kisses growing harder, sucking on my skin more insistently. It vaguely crosses my mind that he could be leaving behind hickeys, but at this moment, I couldn't care less.

I groan as Cole's lips trail back up my jaw toward my ear, where his tongue traces the shell. It's like he's on a mission to find every ticklish spot on my body, every hot button that sends a shudder through me.

"You are spectacular," Cole breathes in my ear, and that, too, has me quivering.

When Cole's hand slips from my pocket and joins the other beneath my shirt, I decide it's time to lose the article of clothing altogether. I grab two fistfuls of my shirt and haul it over my head, leaving me in the deep-purple mesh bra I picked out for this date, though I was not at all expecting this outcome.

Cole's gaze slides to my nipples, peaked beneath the fabric and begging for attention. His lips part as he raises a hand to cover one breast, giving it a slight squeeze. I can tell the moment he feels something harder than my nipple behind the lace because his eyes fly to mine, pupils blown wide. He looks like a kid in a candy store, his lips kicking up as understanding sets in.

I smile back, pleased I could surprise Cole in this way. There aren't many things I can imagine surprising him with in this arena, so I'm counting this as a huge win.

One long finger circles my nipple over the fabric before gently squeezing the metal bar pierced through it. I squeak in surprise, a delighted giggle leaving my lips.

"Goddamn, Rhia," Cole says, his thumb brushing my skin just below my bra. "You are so fucking gorgeous."

My grin widens at the word. Now that I know it's reserved just for me, it feels like the most meaningful compliment of all time.

I press my lips to his, rubbing my breasts against his chest. The lovely friction of my piercings against my bra ramps up the anticipation of skin-on-skin contact. Cole's hands are all over me, tangling in my hair, slipping beneath my bra straps, rubbing up and down my back. Eventually, they land by the clasp of my bra, and he nuzzles his cheek against my jaw.

"Is this okay?" he asks, fingering the clasp.

"Yes," I answer breathlessly. "Please."

He deftly unclips the clasp, and my bra straps slip down my arms. I lean backward just enough to let it slide all the way off.

Cole's hands are on my hips now, kneading restlessly as his

gaze maps my chest, focusing especially on the two little silver bars with spheres on each end that adorn my nipples.

"Fuck," Cole rasps, his fingers digging into my flesh.

"You can touch them," I tell him, glancing at his clenched jaw as he needlessly restrains himself.

I half expect Cole to maul my breasts with that permission, half *want* him to do that, but when his hands release my hips, they travel up my sides all the way to my shoulders, thumbs smoothing over my collarbones. He continues staring at me, his gaze roaming the top half of my body for a few long moments before his hands finally dip down where I want them, cupping my breasts. He brushes his thumbs over my piercings, eliciting what sounds like a purr from my throat.

I'm fully in this moment, but at the same time, it doesn't feel real. I feel wild, my heart is galloping, and there's a flutter in the pit of my stomach reminding me I've never experienced this before, but I'm absolutely desperate for it.

Cole's blue eyes lock with mine. "Do you like these played with?" he asks as he takes one of the metal bars between his thumb and forefinger.

"I...I don't know," I reply, even as I lean farther into his touch.

Cole's brows knit. "Are they new?"

"No." I sigh happily as Cole gives the piercing a gentle tug. "I got them on my twenty-first birthday."

Cole's hand freezes. "No one's tried playing with them in the last five years?"

My heart rate picks up even more. "I mean, *I* have. But, uh...I haven't been intimate with anyone in the past five years." I try to temper my cringe as I add, "Or ever."

Cole's hand falls from my breast like it's a hot potato. *Shit.* Maybe this is something we should have talked about before we got to this point, but I truly wasn't expecting this tonight, and my virginity is not exactly something I advertise. Now I've totally ruined the mood.

"You've...never had sex?" Cole asks slowly.

"I'm sorry," I say quickly, unsure if I'm apologizing for my lack of experience or for not warning him about it. I start to scoot off of him, trying to escape the embarrassment, but Cole catches me by planting two palms on my thighs.

"Please, *please* don't apologize for that." He lifts one hand to run it over his head. "I'm just...surprised."

I cross my arms to cover my bare chest, feeling ten shades of awkward. "You know how terrible I am at dating. Is it really that hard to believe I've never slept with anyone?"

"I know, but...the stuff you read, the stuff you write, the way you *look*...I just assumed..." Cole trails off, tugging on the short strands of his hair.

I slouch back, creating as much distance as he'll let me. "You know what they say about those who assume," I mutter.

"Rhia." Cole rubs his hands up and down my thighs. "I... I don't want to stop, but I don't want to push you too much."

"I don't want to stop either." With the reassurance that I haven't totally turned him off, I release my arms and bare my breasts to him again. "I want this with you."

Cole's hands find my waist, holding me firmly in place. "We'll take it slow," he declares. "Find out what you like."

I nod, liking the sound of that. "I want you to like it too."

Cole's lips kick up. "Trust me, I will." He finds both of my piercings with his fingers. "Let's start with finding out if you like these played with."

CHAPTER 18
COLE

run my thumbs over the cool metal of Rhia's piercings as my palms rest on her heated skin. I'm not sure what was a bigger surprise to me tonight—that Rhia has her nipples pierced or that she's a virgin. To be totally honest, I'm pervertedly pleased with both.

I gently pull at one piercing and then the other, swallowing a groan as Rhia sighs with pleasure. I experiment with different motions, tugging, twisting, and sliding to discover what she likes the best. Once I think I have a handle on her preferences, I dip my head forward, placing kisses over the swells of Rhia's breasts before taking one of her nipples in my mouth.

She gasps as I suck on it lightly, licking the underside and then pulling at her piercing with my lips. Her fingers thread into my hair, and she presses her body toward me, practically begging for more. I take the piercing between my teeth and tug gently, chuckling against the soft skin of Rhia's breast when she lets out a low, "Oh, fuck."

"Yeah," I concur as I move to her other breast to give it the same treatment. By the time I've finished, she's rocking against me, grinding on whatever hardness she can find. My cock is stiff, standing at attention for the raven-haired beauty in my lap. It's already begging for release, but it won't find it tonight—at least not until I get home and hop in the shower. I promised Rhia we would take things slow, and I intend to stick to that. The fact that I'm the first man she's ever trusted with her body is important, and I don't want to do anything to jeopardize that trust.

Releasing Rhia's breast from my mouth, I grab her hips and hoist her to one side so she's riding my right leg, giving her access to all the friction she could ever want. The move seems to make Rhia realize what she was doing, and I barely have a chance to catch the furious blush on her cheeks before she tucks her face into the crook of my neck.

"Don't stop," I tell her, coaxing her hips back and forth with my hands. "Ride my leg."

She remains curled into me for a moment before her nose slides along my neck, and she places a kiss right over my pulse. Her hips pick up again, slowly rubbing against my leg.

"That's it," I whisper. "Does that feel good?"

Rhia nods into my neck.

"Let me see you."

She pulls back so I can see her face, from her rosy cheeks and hooded eyes to her lips, puffy from so many kisses.

"God, gorgeous," I murmur. "You're a vision." I take her breasts back into my hands, massaging them as she finds a rhythm against my leg. Her movements stutter when I find her piercings with my fingers.

"Keep moving," I grit out, jaw clenched in concentration. "Take what you need."

A small shudder moves through Rhia, a miniature indication of what's to come. She regains her rhythm, and I help her keep it, moving my hands to her hips to encourage her to keep riding me. I catalog her soft gasps and moans, taking note of which speeds and angles seem to bring her the most pleasure.

She arches toward me, and I take one nipple between my lips, my tongue darting out to feel the piercing. Rhia mumbles something under her breath, but I don't catch it.

"Let me hear you," I tell her.

"Feels...so good," she chokes out.

"That's it." I tug at her hips when she tries to slow them. "Use me to come."

Rhia groans and moves a little faster as she seeks her release. A couple times, I can tell she's close by her erratic breathing, but each time, something holds her back. The second time it happens, she lets out a frustrated little grunt.

"Keep it up," I tell her, fingers digging into her hips as I swirl my tongue around a nipple. "I'll get you there."

Rhia lets out a whimper, her hips bucking as she rides me with renewed persistence. I'm determined to make her fall apart —to give her this thing that no one else ever has. I move my hands from her hips to her ass, palming it through her jeans and spurring her on. I keep my lips glued to her breasts as I tug her even closer.

"Almost there, gorgeous," I say when I feel her body start to shake.

"I...Cole, I..." Rhia's words devolve into a long moan as I give one of her piercings a good tug. It sets her off, and she comes with her eyes screwed shut and her head thrown back, completely uninhibited. It's the prettiest sight I've ever seen.

Little shivers wrack Rhia's body as the orgasm rolls through her. I keep her moving, helping her ride through every last shock until she's completely wrung out. Then she melts into me, burying her head in my neck, her breaths puffing against my skin.

I whisper sweet nothings into her hair: *you did so good, you are so gorgeous,* until I'm sure she's not hiding from embarrassment, but she's simply sated and satisfied.

"Please, *please* don't tell me that's your first ever orgasm," I say, skimming my hands up and down Rhia's bare back. "Something that pretty should be happening as often as possible."

Her nose grazes my neck as she lets out a ghost of a giggle. "No," she replies, fingers playing with the fabric of my shirt as her cheek lays on my chest. "I've had plenty of those on my own."

Christ. The thought of Rhia making herself come makes me even harder, and I'm already stiff as stone. "Next time, I want you to show me that," I say. Just the prospect of a next time makes my heart thump against my ribs.

Rhia snuggles into my chest. "Only if you'll show me."

"Deal," I reply.

"Mac, you *cannot* drape yourself across the piano shirtless while I do my set," Bailey tells him as we futz with the setup for open mic night. She's opening the show with a Taylor Swift mashup on the piano, and Mac keeps trying to give her ways to spice up her performance.

"Why not?" he whines, shoving a handful of popcorn into his mouth. We decided to have complimentary popcorn for the event tonight, which Tripp is furiously preparing back in the kitchen.

"First off, I'm playing on a keyboard, not an upright piano, and second"—Bailey tosses a piece of popcorn right at Mac's face, hitting him square on the nose—"the sight of your sweaty, hairy body would probably make everyone up and leave before I even finish my set."

Mac grips a hand over his heart as if wounded, and Bailey sticks her tongue out at him. Sometimes I think she tries so hard to hide her crush that it actually makes it more obvious.

"Listen, everyone is keeping their shirts on tonight," I announce.

Mac snorts. "Yeah, except maybe you and your girl."

"Edmond MacArthur," I snap, using his full name to show him I mean business. I was so excited when Rhia texted me that she was coming tonight with a couple of friends that I spilled to Mac about our night together. I didn't give any specifics about what we did, just told him that we'd gotten a lot closer, but he obviously put the pieces together.

"Ew." Bailey wrinkles her nose. "I don't want to hear about my brother's sex life."

I pull her into my chest, giving the top of her head a noogie with my fist. "You're not going to because Mac is going to shut up now."

Bailey swats me away and begins fixing her hair. Mac gives me a devilish grin, raising his eyebrows mischievously and letting me know he'll be giving me plenty of shit later when my sister is not within earshot.

I glance toward the door, waiting for Rhia and her friends to walk in, even though I know the event doesn't start for another half hour. On one of these glances, I see someone I recognize, though it takes me a moment to place him.

"What is he doing here?" I snarl at Mac, who grows wide-eyed when he notices his old pal Jesse entering the space. I apologized to Mac after my episode at family dinner, giving him some bullshit excuse about why someone smoking in my apartment triggered me. He took it well, and he promised he'd whip Jesse into shape before we trialed having him work at the bar. I guess tonight will tell whether or not the whipping has worked.

"I invited him," Bailey cuts in, stepping protectively in front of Mac. "I thought he might like to do something other than sit around in Mac's crusty apartment all night."

I don't have time to respond before Jesse walks up to us and greets Mac with a bro hug then greets Bailey with a regular hug, which makes my skin crawl. Seeing any man's hands on my sister gives me the creeps, but especially a degenerate like this.

I'm not entirely sure what it is about Jesse that makes me dislike him so much. It could be the smoking, or it could be the fact that he's been here for weeks now and hasn't accomplished anything except mooching off of Mac. Or, if I'm being really honest with myself, maybe it's that he reminds me so much of the many boyfriends my mom had over the years.

Jesse gives me a curt nod that I return before sulking back to the kitchen to check on Tripp's progress. Maybe I shouldn't have left him alone for so long, because by the time I find him, he's devolved into making different popcorn flavor combinations. The large bowls are labeled with kitschy song-themed names like Buttersweet Symphony, Cheddar Together, and Running Up That Dill. It's a bit of a risk to stray from classic popcorn, but luckily the different flavors taste amazing.

I help Tripp divide the batches into smaller bowls, and we put together popcorn flights for each table. By the time that's done, a half hour has flown by. I'm still a little edgy from Jesse's presence, but the sight of Rhiannon walking through the front door instantly turns my mood around. She's followed by a redheaded woman walking hand-in-hand with a tall, bearded brunet man.

Rhia's teeth are tucked over her bottom lip as she glances around the space. She breaks into a huge grin when she spots me, and as if that wasn't enough to get my heart thumping, she speed-walks over to me and immediately wraps me in her embrace. I love that she doesn't try to act cool or aloof. She's happy to see me, and she shows it.

"Hi," I say into her hair.

"Hi," she replies into my chest.

For that moment, I forget that anyone else is here, that there are people I've never met watching us, as well as some of the people I'm closest to. I forget that I have an event to run. Nothing else matters except the woman in my arms.

Rhia pulls back and takes my hand, tugging me over to where her friends stand.

"Cole, this is my best friend, Hannah, and her boyfriend, Caleb." She gestures at each of them. "Guys, this is Cole."

I shake their hands, and we exchange pleasantries. Hannah seems really sweet, and Caleb seems just as smitten with her as I am with her friend. I guide them to the best table in the house, tucked away toward the back corner so it's away from the fray and offers an easy escape route should Rhia feel uncomfortable. She shoots me an appreciative grin as she slides into the booth.

"I'll swing back around as soon as I can," I promise. "Once the singing starts, I should be able to clock out."

I make my rounds to check up on everyone—Tripp is behind the bar now, and Mac has just finished sound-checking all the equipment. Bailey is chatting it up with Jesse, which I hate, but I decide to allow it because the thought of having to even get close enough to him to break up their conversation gives me the creeps.

I double-check that everything is stocked up behind the bar, that the bathrooms each have toilet paper, and that the singer sign-up list is gaining momentum. Once I'm sure everything is set up sufficiently for a smooth event, I head over to be with my girl.

CHAPTER 19
RHIANNON

Cole's sister is the opening act for the night, and he slides into the booth beside me just as her set is starting.

"Hey," I greet him with a whisper as Bailey begins playing the opening piano melody of "New Year's Day."

"Hey." Cole presses a quick kiss to my temple, which earns me waggling eyebrows from Hannah. I try to disguise my blush by leaning slightly into him as we watch his sister sing. She's good. Like, *really* good. I mean, I knew she had to be if she was attending music school, but damn. She makes the phrase *voice of an angel* sound like an understatement.

Bailey's performance gains more hoots and hollers each time the music morphs into a new song. Sometimes she plays a few verses of a song, sometimes just the chorus and the bridge. The set goes on for about ten minutes, but I could listen to her sing for hours.

"She's *so* good!" I tell Cole as the audience begins clapping at the end of her performance. Cole is beaming with pride at his sister, and the sight makes my heart flutter.

"She is," he agrees, putting two fingers in his mouth and

ripping out a wolf whistle to cheer her on. "At least all my money is paying off for something."

It takes me a moment to process his off-hand comment. "You're paying for her schooling?"

He glances down at me, a hint of sadness creeping into his eyes. "How did you think she was affording Berklee?"

"I assumed she got a scholarship or something." I shrug. I realize now that while I know how Cole lost his mom, I don't know much about what happened to him after that. Who did he live with? Who supported him? Does anyone support him now? It doesn't seem like it.

The audience's cheers have died down, so Cole leans in to whisper in my ear. "Let's talk more later."

The next singer begins setting himself up at the microphone as Bailey weaves her way through the crowd toward our table. She resembles Cole with her fair, freckled skin and red hair, but she has brown eyes instead of blue and a shorter stature.

"You were amazing." Cole pulls his sister into a bear hug. I can tell by the way Bailey returns the embrace that this is a common occurrence for them.

"Thanks, Coley," she says as she pulls back, smiling warmly up at her brother.

"This is Rhiannon," he introduces me, "and her friends Hannah and Caleb."

Bailey greets us all before settling her gaze back on me. "I *adore* your name," she gushes. "Cole had to talk me out of doing a Fleetwood Mac mashup because he was afraid I'd embarrass you. But 'Rhiannon' is one of my favorite songs of all time."

"That means a lot coming from a music major," I reply. "Obviously, my moms would agree."

Bailey pulls up a chair at the end of our booth, and we all sit down. "Cole tells me you're a writer," she says. "I never miss a chance to connect with a fellow creative."

While talking about writing is one of my favorite topics,

discussing my smutty romance novels with Cole's little sister is *not* something I was prepared for tonight.

"Hannah is a creative too," I deflect. "She writes a blog and does a lot of work on social media."

"Love that!" Bailey exclaims. "I've been trying to grow a following for my music, but I can't figure out which platform will serve me best. YouTube is obviously ideal for posting full songs, but things are so much more likely to go viral on TikTok."

While she and Hannah launch into a conversation about social media, I sneak a glance at Cole. The glow of pride at watching his sister perform has yet to fade, and he's watching her talk with so much love in his eyes. It's obvious she means the world to him.

Cole catches my eye and sends me a wink. His palm finds my thigh and gives it a squeeze under the table. I layer my hand over his to keep it locked there. I love that he's not afraid to be a little touchy even though we're in public and this thing between us is so new. Not that anyone can even see his hand under the table, but it gives me a boost of confidence.

The next performer comes on—an older woman singing Norah Jones a cappella. Our conversation pauses as we listen to her soulful voice. When she's done, I excuse myself to go to the ladies' room before the next singer comes on.

My makeup still looks pretty good, but I still reapply my lip gloss for good measure. When I exit the bathroom, I'm almost immediately caught by the arm and tugged in the opposite direction of where I was headed. I don't have enough time to panic before I register Cole's voice saying, "Come here, gorgeous."

I'm pulled into the back office and pinned against the wall as the door snicks shut behind us. Cole's arms cage me in as he leans his hands against the wall and towers over me. I should feel trapped. Cornered. Instead, I feel nothing but desire.

"I've been waiting to do this all night," Cole murmurs before lowering his head to kiss me. So much for that fresh lip gloss.

His lips meet mine in a slow caress—soft at first but growing hungrier as I wind my arms around his back and pull him closer. His body presses against mine, pushing me into the wall, and I *love* it—the thrill of us sneaking off to make out while the rest of our group awaits our return, blissfully unaware of what we're up to. The fact that we're in public and anyone could walk in here at any moment and find us sucking each others' faces off.

One of my legs drifts up and hooks around Cole's, trapping him to me in my own way. I never want this kiss to end. I wish we were somewhere else, alone, where we could continue without anyone else inconveniencing us.

Cole must feel the same, because he presses his forehead to mine, brushing our noses together, and asks, "Will you come home with me tonight? After the performances are over?" He runs his thumb across my cheek. "I'll make you something better than popcorn to eat."

"I'd like that," I reply, rubbing my foot along his calf. "How many more performers are there?"

Cole snickers. "Probably like five. Why? You eager to get me alone?"

I release my leg and duck out from his imposing figure, playing my best at nonchalant. "No, just a little hungry."

He shakes his head and mimes stabbing himself in the heart. "You wound me."

"We should get back before they wonder where we are."

"You go first." Cole adjusts the bulge in his jeans. "I'm gonna need a minute."

I press my lips together to contain a laugh. "You've got it. I'll let Hannah and Caleb know they don't have to drive me home."

I return to lively conversation at our table. Apparently, we missed an entire performance, and the singer did "Piano Man," complete with harmonica. Caleb is adding one to his Amazon cart as I sit down.

No one comments on my disappearance. Hannah shoots me a sly smile that says she knows something about what just went down, but she has the good grace not to embarrass me by vocalizing it.

Cole saunters over with a fresh round of popcorn, which must have been his excuse for leaving the table.

Bailey looks at him and rubs her bottom lip. "You've got some gloss, bro. Trying out a new look?"

Turns out Bailey, unlike Hannah, is positively ruthless.

Cole wipes his mouth with the back of his hand, and I have to smother a giggle as he makes a face at his sister.

She grins, seeming pleased that she's sufficiently annoyed him. "Well, I'm gonna go check in with some other people, but it was great to meet you all." She meets my eye to address me specifically. "Especially you, Rhia. We should hang out sometime. Talk shop."

"I'd like that," I tell her.

Bailey gives Cole one more hug before wandering off toward the bar where she starts chatting with a skinny guy with dark hair.

Cole gives my thigh another squeeze, but this time it's not accompanied by an affectionate glance toward me. Instead, he's glaring at his sister and whomever it is she's talking to.

"What's wrong?" I ask.

He loosens his grip on my leg. "I just don't like that guy. And I don't like that he's talking to my sister."

"She doesn't seem to mind," I reply. "I think she went over to him."

"That's even worse," Cole mutters.

"How do you know him?" I ask.

Cole sighs and forcibly relaxes, letting his head fall back against the booth. "He's a friend of a friend. I met him a few weeks ago, and there was a little…incident. He just doesn't seem like a good guy. I don't want my sister to have anything to do with him."

I take his hand and lace our fingers together. "Bailey seems like a really smart young woman. If he's trouble, she'll realize it soon enough."

Cole grunts, and I can't tell if it's in acceptance or displeasure. The next performer begins, taking our minds off the issue at hand. This one sings a rousing rendition of "I Will Survive" that garners massive applause at the end.

The rest of the evening passes slowly as I anticipate going back to Cole's place. The time is punctuated by small, seemingly innocent touches on my back and legs, but each time Cole's fingers make contact with my body, my excitement ramps up.

By the time we finally say goodbye to everyone at the end of the event, I'm ready to rip his clothes off right then and there.

CHAPTER 20
RHIANNON

"They're gaining on us!" Veronica shrieked as she peered out the back window of the SUV at the nondescript vehicle that had been following them for blocks.

Damien had been the first one to notice their tail and gently clue her in as to what was happening. One of the damn paparazzi had taken off after them, following them covertly at first before speeding up to try to get alongside them. Veronica normally only rode in vehicles with tinted windows, but in an effort to get away from the mob of paparazzi quickly, Damien had borrowed the keys to her publicist's car, which was closer than Veronica's Jaguar. The paps must have realized they had a chance at a shot through the windows and hurried to follow them.

"Hold on to the grab handle," Damien instructed in a tone much calmer than the situation called for.

"The what?" Veronica screeched, unable to make sense of the command.

"The handle where I hang your pretty little fucking dresses when I pick them up from the cleaners,'" Damien explained. "Hold on to it!"

Veronica pulled down the handle at the last second, keeping her grip on it tight as Damien swung the car in a U-turn that brought them dangerously close to the rumble strips on the other side of the interstate. He maintained control of the car, his steady hands on the steering wheel taking them off the highway at the next exit without even hinting at slowing down.

"I think we lost them," Damien declared as he finally pulled onto a side street, tucking them into a dark parking garage. The SUV screeched to a halt as Damien killed the lights. For a tense moment, he kept his eagle eyes trained on the road, but no cars passed by. "They're gone," he confirmed.

Veronica was unable to respond with her heart in her throat. She didn't dare even take a breath for fear of giving up their location.

"Veronica," Damien said, his tone commanding her attention.

Her gaze snapped to his, taking in the endless blue pools of his eyes.

"They're gone," Damien repeated. "You're alright. We're alright."

When she still failed to respond, Damien reached over the center console and took her hand in his larger one.

"Veronica." He leaned in and tugged her closer at the same time. "We're alright."

"We're alright," Veronica finally replied as she let the words truly sink in. Damien's body was inches from hers now, both of them gravitating toward the center of the car. The thrill of being close to him fused with the adrenaline of the car chase had her heart pounding erratically. "Thank you, Damien."

"Anything for you," he said softly, his thumb rubbing over her wrist. He'd never felt skin so soft. "Anything, Veronica."

Cole's apartment is pretty much what I would expect for a bachelor in his mid-twenties—mostly bare walls, a couch that's seen better days, and a big TV with a bunch of video game equipment in front of it—*except* for the kitchen. He's turned the small kitchen into a chef's utopia with a couple of strategically placed portable kitchen islands that house everything from a food scale to a stand mixer to an air fryer. There's a worn-out old cookbook propped up on the counter with an impressive spice rack beside it. It's clear that this is the space Cole spends the most time in.

I take a seat at the small kitchen table and watch as Cole roots around his cabinets for everything he needs to make chicken saltimbocca. When he discovered on the drive over here that I'd never tried it before, he immediately promised to rectify that. The very fact that this man has prosciutto and fresh sage on hand tells me that he's legit when he says he loves cooking.

"Where did you learn to cook?" I ask as Cole begins seasoning the chicken.

"I basically taught myself," he replies. "Growing up without a reliable influx of food forced me to get creative with what Bailey and I ate. I enjoyed the challenge of testing different flavors together and seeing what worked. When my aunt and uncle took us in, I was able to get my hands on more fresh ingredients, and it opened up my cooking possibilities exponentially. I used to make dinner for the whole family all the time."

"What are your aunt and uncle like?" It's the first time I've heard him mention them, and if they took him in when he was eight, I would have expected them to be a big part of his life.

Cole is quiet as he begins wrapping the chicken in prosciutto. "My relationships with them are complicated," he says slowly. "They took me in when I needed them most, and I'm grateful that I never had to experience foster care, but I never really fit in with their family. Neither did Bailey."

"That must have been tough." I can't even imagine the hardship of an eight-year-old and a three-year-old being thrust into a new family and having to adjust to a whole different life.

"It was," Cole says. "My aunt and uncle sheltered us, fed us, and clothed us, but we never felt emotionally supported by them, you know? To this day, I'm not entirely sure that they adopted us out of the kindness of their hearts. I think my aunt just didn't want to look bad by abandoning her orphaned niece and nephew."

I suck in a gasp. "That's awful."

Cole drizzles some olive oil into a skillet on the stove. "Don't get me wrong—they gave us a decent life, but we were never close to them. My mom and her sister grew up pretty poor, and while my mom stayed in the cycle of poverty, my aunt broke out and married a wealthy businessman, had two kids with him, and lived out the whole white-picket-fence dream. I think when Bailey and I came into her life, we were an unwelcome reminder of her past."

The chicken cutlets sizzle as Cole places them into the pan.

"We never shared any interests with my cousins, Brett and Steven. They were born into a Sunday-dinner, skiing, tennis-playing family, and we were from a grilled-mustard-sandwich, thrifted-roller-skates, lack-of-supervision family. They used to look at us like we were aliens. We always felt less than, and our aunt and uncle made sure to drive home the point when they told Bailey and me that they wouldn't pay for us to go to college."

"Did they pay for Brett and Steven?" I ask, enraged that they would pick and choose between their biological and adopted children.

"Yes," Cole replies. "They claim it's because of the degrees we wanted to get. Brett went to school for criminal justice with plans to go to law school, and Steven went for biology with plans to go to medical school. When I announced that I wanted to go to culinary school, I was told, in no uncertain terms, that it was not a respectable degree or career and that I would receive no help in paying for it. I didn't have the savings to pay for it myself, and I was afraid to take out any loans, so I gave up on the idea."

"Cole," I say softly. "I'm sorry. That's so unfair."

He shrugs and flips each piece of chicken over. "It's probably for the best, honestly, because culinary school would have been a flop anyway. I never considered how much fire is around in a commercial kitchen. They use gas stoves and fryers, and I would have run out of there screaming the second I saw a flame. I grew up with electric stoves, and as long as I can't see the heat, it doesn't bother me, but open flames really set me off."

I watch as Cole removes each piece of chicken and adds butter, wine, and chicken stock to the empty pan. He moves around the kitchen so competently. It's a shame that lack of money and fear of fire keep him from turning this passion into a career.

"I wasn't going to let Bailey give up on her dreams, though," Cole adds. "She was born with a natural talent that most people don't have, and I was determined to get her to music school. Bartending seemed like the closest thing I could do to cooking without having to be around fire, so I got my bartending license as soon as I turned eighteen and started working. By the time Bailey got to college, I had a decent amount of savings, and she got some scholarship money too. At least one of us is going to do what we were always meant to."

Each new piece of information chips away at a piece of my heart, threatening to break it completely. The lack of support from any and all of Cole's parental figures, the lasting trauma from the fire that killed his mother, the selflessness of paying for his sister's schooling...every puzzle piece that makes up this complex man is like another dagger to the chest. He's never gotten a break, and he deserves a shot at his dreams too.

"Have you ever considered trying therapy to help with your issue with fire?" I ask.

Cole shrugs as he returns the chicken to the pan for its final simmer. "I saw a therapist when I was a teenager. I guess that's one good thing my aunt and uncle did, although they probably only did it because I was getting into trouble at school. Couldn't have anyone tarnishing their reputation around town, so they had to whip me into shape."

I picture an angry red-haired boy acting up because his life is so out of control, and my chest aches. "Did it help?" I ask hopefully.

Cole's back is turned to me as he plates our meals. "It helped some, I guess. We never really worked on the fire issue specifically. It was more about the trauma of growing up in poverty and then losing my mom. They diagnosed me with CPTSD. Guess I was too messed up for regular PTSD," he jokes, but it falls flat beneath the heavy weight of that diagnosis.

I sit with it as Cole delivers me my meal. It looks absolutely professional with a drizzle of sauce on the side and some extra sage leaves adorning it.

"This looks amazing, Cole," I tell him, and he grins, pleased. His lips fall when I return to the topic at hand. "If you would ever consider trying therapy again, a different form might suit you better. Have you ever heard of EMDR? It's supposed to be really helpful for healing trauma."

I've done a lot of research into different therapies over the years, and I've found that Jodi's brand of cognitive behavioral therapy is what helps the most with my brand of anxiety. But it very well may not be what Cole needs.

He scratches at his neck as if his shirt is suddenly too tight there. "I don't know. I've never really considered it. I've been able to make my life work by just avoiding fire. Usually, it's not that difficult to do."

"I know," I say gently, reaching over to touch the back of his hand. "But it's exhausting to be hypervigilant all the time. Trust me, I know. And triggers like candles or gas stoves are too common to avoid completely, which means either being uncomfortable by being near them or having to miss out on things by avoiding them. Plus, if the fear is holding you back from a life-long dream, then it's definitely worth working on."

Cole avoids eye contact as he cuts into his chicken. With a soft sigh, I do the same. I don't want to pester him or make him angry, but it's hard to see him struggle when I have ideas on what might help him.

"I'll think about it," he promises half-heartedly.

"Thank you," I say before biting into my chicken. *Damn.* It's delicious, and I tell Cole so.

He chuckles as he swallows a bite of his own. "Saltimbocca literally means to jump into the mouth, because the flavor jumps right out at you."

I nod in agreement. I mostly survive off of takeout, frozen meals, and deli meat sandwiches, often forgetting to eat entirely if I'm engrossed in my writing. The fresh, herbaceous flavor of the chicken is a pleasant shock to my palate.

Bolstered by Cole's willingness to be open to the idea of therapy, I add one more thought. "There's also exposure therapy. I know it's silly to compare our issues, but exposing myself to my fear in small, controlled doses really did help desensitize me to it."

"It's not silly." He pushes his chicken around his plate with his fork. "It's just...really scary to think about purposefully putting myself near fire."

"Of course it is," I agree. "That's why you have to start out slowly. We could even try a version of our own. Start with a candle and work our way up to a stove. I would be with you every step of the way," I promise.

"Maybe we could try that," Cole replies noncommittally. I'll take it. It's not an outright "no."

I scootch to the edge of my chair to get closer to him and lower my voice. "I bet I can think of some good motivators," I say, trailing a finger over his shoulder and down his arm.

He grabs my hand in his as his lips spread into a mischievous smile. "Now you're talking. You still have a promise to make good on first, though."

I frown. "I do?"

"Last time we were together, you said you would show me

how you make yourself come," he reminds me. "And I'm ready to collect."

CHAPTER 21
COLE

fucking love the pretty pink blush that climbs Rhia's neck. She may seem shy, but I know she's got a dirty fucking mind, and that combination is intoxicating.

Rhia straightens in her chair, clearing her throat. "You promised to show me too."

"Hell yeah I did," I say through what I'm sure is a blinding smile. I can't wait to get this woman naked. "I'll clean up the dishes. You go make yourself comfortable on the couch," I tell her, leaving my instructions vague. If I find her stark naked on the couch in two minutes, I'll be thrilled. If I find her fully clothed, I'll be equally thrilled because then I get to strip them off her.

I scrub and dry our plates in record time before joining Rhia in my living room. She's still in her jeans and a white t-shirt, having removed only the burgundy cardigan she had on over it. She's removed her dark hair from its bun so it tumbles over her shoulders in waves. A vision of my fingers fisted in that hair flashes through my mind.

Take it slow, I remind myself.

Rhia's wide brown eyes meet mine. "I'm nervous," she blurts.

And that's exactly why.

"That's okay," I assure her, taking a seat next to her and placing a hand on her arm. "There's no need to be, though. I only want to do what you're okay with. I figured this might ease us into things, but if you're uncomfortable, we can just hang out."

Rhia averts her gaze, grabbing onto the front of my t-shirt like a lifeline.

"No, I…I want to," she replies. "I just feel…awkward."

"Rhia." I cup her jaw in one hand, waiting for her eyes. When they find mine, they're a hazy mix of lust and nerves. "You are so fucking beautiful. You have nothing to feel awkward about."

She snags her bottom lip with her teeth. "I just…you know this is all new to me, and I don't like unpredictability. I feel a little out of control, and that scares me." She pauses before spitting out the rest in a rush. "And sometimes my anxiety medication makes it take a while to…you know, get there."

I can't hold back my smirk. "You didn't seem to have much trouble the other night."

Rhia purses her lips, remembering. I do vaguely recall feeling like something was holding her back, but I was still able to make her fall apart with ease.

"It's okay," I remind her. "You can take as long as you need. I'll enjoy every fucking minute of it. And as for unpredictability, I'll tell you exactly what's going to happen." I run my palm down her arm to her thigh. "We're both going to get naked, and I'm going to try my hardest not to bust at the sight of you. Then you're going to touch yourself and show me exactly how you like it. And I'll do the same." I rub and knead her thigh the way I want to do to every inch of skin she has covered. "And we'll both feel good, and we'll both come. No matter how long it takes."

Rhia listens intently before giving me a small nod. "That sounds good."

I use one finger to tilt her chin up so she meets my gaze. "Yeah?"

Her cheeks are stained pink as she replies, "Yeah."

I dip down to kiss her forehead. "Good." Reaching down, I grab a fistful of my t-shirt and tug it over my head.

Rhia stares at my bare chest and abdomen hungrily. She reaches out a hand, and I grab her wrist to stop her.

"No touching this time. Only yourself."

She nods and pulls her hand back, her compliance making my cock twitch.

I scoot backward into the corner of my L-shaped couch, patting the space in front of me. "Sit here."

Rhia dutifully moves over to sit in front of me on the part of the couch that juts out.

"Turn around," I tell her.

"What—"

"No questions," I cut her off. "Just listen. If you don't like something, you say 'stop.'"

Rhia visibly shivers at the change in my tone. If it turns out she and I share any of the same proclivities—and I think we just might—we'll have to pick a different safe word, but this will do for now. I *may* have taken a calculated guess based on Rhia's bookshelves about what her pen name may be, and I *may* have read a book—or three—by that author. Even if I guessed wrong, I'm hoping I got a peek into her tastes by reading something off her shelves.

Keeping my tone as gentle as possible, I say, "Let's start like this."

Rhia fidgets as she faces away from me. I'm hoping she'll feel less self-conscious if I'm not staring directly at her.

"Take your shirt off."

Rhia barely hesitates before shrugging out of her shirt one arm at a time, revealing the nude bra beneath it. Though I don't have a good view of the front, the mesh and lace that make up the back leave little to the imagination, and I fantasize about what her nipples and nipple rings must look like poking against the other side.

Rhia tosses her shirt across the couch with mine.

"Now your jeans."

She works on the button and zipper for a moment before standing to shuck them off, never looking back at me. I wonder if she's afraid she'll lose her nerve if she does. In reality, if she did, she'd find me unzipping my own jeans to release some of the pressure on my aching cock.

Nude panties barely conceal Rhia's gorgeous ass. They're cinched right down the middle in a way that highlights every lovely curve. I get a much too short glimpse of them before she sits back down, on her heels at first then switching to cross-legged. There's no need to get too comfortable as I'll be having her move soon.

I shift forward and press a kiss to her bare shoulder blade, briefly considering abandoning my entire plan for a moment in favor of kissing her from head to toe until she squirms out of her skin.

"I thought we weren't supposed to touch each other," Rhia chides, and her easygoing tone assures me that she's still with me despite her skittishness.

"With our hands," I reply. "Lips are a different story."

I can hear the pout in her voice as she replies, "Who says?"

I chuckle as I press a kiss to the matching spot on her other shoulder. "Me. I'm making the rules tonight, and you're following them as long as they feel good."

Rhia lets out a small gasp before her breathing speeds up. She's excited. Whether she knows it or not, Rhia likes being told what to do by someone who knows—or at least has a good idea of—what she'll like.

I reach for the clip at the back of her bra, studiously avoiding her skin and brushing my finger over the fabric. "I'm going to take this off," I say. "Nod if that's okay."

Rhia nods eagerly, her hair bouncing up and down. I bite

back a chuckle as I release the clasp. The bra falls down her arms, and she removes it, tossing it to the side with abandon.

All I can see is the smooth plane of Rhia's back, but the thought of her nipples being exposed to the cool air, making them pebble and harden, makes me moan.

"Lean back," I instruct, holding my breath as her bare back presses into my chest. She's warm and smooth against me, and I long to run my hands all over her. "Get comfortable," I add.

Rhia shifts around, scooting backward while avoiding touching my denim-clad legs. Keeping my pants on was a strategic move. I thought Rhia might get intimidated if I was totally naked with her, and I want her to get off at least once before I even think about taking my pants off. In this position, I can at least catch a glimpse of her rosy-tipped breasts as she curls into me.

"There you go," I tell her as she relaxes into my front. I dip my head down to nip at the top of her ear. "Now listen carefully, and do as I say. I want you to touch those perfect tits for me just like I did last time. Feel how soft and lovely your skin is."

Rhia tentatively lifts her hands to her breasts, running her fingers over the globes before taking each one in a palm and squeezing lightly.

"Does that feel good?" I ask.

Her hair tickles my chest as she nods.

"Good," I reply. "Keep kneading them. See how you're such a perfect handful?"

Rhia continues just as I asked her to. She might be even more submissive than I expected. Every book of hers that I managed to read so far contained themes of dominance and submission, whether explicitly stated or not. I've done a little research into the subject at different times in my life. I'm not necessarily into BDSM, and I don't consider myself a dom, but I do crave a certain level of control when I'm with someone else. Any therapist would probably tell me it stems from my trauma, and they'd probably be right. All I know is that I like to be in charge, and based on the looks of it, Rhia likes that too.

One of her thumbs starts idly toying with a nipple ring.

"Show me how you play with your piercings," I say, watching as she twists them lightly. "Remember how you liked it when I pulled on them?"

A soft moan rolls out of her as she plucks at each nipple.

"That's it. Keep that up," I tell her. "Are those pretty tits getting sensitive, baby?"

"Yes," Rhia mewls, her back arching slightly to push her breasts forward. This is exactly how I want her—needy and wanting, forgetting any anxieties and focusing entirely on the sensations wracking her body.

"Maybe we should move on, then," I suggest. "Let's see how you touch that little pussy through those panties."

I hear Rhia's sharp intake of breath as she releases her breasts. Her pert nipples strain, seeking touch as her fingers instead drift down toward her panties. She slowly runs them over the thin material, too high up to be hitting any of the good spots.

"Lower," I say, strangling a groan as her fingers drift downward. It's too hard for me to see anything very clearly from this angle, but I know she's followed my instructions when her body jumps in response to her own touch. I let her continue for a moment before deciding she's ready to move on.

"Are those panties getting all wet?" I ask. "Maybe you should take them off."

Rhia's hand freezes. For a split second, I worry she's going to call this whole thing off. But then she reaches for the hem of her panties and responds with a demure, "Yes, sir."

Goddamn. My cock throbs, straining against my boxers. She might just be the perfect woman.

Rhia wriggles her panties down her legs. All I can make out is a small patch of what looks like well-groomed dark hair as she resumes her position. I grunt as her ass rubs against my erection.

"Put your legs on either side of mine."

She opens her legs wider, hooking them around mine.

"Feel how wet you are," I say once she's settled, and I watch as her fingers disappear beneath the dark hair. "Show me," I demand after a moment.

Rhia holds up her pointer and middle fingers, now glistening with want.

"Bring them closer." I crane my neck forward so I can suck on her fingers, tasting her.

She lets out a mix between a whine and a moan until I release her fingers from my lips. *Delicious.*

"Keep going," I tell her. "Get all your wetness and spread it up to your clit. Show me how you like to play with it."

Rhia complies eagerly, and I mentally catalog every way she touches herself. Her two fingers move in a counterclockwise motion as she strokes her clit. I could feel that circular motion when she was grinding against me last time too. She starts out slowly, but her speed soon increases.

"That feels good, huh?" I ask.

"Yes," Rhia says, a hint of desperation in her tone. She needs more.

"Keep going. Can you usually come this way? Or do you need something filling you up too?"

"I need something," she confirms.

"Use your other hand," I say. "Put two fingers in your pussy while you play with your clit."

Rhia groans as she dips her other hand down, sliding her fingers in.

"Pump them in and out." I want her to keep the momentum up. She's getting close, but if she psyches herself out, she'll have to build up all over again. "Thatta girl," I praise as her legs start to shake the slightest bit.

"Cole," Rhia whines, growing mindless with lust.

Knowing she's getting close, I take a chance. "Please let me see you, baby," I plead, shifting myself out from behind her and moving to the middle of the couch so she has the whole chaise to herself.

Rhia spins to face me, and I get my first real view of her stunning naked form. Full tits tipped with glinting metal bars above a seemingly endless plane of smooth, creamy skin. And beneath that, the prettiest pussy I've ever laid eyes on, partially obscured by dark curls and her hand as her fingers plunge in and out.

I quickly shed my pants and boxers as Rhia continues playing with herself, her body shamelessly draped over the chaise. My cock bobs up to hit my stomach, the head angry and purple. I'm fucking *throbbing* with need.

"Fuck," she mutters at the sight of my erection. I wrap my fist around it and tug, the friction giving me only the slightest relief.

As I continue stroking myself, I quickly realize this somehow seems more intimate than if we were actually touching each other. We're both laid completely bare, unable to hide. Rhia must realize it too, because her hands slow.

"Keep going, gorgeous," I say as I rub my cock up and down, twisting toward the head. "I want to see you come around those fingers. Fucking soak them."

Rhias's eyes drift shut on a moan as she regains speed.

"Open your eyes. Look what you're doing to me." I wring beads of pre-cum to the tip of my cock. "You are so fucking sexy, Rhia. You're going to make me come. I had to keep my pants on until now so I didn't bust all over your back. That perfect body and the way you touch it when you make yourself feel good. *Fuck.* You're the sexiest thing I've ever laid eyes on."

Somewhere in the middle of my monologue, she throws her head back, her mouth forming a little O as she comes, her legs shaking with the force of her orgasm.

I tip over the edge too, squirting cum all over my stomach.

"Keep touching that little clit," I say through the haze of my release. "You can slow down, but don't stop."

Rhia switches to large, slow circles as I grab a napkin from the coffee table and quickly wipe off my stomach before joining her on the chaise.

"I...I can't..." she begs without telling me what for until I realize she's overstimulated, but she's still rubbing her clit because *I* told her to.

"You can stop," I say as I gather her into my arms, tucking her into my chest. She presses her face into my neck, and her entire body melts into mine.

"You did so well," I tell her, peppering kisses along her jawline.

Rhia preens at my words, nuzzling into my skin. After a moment, a small giggle escapes her lips. "I can't believe I just did that."

I place a kiss on her bare shoulder. "Hell yeah you did." What we just did was peak vulnerability, and she handled it beautifully.

Rhia pulls back until she can meet my eyes. "I think...I'm ready for more," she says.

I hide my smirk in her hair. "Greedy little thing, aren't you?"

Rhia gives me a smile that says she knows exactly how to get what she wants. I shouldn't be able to get hard again so soon, but that saucy little grin on her lips has my cock jerking.

"What do you want more of, huh?" I run my hand down her side. "My fingers? My mouth?" I swivel my hips against hers. "My cock?"

Rhia flutters her long lashes up at me. "All of the above, please. *Sir.*"

CHAPTER 22
RHIANNON

oly. Shit. A distant part of my brain is screaming at me that this is too wild, that we should stop here, that I should process what we just did before we do more, but I've pushed all that to the back of my mind. Cole released some wanton creature inside of me from her cage, and I'm not sure she can ever be coaxed back in.

His heated smirk sears me as he arranges my body on the chaise how he wants it.

"Relax," he tells me. "Lie back."

I recline against the back of the couch as he takes hold of my hips and slides a throw pillow beneath my lower back.

"What are you—"

"No questions," Cole reminds me. "Just trust."

Shockingly, I'm finding that much easier than expected. In my everyday life, I prefer to be in control of things. I've found that it's the easiest way to soothe my anxiety. But here, with Cole talking me through everything, I can turn off my wandering mind and just follow along because I feel completely safe with him.

Once I'm propped up to Cole's liking, he sits back on his heels and begins trailing his fingers up my legs, from my calves up over my knees where he begins kneading my thighs. The whole time, he's just staring at my body, gaze roving over every inch as if he's cataloging every little detail.

I don't mind, because it gives me time to do the same. Cole's fair skin extends down his torso, peppered with freckles and a few birthmarks. His red hair gets darker the lower on his body it goes, reaching a dark-brown tint below his belly button where it frames his half-hard cock. It's impressive as is, but based on what it looked like when he first took his pants off earlier, Cole's a grower.

And get this: he has a fucking *thigh* tattoo. It takes me a moment to recognize what it is, but then it clicks. A phoenix rising from the ashes. *Fitting.*

My concentration on the tattoo is broken when Cole's thumbs drift to my inner thighs, mere inches from where I'm wet and wanting.

"So soft," he says as he traces patterns across my skin. One of his hands drifts higher, and he runs a thumb through my slit, making me whimper.

"Wet," he mutters before the tip of his thumb slides just inside of me. He pulls it out before easing it back, all the way to the knuckle this time. "*Shit*, you're tight."

"T-too tight?" I ask. His cock is already growing again, and I worry it won't be able to fit.

Cole gives me an easy grin as he pumps his thumb in and out. "You can take it."

My eyes shut on a moan, and I toss my head back into the couch, surrendering to his ministrations.

"I'll get you ready," he promises as he removes his thumb and replaces it with his first two fingers. "You ever had anything other than fingers in here?" he asks. The way he talks when he's touching me is enough to have me soaking his hand.

"Um…mm-hmm," I reply, opening my eyes just in time to see his light up. He knows damn well I've never had a man inside of me, so that only leaves one option.

"Really?" he asks, drawing out the vowels. "Tell me more."

"I...uh...I have a dildo," I reply as his thumb finds my clit while his other fingers stroke me inside.

"Tell me about it."

"It's...um..."

Cole's thumb and finger still. "You stop talking, I stop touching," he says. "Tell me about your toys, baby." He uses the plural as if he's sure I have more than one.

I mean, he's not wrong.

"It's purple," I spit out, desperate for him to resume his movements. "And...veiny. And it has a suction cup so I can stick it to the wall in the shower and stuff."

Cole's fingers slip in and out of me as his thumb picks up a circular motion. "That sounds nice," he says. "What else you got?"

"I have a vibrator," I reply quickly. "It has a bunch of speeds and settings. And it has...ah!" I cry out as his thumb picks up speed. "It has a piece that tickles my clit!" I shout, out of my mind with the need for Cole to never stop what he's doing.

He chuckles as he slips a third finger in, almost as a reward for my overeager admission. "You like that, don't you?" he asks. "You love having your clit played with while you're getting filled up."

"Yes," I breathe.

"Yes what?" he asks, his demanding tone making my pussy contract around his fingers.

"Yes, *sir*."

"There you go." Cole curls his fingers to hit a new spot inside of me. "Got anything else for me?"

"I have butt plugs," I blurt, not necessarily prepared to admit that but desperate for him to continue. Nothing has ever felt this good—not my own fingers or any of the toys I'm describing. The anticipation of his next move, the excitement of not knowing what it will be. It goes against everything I thought I knew about myself. I shouldn't like it, but I do. I *really* do.

"I knew you were a dirty girl," Cole murmurs as his fourth and final finger breeches my entrance. My hips buck into his touch…so close. If he would just keep this up for a few more moments…

"I think you're ready for me," he decides before retracting his hand, leaving me bereft. I whimper at the loss of his fingers as he makes to get up off the couch. "I need a condom."

"Wait!" I cry, grabbing his wrist and pulling him back toward me. "I'm on birth control."

Cole's brows scrunch together. "You are?"

Heat rises in my cheeks. "I have been for years. Wishful thinking, I guess."

His lips widen in a grin. "Lucky me. I got checked at my last doctor's appointment and I'm negative for any STIs. I haven't been with anyone since."

"I'm negative too," I reply, rather unnecessarily.

"Shit." Cole dives back onto the chaise, gripping my hip as he positions himself before me. "Are you sure you're ready for this?"

I give him my best demure smile. "Yes, sir."

On a long groan, he fists his cock, fully hard now, and runs it through my soaked slit.

"Please, Cole," I beg. I have no patience for teasing right now. "I feel so empty."

"Oh, baby," he croons. "You need me to fill you up with this cock?"

I clench around air and let out a strained, "Yes."

Cole's free hand travels up to rest against the base of my neck. Not squeezing or applying pressure, just reminding me who's in control.

"Yes, sir," he reminds me, but before I can repeat the phrase, he takes mercy on me, pushing into me in slow strokes. "Fuck," he grinds out through clenched teeth as he works on stretching me out. There's a slight burn as he pushes in the final bit, but it's quickly replaced by a satisfying fullness.

"You good?" Cole asks, pausing to drop a kiss on my forehead as he's fully seated inside of me.

"Yes, sir," I reply, squirming as I adjust to his size.

"So fucking hot," he breathes out as he looks down to where we're connected. "You're doing so well for me."

My eyelids flutter shut as I savor his words. He begins to move, sliding in and out in a tortuous rhythm. It feels divine, but it's also not *enough*. I was so close to coming when he was touching me before, and now I just can't. Quite. Get. There.

"More," I plead in a whisper.

"What was that?" Cole asks, though I'm fairly positive he heard my hushed request. His hips slow as if he can't fuck me and hear me talk at the same time.

"More!" I half-shout. "Please, sir."

"Oh, you want more," Cole replies lazily, picking up his pace just slightly. "Well, you *have* been such a good girl for me," he adds before his fingers dig into my waist, and he begins punching his hips, finally giving me what I've been craving. His cock hits every hot spot inside of me as he fucks me, and I know I won't last long now.

"Cole." I reach out, blindly grabbing his lower back to find purchase.

His thumb strokes my neck right over my pulse, which I'm sure is racing. "I know," he croons as he moves in and out of me rhythmically. "I think you like having my cock inside that perfect little pussy. Those toys just can't cut it once you've had the real thing, can they, baby?" He brings his other thumb to my clit, flicking it in perfect little circles, exactly how I like.

"Cole!" I practically scream his name this time as pleasure threatens to overtake me.

"That's it, gorgeous," he mutters as I spasm around him. "Be a good girl and come for me, Rhia."

I can't take it. His dirty words, his hand on my throat, his big cock stretching me. It's all too much and just enough. Exactly what I need. I come on a primal, feral wail, milking Cole's cock with my head thrown back against the couch.

He pumps into me three or four more times before shouting a string of expletives as he falls over the edge himself, his bruising grip digging into my hip as he fills me. A delicious warmth spreads deep inside of me, and I melt into a puddle beneath him, wrapping my legs around his to keep him close.

Cole is panting, barely able to catch his breath, but he still doesn't miss a beat of caring for me. His hands rove over my hips up to my breasts in soothing, feather-light touches as we both come down. He's the first to break our silence with something other than a grunt or a moan.

"Who knew you'd be a screamer?" he asks with a satisfied grin.

I feel my cheeks turn beet red. We both learned something new about me tonight.

Cole takes my cheek in his palm. "Don't worry. I fucking love it," he assures me. His eyes don't leave mine for a few moments as we just breathe together, still connected in the most intimate way. He leans in to kiss me, long, and slow, and sweet, before slipping out of me.

"Don't move," he says. "I'll be right back."

Cole returns a moment later with a warm washcloth and begins cleaning us both up. His gentle care threatens to bring tears to my eyes, but I am *so* not going to be that girl who cries after losing her virginity, especially when the sex was so fricking good.

When we're both clean, Cole disappears for another moment to dispose of the washcloth, and I pull the throw pillow out from beneath me, horrified to discover there's now a huge wet spot on it.

I hold up the pillow as Cole walks my way. "I'm afraid you might have to throw this out."

"Are you kidding me?" he asks as he hops onto the couch beside me, grabbing the pillow from my hands. "I'm going to treasure this thing forever. It's my prized possession now." He hugs it tightly to his chest, cradling it like an infant.

I throw my hand over my eyes. "You're a freak."

Cole tugs at my arm to catch my gaze, giving me a wink. "Takes one to know one."

I dissolve into a fit of giggles because he's right. We both have a freaky side, and I love that we can share that with one another. We may have only scratched the surface at me having nipple piercings, and using butt plugs, and him liking to be called "sir," but that's a damn good start if you ask me.

Cole hands me a pair of black boxer briefs, placing another one in his lap. "I grabbed these for us. They're clean."

"Thank you," I say, grateful not to have to put my soaking wet panties back on. I slide them on as Cole does the same. Reaching for our discarded clothing, I grab my shirt and put it on with the boxers, finding that I feel sexier in them than I ever have in my fancy lingerie.

Cole slips into his pair of boxers, which cut off just above his tattoo. He stays shirtless as he sits back down beside me, and I snuggle in next to him.

"I like your tattoo," I murmur as I trace the phoenix across his thigh.

His lips brush my temple in silent thanks. "Bailey has a matching one on her ribs," he says. "We got them when she went off to college."

My finger lingers on the tip of one of the wings. "That's really special."

"It was," he agrees. "No tattoos for you?"

"No," I reply. "Just the piercings for me."

Cole reaches to pluck one of my nipple rings, making me jump. "Those were a very good call," he says, and then, as if he didn't just get my motor running again, adds, "I'm cooking family dinner for Bailey and some friends and neighbors on Friday. Will you come?"

I don't answer for a moment, more out of the need to recover than actual hesitation.

"It's a small group," Cole promises. "But I'd love for you to meet them properly. My friends, Mac and Tripp, from Marty's always come. They're like brothers to me."

"I'd love to come," I assure him, reaching for his hand to entwine it with mine. "Are you sure I won't be intruding?"

The mention of family in the description of the event gives me pause. I'm certainly not part of Cole's family. I don't even really know *what* I am to him.

"Of course not," he replies. "What would family dinner be without my girlfriend there?"

Well, I guess that answers that.

I beam up at him. "Well, then, I'll be there."

CHAPTER 23
RHIANNON

"We can't," Damien murmured, but the words tasted stale coming out of his mouth. A phrase uttered so many times over the past few months that it had lost its gravity. They'd been dancing around each other since the beginning of this damn arrangement, and his self-control was rapidly waning.

"Why not?" Veronica asked, her fingers dancing over his thigh, swiping dangerously close to his hard cock.

"I'm supposed to be looking out for you," Damien said, prying her hand off his thigh.

Veronica batted her lashes at him. "I can think of some ways you can look out for me," she replied demurely.

Damien's deep groan rattled the car.

***H**allelujah*, I think as my alarm goes off, telling me that my twenty-minute writing sprint is over. My characters are talking to me so strongly right now that I'm actually writing in the morning. Shocking, I know. I had to set the alarm so I didn't miss my session with Jodi in half an hour.

I roll my neck three times each way, pausing at any particularly sore spots, then interlace my fingers and reach my hands overhead. I've done so much writing this week, and apparently my body has forgotten what it feels like to twist itself into a pretzel while hunched over a laptop.

I spend the ride to Jodi's office thinking about what I should bring to Cole's family dinner tonight. He told me not to bring anything, but it feels weird to show up empty-handed. He mentioned that Mac will bring bread, Tripp usually does dessert, and his elderly neighbor, Louisa, likes to make different alcoholic concoctions. As a broke college student, Bailey usually doesn't supply anything.

As I pull into a parking spot, I realize that no one is on salad, and that's about the extent of my cooking abilities, making it a perfect fit. I make a mental note to stop on my way home for the ingredients to make my favorite goat cheese and walnut salad. It's crunchy and chewy, nutty, and sweet from the craisins I throw in. I know some people are weird about soft cheeses, but hopefully there will be some takers.

I'm only in the waiting room for a couple of minutes before Jodi pokes her head out and tells me to come back to her office. She's in one of my favorite outfits of hers—a purple power suit complete with a thick, silver-buckled belt around her waist. As we sit down, I clock the lavender wiener-dog socks tucked into her booties.

"How has this week been?" Jodi starts off as we get settled.

"Good," I reply. "Really good, actually."

Her brows draw up in a shrewd expression, silently asking me to go on.

"I've been really inspired, so I'm writing a lot," I explain. "It feels good to be in the flow of it again. I was really slogging along for a while there."

"Anything in particular inspiring you?" Jodi asks.

I pick at the hole in my jeans, almost afraid to admit how well things are going. "I had a really good time with Cole at the open mic night," I reply. "And we went back to his place after. We...had sex," I add.

It doesn't feel as weird as one might think to talk about my sex life with Jodi. I've told the woman nearly everything about myself. We've discussed the intricacies of my deepest anxieties, all my childhood traumas, and the entire extent of my (limited) romantic history. Sex is menial compared to all that.

"That's huge for you, Rhia," she replies. "How did you feel about it? And how are you feeling about it now?"

"Really good," I answer both questions at once. "Cole was great, going slowly and checking in with me. I have no regrets."

Jodi breaks into a wider grin. "I'm very proud of you for taking that step. I know a sexual relationship with a partner is something you've desired for a long time, and it sounds like you're in a really good position right now."

I nod in agreement, and although everything I said is true, there's something that's still bugging me.

"I did learn some details about him recently that made me kind of nervous, though," I admit. "Not nervous to be around him or anything, but nervous that he might have some stuff he needs to work on that he's in denial about."

Jodi leans in slightly, letting me know she's ready to listen. I go through Cole's backstory, from growing up in poverty to losing his mom and moving in with his aunt and uncle, then forging his own path without any support and giving everything he has to his sister. Finally, I launch into what really worries me —Cole's fear of fire and how it's holding him back from living the life he really wants.

I don't care specifically about him being afraid of fire—I would happily throw out all my candles and never light a flame again if it meant getting to be with him—but the fact that he has this unresolved issue and untreated trauma that he has no plans to address worries me. I've worked so hard to get to where I am mentally, and I know you can't help someone who doesn't want it, but I care about Cole, and I want to make sure he is healthy and whole.

"I was encouraging him to try therapy the other day, and he said he'd consider it, but I don't know how serious he was," I finish as Jodi scribbles down a few notes. I realize I'm biting at my thumbnail, and I lower my hand to inspect the chips I've created in my black nail polish.

Jodi waits for me to meet her gaze before responding, "It sounds like Cole had a very hard upbringing, and he's made remarkable progress since venturing out on his own." She crosses her legs and sits back slightly. "But you're smart to take his background and the parts of it that still haunt him into account. I want to be very clear that two people with histories of mental illness can absolutely have a healthy relationship, but you're also correct that it takes work on both parts. It doesn't necessarily mean that he absolutely needs therapy for his PTSD and pyrophobia, but I imagine it would be very difficult to navigate those issues on his own."

That's exactly what I thought. I hope to help Cole in my own ways—in fact, I have a plan I'm going to propose after family dinner tonight to get the ball rolling—but he also likely needs professional help.

"It's still quite early in your relationship," Jodi adds. "It's great that you've floated the idea of therapy past Cole, but I understand why you wouldn't want to push it too much quite yet. If he's not comfortable trying therapy on his own, I would also highly recommend you two try some couple's therapy. I always advise couples to begin therapy when they're happy, before any issues arise. Again, it's early, but it wouldn't be a bad idea to have some sessions to navigate the basis of the relationship."

I had never considered the idea of us going to therapy together, but it's actually brilliant. Cole would probably be way more open to the idea if we did it together, especially if I said coming to therapy with me would help me. That way, it would feel less like me telling him *he* needs help and more like me telling him *I* need him to get help.

I leave my session with Jodi feeling relieved that this relationship isn't doomed to fail. After my amazing night with Cole, my anxiety started to run a little wild. Not seeing him for a few days allowed my brain to start ruminating on all the ways this might not work out.

Now, I'm bolstered by Jodi's reassurances and the fact that I'll be seeing Cole in just a few hours. Plus, I have a plan for us after dinner that I can't wait to play out.

CHAPTER 24
COLE

The scent of red sauce and melted cheese permeates my kitchen. I have a lasagna stuffed with meat and veggies cooking in the oven. Ever since I made Rhia that chicken saltimbocca, I've been on an Italian kick. She texted me a few minutes ago that she's on her way with salad, which reminds me—I should really have told Tripp to keep dessert normal tonight. His Jell-O salad from last month still plays a starring role in my nightmares.

I wipe my hands over my black jeans then curse, quickly inspecting to make sure I didn't get food on them. It's not that I want to impress Rhia tonight. It's just that...I want to impress Rhia tonight.

I give my table setting a final inspection. It's not something I usually give much thought to for family dinners, but I want everything to be perfect tonight. I laid out a cream tablecloth and some festive disposable napkins with multicolored leaves on them. I even bought a few of those tiny pumpkins when I was at the grocery store the other day, and I have them lined up in the center of the table. I'm sure some candles would look great nestled in there with them, but that's not going to happen tonight.

I've been thinking a lot about Rhia's therapy suggestion. I even started to do some research before panicking and shutting my laptop. Exposure therapy seems so extreme. I could try talk therapy again, but it took everything in me to tell my story to Rhia. I don't know if I could open up about it to a complete stranger. Plus, from the miniscule amount of research I did, I gleaned that therapists are near impossible to get appointments with, which means I'd probably have to go at the most inconvenient time and potentially have to miss work. I can't afford to miss any shifts when Bailey's college tuition is on the line.

I want to be better for Rhia. I know it would please Bailey if I got help too. She gave up on pushing me a long time ago, but I know she still worries about me. After the cigarette incident at last month's family dinner, she checked in on me every day for the rest of the week. Her daily texts were seemingly innocent— updates about her own days or random musings on current events—but I knew they were a front for making sure I wasn't spinning out.

I want to be the best version of myself for them, but it doesn't seem like therapy is in the cards right now.

A knock at the door pulls me from my thoughts, and I instantly crack a smile at the realization that Rhia is right outside. I head for the door and pull it open, and I think I literally stop breathing for a second at the sight of her. She's in a long black coat, but it's unbuttoned to reveal a ruby red dress that hits her mid-thigh. To my chagrin, black tights cover her gorgeous, creamy thighs, but the sexy, knee-high, black heeled boots on her feet make up for that. Her hair is down, flowing around her shoulders in a glossy black waterfall that I long to wrap my fist in.

"Hi," she breathes, her gaze heated at my obvious appraisal.

I pull the door open wider and duck out of the doorframe. "Get in here."

Rhia steps in and places her salad on the kitchen counter before I sweep her up in my arms, pressing my lips to hers in a hungry kiss. In two seconds flat, I have her pinned against the fridge as I ravage her mouth, pulling moan after moan from her lovely little throat. I lift a hand to bracket it, running my thumb along her pulse as she catches her breath.

"Wow," she says softly, as if she can't believe how desperate I was for her. I haven't seen the woman in days, and I haven't been able to stop thinking about everything that happened last time we were together. Of course I'm desperate.

"Let me take your coat," I say, remembering my manners.

Rhia shrugs out of her trench coat and hands it to me. I take it over to a chair in the living room and carefully drape it over the back. When I return to the kitchen, Rhia is sitting at the table, rifling through her purse. I pause to admire her for a moment, wondering if she's got sexy lingerie under her dress like she did last time. I wouldn't mind a little sneak preview before the others get here.

Rhia looks up and catches my gaze, her cheeks turning a pretty shade of pink. She zips up her purse and slings it over the back of the chair. "It smells great in here," she says.

"Thank you." I head to the oven and flick the light on to check on the lasagna. The cheese is browning and bubbling to perfection on top, so I pull it out and set it on the stove. It should be cool enough to cut into once everyone arrives. I gave Rhia an arrival time half an hour earlier than everyone else. I'm hoping she'll stay after too, but this way I ensure we have some alone time together.

I join Rhia at the table and set my palm on one of her thighs. "How has your week been?" I ask.

Rhia places her hand over mine and weaves our fingers together. "Good," she replies. "I've been writing a ton, thank God."

"Ooh." I give her hand a squeeze. "Tell me about it."

"Um." Rhia tugs at her bottom lip with her teeth. "I'm working on a companion novel for one of my bestsellers. I think it's partially freaking me out that the first book did so well, and

I'm afraid that this one will bomb. It's about this heiress, Veronica, who's writing a tell-all book about her family's juicy secrets, but an anonymous family member is threatening her life in retaliation. She hires a bodyguard to protect her, and they fall into a steamy love affair. I really like the main character, and I want to make sure I do her justice."

"Oh, that's Vincent's sister, right?" I ask before I can help myself.

Rhia rears her head back. "What? How did you know that?"

I cringe at her shock, hoping she's not totally pissed at me. "I *may* have studied your shelves when I was at your place, and you have a whole row of multiple copies of the same books by the same author. I took a guess that it was your pen name, and I *may* have read a few of her titles."

"Damnit," Rhia whispers, her eyes narrowed. "Which ones did you read?"

I list off a few titles, and my stomach sinks as Rhia's gaze falls to her lap. "Don't be mad," I plead. "They were *so* good. I really enjoyed them."

Her eyes widen as they lift to meet mine. "Really?"

"*Yes*," I reply. "They were heartfelt and sexy, and I couldn't put them down." I shift a little in my seat. "And they made me *really* horny."

Rhia's expression turns sultry. "*Really...*" she repeats in an entirely different tone, her hand creeping up my thigh.

"Mm-hmm," I hum as I lean toward her. "They gave me lots of...ideas."

"Yeah?" she asks in that same husky tone, her fingers clenching my denim-clad thigh.

"Oh yes." I press my cheek to hers, taking a moment to inhale the soft scent of roses from her hair before whispering in her ear, "I was hoping we could try some of them out tonight."

I swear I feel her cheek heat beneath mine.

Rhia pulls back just enough to meet my gaze. "I'd like that." She squeezes my leg, her fingers tantalizingly close to where I'm growing more aroused by the second. "I had some ideas of my own," she adds. "I actually brought a surprise for you."

My brows jump. "A surprise?" I ask, interest piqued. "I like the sound of that."

A look of uncertainty passes over her face, and I wonder if there's something she wants to try that she's nervous about. Based on her books, I'm guessing Rhia has some kinks she'd like to explore. And let me tell you, I am *down* for it. I'll try anything once.

"I'm sure I'll love whatever it is," I tell her.

"I hope so," she says, a small smile returning to her supple lips.

I can't resist leaning in to kiss them. As soon as I do, Rhia's hand is sinking into my hair and pulling me closer. Her candor assures me that she's been missing me as much as I have her these past few days.

Rhia's soft lips surrender to mine, yielding as a muted moan escapes her. I coax her lips apart to slip my tongue in, drawing out another moan. I fucking *love* that she's vocal. That she can't help the sexy little sounds that spill out of her. That I make her lose her tight grip on control.

I wrap my arms around Rhia, sliding one hand under her ass and tugging her closer until she's forced to rise from her chair and straddle my lap. We never break the kiss, and I pour everything I'd otherwise be saying into it. *You're gorgeous* and *I've missed you* and *Let's do this all the time for the rest of our lives.*

Rhia rocks against me, feeling how hard I already am for her. My cock strains against my zipper, begging to be released. I'm contemplating a quickie and mentally calculating if I have enough time to adequately satisfy Rhia when a knock sounds at the door.

Rhia startles, breaking the kiss, and drops her head to my chest with a soft groan.

"Fuck," I mutter. "Someone's early."

Rhia begins to dismount me, and I keep my hands on her

hips until she's steady on her feet. I begin to stand, and I'm quickly reminded of my predicament.

"Wait. Shit." I adjust myself to try to ease the ache in my cock. "I can't answer the door like this."

Rhia looks down and stifles a laugh with the back of her hand. God, she's gorgeous. Cheeks flushed, hair slightly mussed, eyes still a little hazy. I want nothing more than to ignore the door and lose myself in her, but I have a huge lasagna waiting on the stovetop, and I would never live it down if I cancelled a family dinner for sex.

"I can let them in while you…settle down," Rhia offers with a bright smile.

"Would you mind?" I ask. "You can just tell them I'm in the bathroom, and I'll be out in a couple of minutes."

Rhia nods and heads for the door. I pivot toward the bathroom and lock myself inside, grabbing the porcelain sink in a white-knuckled grip and hunching over it as I try to talk myself down. *Think bad thoughts*, I tell myself. I force myself to picture freaky clowns and old people's feet. When all else fails, I pull out my phone and watch an ASPCA commercial, my dick deflating as Sarah McLachlan croons "Angel" while photos of emaciated dogs flash over the screen.

Once I'm no longer pitching a tent, I flush the toilet and run the sink in case anyone is paying attention and head back out to the kitchen. Rhia and Bailey are engaged in a lively conversation, and the sight is so heartwarming that I don't notice the other presence in the room at first. Jesse is lurking by the door as if he's not one hundred percent sure he wants to be here.

I'm one hundred percent sure I *don't* want him to be here.

"Hi, Bails," I say, giving her a side hug as she continues talking to Rhia. "Hey, Jesse," I add with a small wave as an afterthought. I scan the room, but I don't see Mac, and I'm confused as to why Jesse is here. Did he think my invitation last month was a standing invitation? Because it most certainly was *not*.

Bailey turns to me. "I hope you don't mind that I invited Jesse along. He wasn't doing anything tonight, and he *loves* lasagna." She gives the guy a brilliant smile, as if his love for layered pasta is revolutionary.

I shrug in response. "Sure." Bailey and Jesse chatting at last month's family dinner or open mic night is one thing, but her being close enough to him to invite him to an event turns my stomach. And how does she know his food preferences?

"He brought JW blue," she says, elbowing Jesse lightly in the ribs. He pulls a bottle from his inner jacket pocket and presents it to me without flourish.

I take it and say, "Thank you," but the words taste sour in my mouth. Bailey knows that's my favorite whiskey. She's definitely trying to butter me up. But bringing me a nice bottle of whiskey doesn't make up for Jesse's bad behavior. And where the fuck did this dude get two hundred dollars for a bottle of whiskey, anyway, when I know for a fact he isn't currently working?

We move toward the table, and Bailey raises a brow.

"Fancy," she says as she gazes at my table settings with a smirk. She shoots a glance between me and Rhia, and I hear her unspoken teasing words about me trying to impress my girl.

"I guess I'll set another place for Jesse." I move woodenly as I set out another plate, napkin, and set of utensils before returning to the kitchen to check on the lasagna.

"Hey," Rhia says over my shoulder, wrapping her arms around my waist as I stand before the oven.

"Hi," I reply, my shoulders instantly relaxing at her touch.

She stamps a kiss on my shoulder blade. "That's the guy you don't like, right?" she asks. "The one your sister was talking to at the bar?"

"Yeah," I respond. "I didn't know he was coming tonight."

Rhia unwraps her arms to run her hands up and down my back in a soothing gesture. "Don't let it ruin your night." Her hands dip to squeeze my ass quickly. "Just keep thinking about your surprise."

I muffle a groan and turn to catch Rhia in my arms. "I can't *stop* thinking about it," I complain. "Will you at least give me a hint what it is?"

Rhia shakes her head with a devilish grin. "You're just going to have to wait and see."

"Wicked woman," I taunt, leaning in to kiss her, when there's another knock on my door. *Damn.*

My friends are total cockblocks.

CHAPTER 25
COLE

Rhia pats my chest and pushes me toward the door. I open it to find both Tripp and Louisa standing there, deep in conversation about a recent potential U.F.O. sighting.

"Come in, guys." I usher them through the doorway. "This is Rhiannon. Rhia, this is my friend, Tripp, and my neighbor, Louisa."

Louisa plunks a gallon-sized tub of hooch on my kitchen counter and reaches out to shake Rhia's hand. "Great to meet you," she says. "You know, I shared a joint with Stevie Nicks once. Cool chick."

Rhia's brows lift, as do the corners of her mouth. "That's… actually really cool," she replies.

Tripp grabs Rhia's hand next. "I once took a hit of Joe Jonas's bong," he boasts. "During the purity years," he adds in a stage whisper.

Rhia lets out an adorable giggle. "Also very cool," she tells him, and I send up a silent prayer of thanks that my weird-ass friends aren't totally scaring her off. Tripp unveils his dessert offering—completely ordinary-looking brownies—and my gratitude continues.

Mac arrives a few minutes later with a loaf of warm bread in hand. He seems genuinely surprised to see Jesse here, and I don't miss his look of concern when I tell him that Bailey brought him. I'm glad I'm not the only one who's worried about what's going on there.

By the time we're seated at the table and I'm cutting into the lasagna, it seems like my friends have known Rhia as long as they've known me. Conversation flows seamlessly, Rhia laughs at everyone's ridiculous jokes, and I breathe a big sigh of relief.

"How's school going, Bails?" Mac asks around a bite of lasagna.

Bailey lifts her shoulders with a sigh. "Just trying to make it to Thanksgiving break."

"Only another couple of weeks," he replies. "You've got this." He reaches out a fist, which Bailey half-heartedly bumps with her own.

"I hope so," she says miserably.

"What are you two doing for Thanksgiving?" Tripp asks, his gaze flitting between Bailey and me.

Bailey's gloomy tone turns bitter. "Aunt Jen and Uncle Tom are hosting." She stabs some lettuce in her salad bowl with more force than necessary. "I can't wait to be told how impractical my major is. *Again.*"

We don't see Jen and Tom often, but when they invite us for major holidays or events, we feel compelled to go. I know we don't owe them anything, but it still feels like the right thing to do. They never miss an opportunity to tear us down, though.

"Don't listen to them," I remind her. "They don't pay; they don't get a say." That's the catchphrase we made up when I told her I would be paying for Berklee.

A smile blooms on Bailey's face, and she reaches out to me for a much more enthusiastic fist bump. "Hell yeah."

"What do you do for Thanksgiving, Rhia?" Tripp asks.

Rhia finishes chewing her bite with a shrug. "I don't have any plans this year. My moms travel a lot, and they're doing an extended stay in Peru right now. I don't have any other family around here, so I'll probably just lay low."

I frown at the thought of her spending the holiday alone. I may not be looking forward to my plans this year, but Thanksgiving is one of my favorite holidays because it centers around one of my favorite things: food. I've seen Rhia's pantry. If she spends Thanksgiving alone, she'll end up eating peanut butter and jelly and microwave popcorn instead of turkey and all the fixings.

"You're welcome to join us," I tell Rhia. "I know I didn't make our plans sound very enticing, but Bailey and I always make the most of it. At least you're guaranteed a good meal."

Bailey nods enthusiastically. "Yeah! It would be so much more fun with you along."

Rhia catches her bottom lip with her teeth, hesitating.

"No pressure," I assure her. "You don't have to decide right now. But we'd love for you to come with us."

Her shoulders relax. "I'll think about it," she promises.

Now that the idea is in my head, I can't help but hope that she'll agree to it. Part of me never wants Rhia to see that side of my life, but a bigger part knows she would make the day infinitely better.

After another hour or so, dinner winds down, and dessert is brought out. Tripp proudly presents his brownies, and they're a huge hit with everyone. Turns out they have an Oreo center that adds another layer of chocolate decadence. Louisa's mystery liquor is less of a winner, and I only take the slightest sip out of courtesy. She pours Rhia a hefty glass of it that I have to surreptitiously dump into a plant when Louisa isn't looking.

Tripp is the first to excuse himself for the night, claiming he has to be up early for a sunrise yoga session. I've never heard the man mention doing yoga in his life, but somehow it tracks. Louisa leaves next because she can't miss *The Late Show*, professing that Stephen Colbert is a "dreamboat of a man" that she'd "do any day of the week and twice on Sundays." Bailey departs with Jesse in tow, and Mac quickly takes the hint that Rhia and I want to be alone.

We clean up together in relative silence, the way we flow as we do the domestic task making it feel like something we could be doing together for the rest of our lives. Delicious tension builds within me as clean dishes pile up in the drying rack. As soon as we're done, we can get to this damn surprise that's been plaguing me all night.

"Do you want to save the…whatever this is?" Rhia holds up the jug of alcohol from Louisa.

"No, just dump it," I reply as I finish wiping down the stovetop and counters. Everything is just about done, and I'm dying to get a move on to the next thing on the agenda. "So, about this surprise."

Rhia spins from the sink, where she's left the jug sitting upside down. A glugging sound fills the air as the alcohol pours down the drain.

"Are you ready for it?" she asks, her eyes bright. "You've been very patient."

"I have been," I agree, stepping forward to place my hands on her hips. "And I think patience should always be rewarded."

"Oh, it will be." Rhia gets up on her tiptoes to place a quick kiss on my lips. "Let me get my bag."

I watch with curiosity as she grabs her purse and takes it to the living room. If this surprise involves some kind of toy, I might just combust on the spot.

I join Rhia on the couch and watch as she sifts through her bag, pulling out a tall, tapered black candle and a small, lip-shaped lighter. *Oh.* This is *not* where I saw my special surprise going. I was thinking maybe she'd pull out a vibrator or one of those dildos—or, if I was *really* lucky, a butt plug—that she talked about.

I wasn't expecting my exposure therapy to be starting now.

Rhia sets the candle into a simple little base before placing her palms on her thighs. She gazes at me with those big brown eyes that could probably get me to do just about anything, but she doesn't speak.

"What's all this?" I finally ask.

Her tongue swipes out to wet her lips, and she swallows. "I was thinking we could practice having you tolerate a lit candle tonight."

"I don't know," I reply quickly. "I really just wanted to relax tonight."

As much as I want to please Rhia by humoring this whole exposure-therapy thing, all I want right now is to sink deep inside of her and get lost in pleasure. We can save the hard stuff for another day when I haven't been aching for her for hours.

"That's fine," Rhia says. "I'd be down for that too, but I think you should hear me out."

I give her an unenthusiastic nod and wait for her to go on.

"This is a paraffin candle," she explains. "It has a low melting point, so it will burn quickly and collect a decent amount of melted wax." Rhia shifts closer to me, her leg brushing mine. "If you can tolerate it for half an hour, I'll let you drip the wax on me...*anywhere* you want."

My cock is instantly rock hard. This idea just went from zero to one hundred *real* quick. I'm not sure how I'll be able to keep it together for thirty minutes, but the lure of getting to watch that dark wax drip over her porcelain skin is too strong to deny.

I stare at the unlit candle like it's my opponent. "I can try," I say.

Rhia grins and leans in, brushing kisses down my jaw and over my lips. "That's all I'm asking." She grabs the lighter and holds it between us. "Do you want to light it, or should I?"

"You," I say. We're taking baby steps here.

Rhia nods and holds the lighter over the candle's wick. "Are you ready? You can blow it out at any point if you need to."

"Ready," I reply, eyes glued to the process as she flicks the lighter open to produce a small flame and sets it to the wick, which catches easily. The flame dances to life before my eyes, making my gut twist and my eyes water. I swallow hard as pure agony threatens to overtake me. It's such a small flame compared to the blaze that changed my life, but it serves as a powerful reminder of how destructive fire can be.

What if the flame catches on something and the fire spreads like it did back then? I can't afford to lose this apartment. What if the whole building goes up? Louisa can't do stairs very well, and she might get trapped. Oh God, what if Rhia gets hurt? There are too many painful possibilities, each one harder to bear than the last. They make my stomach churn and my chest feel tight.

There's no way I can handle this for another second, let alone thirty minutes.

Leaning forward, I let out a puff of air, instantly blowing the flame out.

"I…I'm not ready," I confess as I watch a plume of smoke float away from the candle's wick. Relief washes over me the second the flame is gone.

Rhia tucks herself into my side, wrapping me in her arms. "It's okay, baby," she soothes. "I'm so proud of you for trying."

I sag into her embrace, feeling more like a failure. Why can't I do this one fucking thing? It shouldn't be that hard. Half an hour of discomfort for the reward of a lifetime.

I think about how brave Rhia has been about facing her fears. It wasn't easy for her to go on all those dates, but she pushed herself because she was staunch about her end goal. She knew what she wanted, and she was relentless in her pursuit of it.

If I can take this one small step tonight, not only do I get my immediate reward, but I take a step on the path to freedom to pursue a life I've always dreamed of. I may not be ready to dive into the world of traditional therapy, but doing this one little exposure in the safety of my apartment, with Rhia by my side, feels more attainable. It's a step I want to take.

"I want to try again," I declare.

Rhia pulls back to meet my gaze. "Yeah?"

"Yeah," I respond before I can think better of it.

She grins, pleased. "Okay." Scooting over a little, Rhia puts some space between us again. "You have a fire extinguisher, right?"

Who is she kidding? I have five—one in every room of my apartment.

"Yes," is all I reply.

"Why don't you bring one over so it's right here in case you need it?" Rhia suggests. "I don't think you will, but it might make you feel better."

I nod. "Good idea." I grab the small fire extinguisher I keep tucked behind the television and set it on the coffee table so it's ready to go. "Now what?"

Rhia picks up the lighter. "Now, I'm going to light the candle again, and we're going to breathe together."

Sounds like a good enough plan to me. "Okay."

Rhia lights the candle again, and I watch just as vigilantly as I did last time. The flame produces the same response in me, but this time, Rhia starts coaching me before I can panic and blow it out.

"Breathe with me," she instructs. "Like we did last time. In through your nose, nice and deep." She takes an audible inhale. "And out."

I follow along as she guides me through a round of deep breaths that settle the immediate discomfort in my body. I find it's not so bad once I've gotten over the initial panic. I'm not comfortable by any means, but I can at least tolerate it.

"Doing okay?" Rhia asks after a minute or two.

"Yeah," I reply. "I think I am."

"Good. Just keep breathing, and if panic spikes, try and deepen your breaths."

That doesn't sound too difficult. I guess I can do it.

Rhia sits back on the couch, her red dress hiking up higher on her thighs. I'm dying to tear those black tights off her legs and see what's beneath them, but I can't let anything hinder my alertness while there's a lit candle nearby.

"Now what?" I ask, allowing myself to relax just a bit into the couch. The flame and fire extinguisher are both still in my sight line, so I feel secure enough.

"Now we just hang out." Rhia reaches for my hand and starts playing with my fingers. "I think I'd like to come to Thanksgiving with you," she says, surprising me.

"Really?"

Having Rhia with me would make me so much more comfortable. She'd be a great buffer, and maybe she would even prevent some of my family's choice comments. Plus, I'd *love* to see their reactions to the fact that she's an erotic romance author.

"Yeah." She laces our hands together. "I tell myself I don't mind that my moms have this whole big life with all these travel plans that make them miss things sometimes, but really it makes me kind of sad. It's not like I want to be traveling with them, but I still can't help feeling a little left behind."

I squeeze her hand. "That makes sense. I would love to take you to Thanksgiving. I'm not promising it will be fun, because I can almost assure you that it won't be, but they always have a great meal. And I'm planning to make my famous apple-and-sage stuffing, so that will make it all worth it."

Rhia beams at me. "I can't wait to try it."

Her beautiful smile and rosy cheeks draw me in. She's like the sun, and I'm just a lowly plant that craves her warmth, needing her for my mere survival.

"Maybe you could come over and help me make it," I suggest.

Rhia's lips are just inches from mine as she replies, "I'd like that."

Her breath is hot on my skin, tickling my lips. Her eyes are already half closed as she hovers just out of reach, waiting for me to make a move.

Fuck the fire. I need to kiss her.

I seal my lips to hers, catching the little gasp she lets out just before I do. Fuck, she tastes so good. I detect a hint of the two chocolate brownies she ate, which only serves to enhance her natural sweetness. I can't get enough, and I lick the taste out of her mouth like a man starved.

Rhia responds in kind, climbing halfway into my lap as she meets every impassioned kiss with her own fervor. I start to trail my fingers up her leg, and she swiftly hoists her leg over me to straddle my lap. Suddenly, we're back where we started on my kitchen chair all those hours ago, only this time there's no one around to interrupt us.

CHAPTER 26
COLE

'm about to tear my shirt over my head when my gaze catches on the candle from the corner of my eye, abruptly bursting our sexy little bubble. I stare at the flame for a moment, rubbing the back of my neck. I can't believe I forgot it was there for a second.

Rhia responds right away, nuzzling her face into my neck. "You're doing such a good job, baby," she purrs. "Take a breath."

I do, and then I take another one for good measure. The flicker of alarm subsides.

"I have another surprise for you." Rhia stands and begins stripping off her dress.

My eyes widen as I realize that she wasn't wearing black tights beneath it. They're stockings, complete with strips of black lace at the top of each. And not just that, but they're clipped to a matching, lacy black garter belt that accentuates her hips. A little black bow adorns the center of the belt, as if presenting me with the gift beneath it.

My lips fall open with a grunt. "Spin," I order. "Slowly."

Rhia obliges with a sexy little smirk on her lips. The back of the outfit—if it can even be called that—is as enticing as the front, with its G-string thong and thin black straps that bisect each luscious ass cheek.

"This stays on," I tell her.

Rhia quirks a brow. "All of it?"

I take a quick inventory of her lingerie.

"Just the stockings," I amend. I'm going to need access to the rest of her skin.

She reaches back to unclip her bra. "As you wish."

"Fuck," I mutter as her bra falls open and slides down her arms. She's changed out her nipple rings for a set of barbells with chains dripping below each nipple, framing them like the perfect pieces of art they are.

Rhia really pulled out all the stops tonight. Then again, she probably knew she'd need every distraction technique at her disposal. While her outfit certainly helps numb some of my angst, I'm also gaining confidence each time I look at the candle and find the flame completely in control as wax steadily pools around the base.

Rhia reaches for the top of her stockings where the garter is clipped, and I grab her wrist to stop her.

"Let me."

She clasps her hands primly behind her back as I flip open the clips at the front and back of each stocking. I feel like I'm unboxing a much-anticipated present. With one flick, the back of the belt opens, and the piece of fabric falls to the floor, leaving Rhia in just her lacy black panties. I tease a finger below the elastic band of them.

"I think I'll leave these on for now so you can grind that pretty little clit against the lace."

The fierce blush that creeps into her cheeks tells me she likes that idea.

"You're a goddess," I tell Rhia, skimming my hands down her hips to the tops of her stockings.

She lets out a soft chuckle as she climbs back into my lap. We make out like horny teenagers, and it brings me back to the first time I got Rhia off, when neither of us even had to remove a stitch of clothing. Still pretty proud of that one.

After an indeterminate amount of time, she pulls back and curls her fingers through my hair. Her lips are puffy from my kisses, her cheeks still tinged pink.

"The wax is probably ready."

It dawns on me that I haven't set eyes on the flame in minutes, and I feel much calmer than expected about that.

"How do you want to do this?" I ask. "Should I grab a towel or something?"

Rhia nods. "Probably."

I hustle to the bathroom for a towel and drape it over the long part of the couch. There's a deep well of melted wax at the bottom of the candle. I've never done this before, but I understand the concept, and if anyone is going to handle this safely, it'll be me.

"You ready for this?" I echo Rhia's earlier question to me. This may have been her idea, but that doesn't mean she can't change her mind.

In lieu of a response, Rhia lays herself on the towel, adjusting her hair so it splays out around her head like black sunbeams. Her stocking-clad legs are slightly bent with her feet planted on the couch. I place a hand behind each of her knees and spread them, making space for myself between her open legs.

"Comfortable?"

Rhia nods, and it registers that her eyes are full of devotion. The trust it takes for her to let me do this mirrors the trust it took *me* to let her light that candle. We're both pushing each other, but it works because of the amount of trust we've built.

Chest filled with pride, I blow out the candle. I fucking *did* it. There's still a sense of relief when the flame is eliminated, but it's not nearly as powerful as it was before, and I think that's a good sign. I wasn't paying enough attention to the actual amount of time I kept the candle lit for, but it was enough to create a healthy pool of wax.

I settle myself between Rhia's legs, ready to reap my reward. "Relax," I tell her as I run a hand down her sternum.

Her knees fall open slightly wider at my touch.

"Good girl," I tell her, and they spread even wider.

I run my fingers along her curves, deciding where to start. Without warning, I let a small drop spill just above her belly button.

Rhia lets out a small gasp as her entire body jolts.

"Okay?" I ask.

"Yes," she replies as the wax begins to harden into a little bead. "I like it."

I hum my approval as I move higher up her torso. "I knew my naughty girl would enjoy this."

I deposit a drop of wax on the swell of her left breast, and Rhia hisses with pleasure. We might have to make this a regular thing if she's going to keep making noises like that. My cock is already rock hard, and each sexy little noise she lets out is like a bolt of lightning straight to it.

I drip the wax down closer to her nipple, and Rhia pushes her chest into the sensation.

"What does it feel like?" I ask, fascinated by her reactions.

"Warm," she replies in a dreamy voice. "Perfect."

I let a drop spill directly onto her nipple, and she shivers.

"Just like you," I muse, my free hand gripping her waist as I add some wax to her other breast. She continues to wriggle and squirm with every drop. Her core muscles flex and strain as I rain dots of wax down her sternum.

"Cole!" she cries out as it nears her belly button, her stomach hollowing.

I pat her side soothingly. "Yes, gorgeous?"

"This is more of a tease than I expected it to be," she whines.

I drip wax a bit further down her stomach with a chuckle. Ironically, it's more of a tease for *me* than I expected it to be too. Watching the dark wax drip and pool over her pale skin is so unexpectedly sensual.

Rhia grabs two fistfuls of the towel beneath her, her knuckles turning white with the force of her hold.

"You're doing such a good job," I tell her, allowing the wax to coast down over the crease of her thighs. Goosebumps crop up over the tops of her legs. "Is that pretty little pussy aching for me?"

Rhia's hips buck as she lets out a strangled moan. "Yes!" she cries.

I'm almost out of wax, so I quickly move to the other leg, trailing wax down her inner thigh. "Yes what?" I prompt.

"Yes, sir," Rhia wails, her eyes sealed shut as she arches her back, putting those gorgeous, wax-covered tits on display.

"That's my gorgeous girl." I let the last drop of wax fall before setting the candle on the table and taking a moment to admire my work. Rhia is a writhing mess of dark hair, flushed cheeks, and black wax hardened onto soft, creamy skin. When she opens her eyes, I see that her pupils are blown wide.

"Oh, baby," I croon. She looks like a fallen angel, some innocent I've corrupted, and I perversely love that.

"Please," she murmurs, begging for something unnamed.

"I've got you." I skate my fingers up and down her sides so as not to disturb the wax. "Just relax," I tell her before diving face first at the apex of her thighs.

Rhia's sudden intake of breath makes me smile against her pussy. I don't waste any time, licking right up her center to the hardened nub at the top. She's already soaking wet for me, and her taste is divine. I can't believe I haven't had her like this until now. I've eaten a lot of delicious dishes in my lifetime, but this has to be the finest delicacy I've ever had the privilege of tasting.

I repeat the motion, wringing a long moan out of Rhia. One of her hands dives into my hair as her legs open wide for me, cracking some of the wax along her inner thighs.

"You taste," I say as I lap at her wetness, "so fucking good."

"Fuck!" Rhia screams when I turn my focus entirely to her clit, suctioning my lips around it. I can tell she's close, already having learned her signals, so I slide a finger into her pussy, feeling its tight grip. I moan around her clit as her pussy squeezes my finger.

"Cole!" Rhia spasms around me as I add another finger, brushing against her inner walls as I suck on her clit. Her grip on my hair tightens almost to the point of pain, but it barely registers as she comes all over my hand and mouth. Her legs start to shake as a groan rattles out of her, long and ragged.

I bring her down from her orgasm with long, slow licks, cleaning her up as her body melts into the couch.

"Holy. Shit," she utters.

"Yeah," I agree, lying down beside her so I can reach her lips. I thread my fingers into her mess of hair and kiss her softly and slowly. "You did amazing," I tell her.

Rhia smiles softly at me. "So did you." She glances over at the candle, now short and stubby. She starts to sit up, and bits of wax crack onto the towel beneath her.

"I fucking love it when you're messy," I admit. Much of the wax still clings to her skin in a patchwork of our passion.

"I'm honestly not sure how to clean this up," she says.

"I'm thinking a long, hot shower," I suggest. "Together, of course."

Rhia beams at me. "What a great idea."

CHAPTER 27
RHIANNON

Damien's fingers sifted through Veronica's hair as he lay beside her. After their romp in the car, they'd spent the night together in her bed. And the next night after that. And the one after that.

Being together was becoming a habit that was hard to break.

"Veronica," Damien whispered, pressing a kiss to her bare shoulder. "It's morning."

She mumbled something incoherent, still half asleep.

"Your book comes out today," he reminded her. "Today, the world finds out the truth about your family."

That woke her up.

"Today's the day," Veronica murmured. "What will people think of me?"

"It doesn't matter what people think," Damien replied. "I think you're spectacular."

Two days before Thanksgiving, I get a text from Caleb, asking me to meet him for coffee. It's not necessarily unusual for Caleb to text me, but it *is* out of the ordinary for him to ask to meet up without Hannah along. After making him promise me there's nothing urgently wrong with either of them, I agree to meet up. Even then, my mind races with all the adverse possibilities.

When I arrive at Waffee, Caleb is already sitting at a table. His leg bounces beneath it in a nervous gesture. I've never known him to be a fidgety guy, so this kicks my anxiety up a notch. I can't possibly imagine what he might need from me that he doesn't want Hannah to know about. My stomach twists at the sudden thought that he might be breaking up with her, and I rush over to the table to meet him.

"Hey, Rhia." Caleb greets me with a warm smile as I sit down, pushing one of two green teas across the table to me. He's not a coffee drinker either, much to his girlfriend's dismay.

"Hi," I reply, his warm welcome doing nothing to appease my anxiety. "What's going on?"

Caleb's brows draw together. "I'm sorry if I worried you—I promise it's nothing bad."

I hold the paper cup of tea, allowing its soothing warmth to seep into my hands. "I know you said you two are both fine, but my mind is kind of running away with me," I admit.

Caleb takes a sip of his tea and runs a hand over his beard. "I'm sorry again. I actually asked you here because..." He pauses, and I want to reach across the table and shake him until he spills.

The corners of his lips tip up in a shy smile. "I'm planning to ask Hannah to marry me."

The squeal that escapes me is part cat yowl, part whistling tea kettle, but it's *all* excitement.

"For real this time," Caleb adds. Last year, Hannah and Caleb got legally married at the courthouse so she could get on his health insurance plan. She was turning twenty-six, and as a self-employed chronically ill woman in America, her healthcare options were grim. Caleb never planned to marry, so he didn't see it as a big deal—just a favor to a friend in need.

Once they started actually dating, though, they decided to

get divorced so things didn't get too messy. Hannah also got a job at Caleb's company that gave her amazing health insurance, so the sham marriage wasn't necessary anymore.

The whole thing had my romance-author heart jumping for joy.

"Caleb, I am *so* excited for you! I know she'll say yes. Obviously. But I'm so happy! Now you two can have a real wedding!" I start picturing all the things I want Hannah to have at her wedding. She was never a huge dreamer about her big day, but I've done enough fantasizing for the both of us. I may or may not have a separate Pinterest wedding board for her in addition to my own.

Caleb lets out a low chuckle "I'm going to take her up to the lake house and pop the question in our favorite spot at sunset," he says. "I'm telling you because I'd like to ask you to be there afterward, like a little surprise for Hannah. I don't necessarily think she would want to celebrate her engagement with her family, although they're on good terms now, but I know she would want to celebrate with you."

Tears sting the backs of my eyes at his thoughtfulness and at the fact that he would want to share their special moment with me.

"Really?" I ask, worried I would be a nuisance. Who wants to get engaged and then have to host their friend? They're probably just going to want to go bang each other's brains out.

"Of course," Caleb replies. "You've been her best friend since you were young. You're like a sister to her. If you're not there, Hannah would probably insist we drive right home so she could tell you."

The thought makes me smile. Hannah knows how much of a hopeless romantic I am. She would definitely be dying to tell me about her engagement.

"I would love to be there," I say. "I'd be honored."

"Good." Caleb seems genuinely happy I've said yes, so I feel secure that my presence won't annoy them. "You can bring

Cole if you'd like," he adds. "We could make a whole weekend of it."

The offer gives me pause. I would obviously love a weekend away with Cole, but is it too much too soon? And is celebrating my best friend's engagement too serious an occasion? Although, I *am* going to his family's Thanksgiving dinner, and that seems pretty serious.

"I'll ask him," I say.

Caleb gives me the dates, and we go over the plan—he'll text me when they're leaving the house for the beach, and that's when I'll arrive and set up a mini surprise engagement party for them—and I ask him for one little favor in return.

Hannah's and his apartment has a gas stove, and since I know they're going to his mom's house for Thanksgiving, I ask if I can borrow their kitchen that morning. Caleb agrees easily, and we say our goodbyes. I get a little teary again at the thought that the next time I'll see him, he'll be engaged to my best friend.

Before I leave, I text Cole to ask if we can make a slight change to our Thanksgiving morning plans, explaining that I got us access to a gas stove if he wants to continue his exposure therapy. I don't get a reply until a couple of hours after I've returned home, but luckily, it's him agreeing. I have some more tricks up my sleeve, so I'm hoping I'll be able to keep him just happily distracted enough while he works on facing his fears.

have most of what I think we'll need set up in Hannah and Caleb's kitchen, including a large skillet for sautéing the vegetables and a glass baking dish for the final product. Cole is bringing all the ingredients, so I didn't have much prep work to do.

He knocks on the door right on time, and I open it up to let him in.

"Did you…just wake up?" Cole asks, scratching his head as he takes in my long, silk bathrobe.

"Not exactly," I reply with a giggle. "Come in."

He enters the kitchen and places two bags on the counter. Once I have the apartment door closed, I shrug off my robe and hang it over a kitchen chair, revealing the sexy chef costume I bought for Halloween a few years ago and then was too chicken to wear out in public. I'm rather pleased I have an opportunity to use it now.

Cole drinks me in with hungry eyes, his gaze roaming over the fishnet stockings and frilly little black-and-white dress with buttons all up the front. I grab the matching chef's hat off the counter and plop it on my head to complete the look.

"Goddamn," he mutters, taking two long strides to reach me and pulling me in for a long kiss. "And all I brought was this." Cole pulls out an article of clothing and unfolds it before placing it over his head. It's a "kiss the chef" apron with a big pair of juicy red lips on the front.

With a wide grin, I lift up on my tiptoes and comply with the order written on his apron. We kiss for a long moment before Cole backs me against the counter, gearing up for more. I grasp his apron in my fists to wrench his lips off mine.

"Don't think you're going to distract me from our task," I chide. "We can't show up to Thanksgiving empty-handed."

"You can't show up to Thanksgiving like this at all. His gaze rakes up and down my body.

"I have an outfit packed," I assure him with a pat on his chest. "Now, I want to learn how to make this stuffing."

Cole sneaks one more quick kiss before unpacking all the ingredients. The counter comes to life in a rainbow of colors as he sets a bag of fresh cranberries beside a couple of carrots, a few stalks of celery, an onion, and a large Granny Smith apple.

"The first step is chopping all this shit up," Cole explains as he sets up two cutting boards side by side. He places a loaf of sourdough on one of them and the carrots and celery on the other. "I'll work on dicing up the bread, and you can do some of the veggies."

"How big?" I ask, picking up a sharp knife.

"About half an inch should be good." Cole dives into the sourdough loaf while I move a little more slowly, deciding if I want to slice the long vegetables lengthwise first before dicing them up or just start chopping them. By the time I've made my decision to do the former and gotten the celery cut lengthwise, Cole is practically halfway done with his task.

I try to speed up my process, but I'm too clumsy with the knife, and I have to slow back down so I don't chop a finger off. Cole notices I'm struggling and pauses what he's doing.

"Here, let me show you." He steps behind me, taking my knife in one hand and the celery in the other, gripping it with his fingertips pointed back toward his palm. "If you're worried about catching your fingertips, you can hold them like this." Switching his grip, he uses the pads of his fingers to grip the stalks. "But the real key is controlling the knife." He picks up my knife, showing me how he holds it with the base of the blade pinched between his thumb and forefinger. "You want to have a grip on the blade, not just the handle," he explains. "You try."

I can't help but wiggle my ass against him as I take the knife, imitating his grip on it. I definitely feel less likely to lose a digit this way. "I think you need your own cooking show," I muse as I resume my chopping. "You could call it 'Cooking with Cole.'"

He chuckles as he moves back over to his own cutting station. "Now there's an idea. If you played my sous chef dressed like that, I'm sure we'd get tons of viewers."

"You think?" I ask, purposefully knocking a small piece of carrot on the ground. "Oops." I bend over to pick it up, my dress riding up to reveal the thong I'm wearing beneath it.

Cole groans, leaning over to give my ass a light swat. "I, for one, could watch you like this all day."

I toss the piece of carrot into the garbage. "Yeah? Is roleplay your thing?"

"*You* are my thing," he replies.

I turn to find him watching me, his gaze soft. I reward his sweet statement with a quick kiss before we get back to our prep. Cole pulls out a stick of mint gum before chopping the onion, informing me that the chewing motion helps make you cry less.

Once everything is chopped up, I ask Cole for our next step.

"Now, we sauté," he says, staring at the skillet I have set up on the stove. He tosses a hunk of butter into the skillet and approaches the dials to turn on the stove.

I sidle up next to him to offer my support. "You want to do the honors?"

His hand hovers over the dial for the largest burner. "I'll try."

Cole takes an audible deep breath and twists the dial just enough for the burner to light. Almost as soon as the flame flickers on, he turns the dial back off, his entire body jerking away from the stove.

"That's okay." I wrap my arms around him, pressing a hand over his rapidly beating heart. "Take a second and breathe."

I try to synchronize our breaths, and after a minute or two, I feel some of the tension unravel from his muscles.

"You want to try again?"

He nods, and I let him go. Cole cracks his knuckles and places his hand on the dial again. This time, he gets the burner lit, and the dial makes it all the way to medium. We both stare for a second as the flame crackles beneath the skillet.

A proud smile stretches over my lips. "You did it."

Cole tears his gaze away from the flame, his eyes finding mine. A soft grin pulls at the corners of his lips. "I did."

"Now show me the right way to sauté vegetables," I instruct. Cole coaches me through the process, and I ask loads of questions to help keep his mind off the flame. He stays vigilant, never turning away from the stove, but I suppose that's basic kitchen safety.

Just as the onions start to become translucent, Cole turns off the stove and moves the skillet away from the heat.

"You did it," I tell him once again, wrapping him in a hug and pressing my cheek to his chest. Any residual tension in his body melts away as he rests his chin on the top of my head.

"Only because I have you by my side," he tells me quietly. "After that first try, I probably would have just chickened out if I was on my own."

"That's what I'm here for," I remind him. "You don't have to do this alone. You've helped me gain so much confidence in myself since we met. I want to do the same for you."

Cole gazes fondly down at me, brushing some of my hair behind my ear. "Thank you." He presses a sweet kiss to my forehead before we finish out the non-stove related tasks, adding the sautéed veggies to a bowl with the bread, apple, cranberries, and some chicken broth and spices. Once everything is combined, Cole pours it into the baking dish, covers it with tin foil, and places it in the pre-heated oven.

"How long do we have?" I ask.

Cole sets a time on his phone before dropping it into his pocket. "Half an hour until I have to uncover it."

"Perfect." I reach behind him to untie his apron and tug it off over his head. "Your apron says "kiss the chef," but it doesn't specify where," I say, dropping down on my knees before him.

CHAPTER 28
RHIANNON

I relish Cole's sharp intake of breath as my knees hit the kitchen floor. I haven't had the opportunity to try this out yet. After Cole ate me out, we had sex in the shower, but I never got the chance to taste him. That changes now.

"Fuck," Cole hisses as I pop open the button of his jeans and yank down his zipper. "Rhia, you don't have to–" he starts.

"I want to," I assure him as I grab fistfuls of his jeans and begin dragging them down his legs. Cole helps me out, using his feet to push the pants down before finally stepping out of them. His boxer briefs do little to hide his growing erection, which gets even harder when I palm it through the fabric.

"You did such a good job today," I tell him as I trace his cock through his boxers. "I think you deserve a reward." I draw his boxers down until he can step out of them. His hard cock springs free, and I grasp it in my palm.

"Shit," Cole mutters as I give it a firm tug. I know this is what he likes, because I've seen him do it to himself. Even if I have no idea what I'm doing with my mouth, at least I know how to use my hands on him.

I trace the vein running along his cock with my fingertip.

"You'll have to tell me what you like." Leaning in, I use my tongue to follow the same path I just drew.

"I–I like *that*," he says.

I repeat the movement before lifting his cock to access the underside, flicking my tongue beneath the head of it. Any erotica author worth her salt knows that's the most sensitive area.

Cole lets out a grunt, his hips pushing forward. I take that as an invitation to take him fully into my mouth, wrapping my lips around the head of his cock. Once I get a feel for that, I take him deeper, experimenting with long, slow sucks, swirling my tongue around the end each time.

"That's so good." Cole tears the chef's hat I've forgotten all about off my head and tangles his fingers into my hair. "Fuck, that's perfect, gorgeous."

Spurred on by his praise, I take more of him, accidentally going too far too fast and gagging around his cock. Cole gently pulls my head back, his finger stroking my cheek.

"I'm okay," I murmur before trying again. This time, I'm more prepared, and I manage to take a good amount of his erection without triggering my gag reflex.

"Good fucking girl," Cole growls, pulling slightly on my hair. I repeat that exact movement a few more times before trying something new. There's so much I want to experiment with—so many things I've read about or watched and want to try—but I know I need to start slow.

On my next suck, I reach down to cup Cole's balls. His hips lurch forward, and I gag again before pulling back.

"Sorry, baby," Cole says quickly. "Wasn't expecting that," he adds with a soft chuckle. "But I like it. A lot."

"'S'okay," I murmur, almost swallowing the excess saliva he created before remembering how he said he loves me messy. Instead, I let some of it drool out onto his cock before resuming.

A groan pours out of Cole, but he's more controlled when I touch his balls this time, gently rolling them in my hand. I marvel at how soft they feel and how sensitive they are.

"I, uh…I like them licked too, if you want," he says. "No pressure, though."

I can't help but smile around Cole's cock. Does he not realize how much I aim to please him? I'd do just about anything if he said it made him hot.

Gently lifting his erection out of the way, my nose brushes against it as I lap at the smooth skin that stretches over his balls. I stroke my tongue experimentally, getting a feel for which areas are the most sensitive, before sucking one side of his sac into my mouth.

Cole hisses with pleasure. Half of me wants to get him off as quickly as I can, because I love watching him come undone, while the other half wants to draw this out until I've gotten a chance to explore everything I want to.

I release him with a slight pop before drawing a teasing line with my tongue up the seam of his sac and the underside of his cock. I take Cole back into my mouth for a long, deep pull, drawing another garbled noise from him. I'm about to go in for another when he gently pulls me back by my hair.

"That's enough," he barks, tugging me upward. I take the hint to stand, and Cole crushes his mouth to mine, uncaring that my lips were just stretched around his cock. His erection gets sandwiched between us, and he feels hard enough to cut diamonds.

"Why didn't you let me finish?" I ask breathlessly.

Cole takes me by the hips and backs me against the counter. "I had other ideas about where I want to come." Reaching beneath my mini dress, he hooks his finger into my panties and slides them off. "Turn around," he instructs. "Be a good girl and bend over."

Cole guides me onto the counter with a hand on my upper back until my cheek presses into the cool marble. He flips up the bottom of my dress, and the sensation of the air in the room whispering over my bare bottom raises goosebumps up and down my arms.

"I've been thinking about doing this ever since you took off that damn robe," he grumbles, palming one cheek in his big hand. "Did sucking me off get you nice and wet?" His fingers slip lower, sliding through my soaked slit. "Oh, baby," he murmurs as he gets the answer to his question.

I squeak when his fingers slip inside of me, effortlessly gliding through my wetness.

"You've been such a good girl," Cole murmurs as he dips his fingers into my pussy and drags the moisture up to my clit. "Sucking my cock. Licking my balls." He swirls the pad of his finger around the hard nub. "Being a naughty girl for me."

With a moan, I push my ass back against him, grinding it on his erection.

Cole gives it a light swat. "Greedy girl."

"I want you," I say, still seeking friction.

Cole takes me by the hips and lines himself up behind me. "Where do you want me, baby?"

I let out an irritated grumble. "Inside of me."

He brushes the tip of his cock through my slit. "You've already had me inside your mouth. Where do you want me now?" he teases as he pets my hips and thighs, teasing strokes over my sensitized skin.

"In my pussy!" I cry. "I want you in my pussy. *Please*, sir."

A breath whooshes out of Cole. "My good girl gets what she wants," he whispers in my ear as he drives into me in one swift stroke.

We let out twin moans as he fills me, deliciously stretching me out. The sound of slapping flesh fills the kitchen as Cole sets a brutal rhythm that's exactly what I craved. His fingers reacclimate themselves with my clit, and he works it in tight little circles that have me moaning.

"Fuck, Rhia," Cole grits out. "I'm not going to last. Are you close?"

I'm so fucking turned on right now, and he's touching me

exactly how I like, but my body just doesn't want to cooperate. Damn those SSRIs. Little lifesaving losers.

"I might not be able to...but I want you to come, Cole." I grind back into him. "Come inside me," I say. "Fill me up. Show me how good I make you feel."

With a long string of curses, Cole empties himself inside of me, his hips punching until he spills every last drop. He bends over me and presses a kiss into my neck before slowly sliding out of me. As soon as his cock slips out, he thrusts two fingers inside of me, catching our combined wetness and dragging it upward.

"Come here, baby." He tugs on my shoulder until I stand, my back to his front. He wraps his arm around me and slowly walks us backward until he hits the other set of counters.

"Can I try to get you off like this?" he asks as he continues to toy with my clit.

"Cole, you don't have to—"

"It's okay if you can't, but I'd like to try," he insists. "I'm not in any rush."

"Okay," I reply, craning my neck until he lowers his lips to mine. Cole kisses me soundly while his fingers play over my clit, periodically dipping back inside of me to gather more moisture. My pleasure builds, still not quite reaching the heights I need it to.

Cole taps my inner thigh. "Spread a little wider."

I do, and the new angle helps, but it's not enough. Damnit. This is one of the hottest moments of my life, and I can't manage to get there despite how turned on I am. As if he can sense my frustration, Cole grabs my left leg behind the knee, hiking it up and draping it over his elbow. The movement opens me up obscenely wide. I'd lose my balance if it wasn't for Cole's hard body behind me and his strong arms holding me up.

I feel his breath coast over my ear. "I want my gorgeous girl to feel as good as she made me feel," he whispers, nipping at my earlobe. "I'll do whatever it takes to get you there, baby. You want my mouth on your pussy, sucking on that little clit? Done. You want me to rip this dress off and play with those pierced nipples until you scream? Done. You want a finger in your ass while I fuck you? Done. Whatever it takes," he promises.

As it turns out, his dirty words are all it takes. Visions of his fantasies float through my mind as his fingers play my clit like a fiddle, and a switch flips inside of me. I cry out as I come all over his hand, soaking it in my pleasure.

"Thatta girl," Cole murmurs as he slows his strokes to long, drawn-out circles. "You did so good for me."

I sag against him, unable to hold myself up any longer. He wraps me in his arms and holds me, stroking my skin wherever he can reach, until the timer beeps behind us. I jump, startled, and Cole drops a kiss on my temple before releasing me with a chuckle.

"Let me just uncover this." He turns to open the oven.

"I'll go get cleaned up." I grab my discarded panties off the floor and shove them into my bag, trading them for the extra outfit I brought. By the time I've cleaned up and changed, Cole has removed the stuffing from the oven, and it sits steaming on the counter. The aroma of baked apples and sage winds through the air, making my mouth water.

Cole is scrubbing the counter he bent me over, but he pauses to take me in. I'm hoping my long-sleeved beige turtleneck and brown plaid pinafore are appropriate for his family holiday. The outfit is cute but comfortable, and everyone knows you don't wear something tight to Thanksgiving.

"Okay, this is giving me sexy schoolgirl vibes," Cole says, dropping his washcloth on the counter.

"That's not exactly what I was going for, but whatever works." I give him a little spin. "Is this good enough?"

Cole grabs me into a big hug. "This is better than good enough." He runs a hand over my backside. "I'm afraid I won't be able to keep my hands off of you."

"You're going to have to." I glance at the clock on the wall. "What time are we picking up Bailey?"

Cole groans. "I said we'd be outside her dorm at noon."

I pull out of his embrace and swat his hands away. "We're running behind!"

Cole hangs his head. "Do we have to go?"

His sudden hesitance stops me in my tracks.

"No," I reply softly. "We don't have to do anything you aren't comfortable with." I reach up to sift my fingers through his hair. "We can cancel if that's what you really want, but I don't want you to have any regrets."

Cole presses the heel of his hand to his forehead. "No, we should go," he decides. "Plus, we're Bailey's ride, and I don't want to make her miss a family holiday."

"Let's get going, then." I pull a large piece of tin foil out of the box on the counter to cover the stuffing. "The faster we get through this, the faster we get back here. And I *may* have even more surprises in store."

Cole's bright grin stretches wide. "I'm learning to really love your surprises."

CHAPTER 29
COLE

My stomach bottoms out as we pull up to the familiar Victorian with its light-blue siding and white trim, complete with a goddamn white picket fence bordering the yard. It's the very picture of the American dream, and yet I know that, within those walls, live the ghosts from my childhood that still haunt me to this day.

Don't get me wrong; this house is home to many good memories. It's the place where I watched my first cooking show because I'd never had a television before. It's where I had my first kiss under the big tree in the backyard. It's the first place I ever existed where I wasn't worried about where my next meal would come from.

But it's also where I was told over and over again that my aspirations weren't enough. That *I* wasn't enough. It's where Bailey and I tried endlessly to stuff ourselves into the neat little box the rest of the family resided in until we were old enough to decide that we wanted to break free of it.

It took years for me to realize that my aunt and uncle weren't the heroes they saw themselves as. We saw them that way for a while, until we matured enough to realize the truth. When Bailey and I first arrived here, we saw Jen and Tom as our saviors. They rescued us from poverty, food insecurity, and constant emotional turmoil. They provided us with our own bedrooms, an endless supply of food, and access to anything money could buy.

They had a refrigerator with a built-in ice machine and a water tap. They had a flat-screen television with multiple video gaming systems attached to it. They had a finished basement with a ping pong table and a grand piano that lived in its very own room. Coming from a one-bedroom apartment shared by two children and their unpredictable alcoholic mother, it felt like paradise.

But other than the bare necessities for survival, what Bailey and I really needed was love. Warmth. Acceptance. Support. And we received none of that here.

"Wow," Rhia murmurs as I put the car in park. She's taking in the house, which I'll admit looks quite impressive. The covered porch is decked out for fall, with corn stalks standing tall on either side of the front door and pumpkins lining the front steps. There are tin buckets full of mums and even a little stack of decorative hay bales adorning one corner of the porch.

"Jen's a big decorator," I explain, recalling the many events she went all out for over the years. Particularly clear in my mind is the camping-themed birthday party she threw me when I turned nine. I longed for a party at the local roller-skating rink, but I got a camping one in our yard instead because Jen was inspired by something she'd seen in *Better Homes and Gardens* magazine. I had never been camping once in my life.

Jen set up tents in the yard with little lanterns and activities that would put Pinterest to shame in each, and she insisted that we make s'mores over a tabletop fire pit. I spent that whole portion of the party huddled in one of the tents. My mom had died in the fire less than a year earlier. When I pretended to blow out the candles I had insisted remain unlit on my forest-themed cake, all I wished for was her to come back.

Rhia takes my hand as we walk up the front steps—a silent show of support. Bailey trails behind us, taking her sweet time.

Aunt Jen answers the door in a crisp white apron, looking much the part of the happy housewife. There's the slightest hint of surprise in her eyes, as if she didn't actually expect us to come, even though we confirmed our plans via text just a few days ago.

"Hi, kids," Jen says, her social smile snapping into place.

"Jen," I reply, greeting her with a half hug. "This is my girlfriend, Rhiannon."

Jen gives Rhia a not-so-subtle onceover before reaching out her perfectly manicured hand to shake Rhia's.

"It's very nice to meet you, Mrs. Aster," Rhia says, scoring points, I'm sure, for using an honorific instead of her first name. I'm so glad Jen and Tom's last name happened to come up in conversation on the way over. "You have a beautiful home," she adds, flashing Jen a demure smile.

Jen nods, satisfied by Rhia's praise. "Thank you. Why don't you all head into the kitchen?" She uses a sweeping gesture to welcome us in, and we begin our trek through the house.

Rhia takes note of the family photos that line the long hallway, slowing slightly to get a closer look at each. I don't have to look to know that Bailey and I only appear in exactly two of the approximately twenty photos present. One picture in particular seems to catch Rhia's eye, and I glance over to see which one it is.

Ah, our first foray into the annual family vacation on Cape Cod. The first summer we stayed with Jen and Tom, they brought us along on their yearly trip. Bailey and I had never seen the ocean before, despite growing up in a coastal state. As it turned out, Bailey was terrified of the water and wanted nothing to do with the beach.

In the photo, we all wear matching khaki pants and white tops—the classic uniform of the perfect family. There's a long expanse of sand in the background, with the ocean a tiny sliver right at the very edge of the photo. Jen, Tom, and their biological children stand arm in arm wearing wide smiles, while Bailey and I stand off to the side like our own little island. The professional photographer kept encouraging us to get closer to the rest of the group, but Bailey wouldn't let me out of her grasp for fear that the ocean would whoosh all the way up the beach and suck her into its swirling depths.

The photo is an impeccable depiction of the nature of our relationship with the family. Each year after that first one, we stayed behind for the "family" vacation. Tom's mom would watch us for the week, but she mostly kept to herself and didn't really want much to do with us. I remember loving it because it felt like the old days when it was just Bailey and me alone together, minus the threat of our unpredictable mother returning home at any time.

We reach the kitchen and find my cousins, Brett and Steve, as well as my uncle Tom, sitting at the kitchen island, sipping on beers and shouting at the football game on TV while Jen pokes her head into the oven.

"I would love to give you a tour, Rhiannon, but I have to check on my bird first."

"No worries," Rhia replies as she looks around the kitchen.

The boisterous men turn their gazes from the TV to study her.

"Hey, everyone," I say with a wave. "This is Rhiannon."

Like the well-raised young men they are, Brett and Steve each stand up to introduce themselves and shake Rhia's hand. Tom does the same before they quickly return to their perches at the island.

Brett and Steve are a couple of years apart, but they could pass for twins with their matching brown undercuts, brown eyes, and olive complexions. Their likeness is so starkly different from Bailey's and my red hair and blue eyes that it always automatically set us apart. Growing up, people could tell before even speaking to us that we were separate. Different. Outcasts in our own family.

At least we had each other.

I set my stuffing down on the counter, and I'm just about to find the three of us a place to sit when Jen shuts the turkey safely back in the oven.

"How about that tour?" she asks.

Rhia graciously accepts the offer, and Bailey and I tag along, even though we know this house by heart. Jen glides through the kitchen, which opens right up to the living room, and then the dining room, showing off its perfectly set table, laying in wait for us to feast. She points out the half bath for guests to use and the study, opening the door just long enough for us to get a glimpse of the computer, chess table, and antique bookcases before sealing the room shut again.

We end in the piano room, congregating around the edge of the black baby grand that shines like a jewel at the center of the room.

"Oh, Bailey, why don't you play us a song?" Jen suggests.

"Oh, I—" Bailey begins to argue.

"Oh, please, sweetheart," Jen pleads. "Just one song."

Bailey takes a seat on the bench with a soft sigh. She knows as well as I do that Jen only likes using her talents for show. My aunt loves the thought of impressing house guests with her adopted daughter's talent, yet she refuses to fund or support Bailey's efforts to use that talent as a career. It's the very definition of hypocritical.

I immediately recognize the opening notes of "Pink Pony Club" as Bailey's fingers dance across the keys.

"Isn't she wonderful?" Jen stage whispers to Rhia, oblivious to her song choice.

"She sure is," Rhia agrees with a conspiratorial smile toward me.

Jen's mouth flattens into a thin line as Bailey launches into the lyrics, but she refuses to be embarrassed in her own home. We listen in silence as Bailey belts out the words about leaving your hometown and finding a safe space to be who you are. Jen indulges her with a lackluster golf clap when she's finished playing, while I dog whistle and Rhia whoops her praise.

We're soon ushered back to the kitchen so Jen can check on her food again. Tom comes over to pick at the charcuterie board on the counter that was obviously dug into long before we arrived.

"What did you bring, kid?" he asks, his mouth full of salami as he points at my still-covered stuffing.

"It's an apple, sage, and cranberry stuffing," I reply, gently prying the tin foil off the top of it.

Jen turns her nose up at the dish. "That sounds…like a lot of carbs."

Tom leans in to sniff it, his lips puckering as if he's eaten something sour.

"Isn't that what Thanksgiving is for?" Rhia asks with a cheery smile.

Neither my aunt nor my uncle responds, instead returning to their respective jobs of cooking and watching football. Rhia reaches for my hand, giving it a comforting squeeze as we make our way to the window seat. It's the only open area for us to sit down, and we stay there chatting amongst ourselves until dinner is ready.

The dinner spread is a true feast—a huge, steaming turkey, a vat of fluffy mashed potatoes, side dishes of blanched green beans, roasted carrots, and tart cranberry sauce, and, of course, my stuffing, which sits untouched on a far corner of the table. All the other dishes have been passed around for people to take from, while the one I made was ignored and pushed to the side like it's made of nuclear waste.

Rhia must notice my sideways glance at the dish, wondering if it'll get passed around last or if everyone is truly just going to act like it's not there.

"Brett," she addresses my cousin who sits closest to the stuffing. "Could you pass the stuffing please?"

Brett—whose mouth is already full of mashed potatoes

despite dinner not yet being completely served—meets her gaze with wide eyes, as if he's shocked she would deign to ask him for something.

"Uh, sure," he says, fumbling for the dish before handing it to Steve, who hands it to Bailey, who finally passes it to Rhiannon.

"Thank you," she says. "I've been dying to try this!" She might be selling it a *little* too hard, but I can't help but love her for it. And when she cuts herself a serving of stuffing that's literally a quarter of the dish and plops it on her plate with an audible *thunk*, I truly don't think I could love her more.

Love? The word startles me as it pops so naturally into my mind, but I have to admit it's the closest fit for what I'm feeling at the moment.

"Wow, you must be hungry," Jen remarks.

"Starving," Rhia replies, unbothered by my aunt's snootiness.

"I'll take that next," Bailey pipes up once Rhia is finished serving herself. Rhia passes the dish to Bailey, who scoops herself a similar-sized helping.

"Damn. You two must be on your periods or something," Steve says with a derisive snort.

"Steven," Jen warns.

"What?" he asks. "Doesn't it make you crave, like, comfort food?"

Bailey sticks her tongue out at our cousin.

"Shut up, son," Tom pipes up.

"Sorry," Steve mumbles under his breath, shoveling a forkful of turkey into his mouth.

"The carrots are fantastic," Rhia says, obviously determined to get this dinner back on track. "Is that brown sugar I taste?"

"Yes," Jen replies. "And maple syrup."

Rhia hums. "Delicious."

The rest of the dinner passes in a similar vein—thinly veiled barbs from my extended family and valiant attempts from my girlfriend to smooth them over. While I appreciate her efforts, I can tell that my family's attitudes are eating her up inside.

I'm sure no one else notices the way her shoulders have gradually hiked up higher as she grows more and more tense, or how her smiles have grown tighter, or her patience has thinned. But I know my Rhia, and I can tell she's ready to get out of here, so I rush to wrap up dinner and make our escape.

CHAPTER 30
COLE

"Glad that's over," Bailey mutters as she pulls the car door shut behind her on our way home.

A heavy sigh gusts out of me. "Same," I agree.

Rhia shifts in the passenger seat beside me. "Guys," she says as I peel out of the driveway. "I'm going to say something, and I want you to really hear me when I say it. Bailey, I don't know for sure about you, but I know that Cole feels beholden to your aunt and uncle for taking you in, and that's a big part of the reason he felt like he had to go today, but adopting you was Jen and Tom's choice to make. Not yours. You don't owe them anything but the respect they've given you, which isn't much. So while I admire your dedication to staying in touch with the family who took you in, I just want you to know that you shouldn't ever feel like you have to pander to them."

Bailey and I are both silent for a moment as we let Rhia's words sink in. Everything she said makes so much sense without the emotional charge my brain has always added to the situation. My gratitude for not ending up in the foster care system always made me feel obligated to keep my aunt and uncle in my life, but the truth is that they're toxic, and they don't really *deserve* a place in my life.

To be honest, Rhia's strong words feel like the permission I've always needed to cut that toxicity out of my life.

"Amen, sister," Bailey drawls. "I'm down to never see them again. How about you, Cole?"

"We can't cut them out completely," I reply, trying to be a voice of reason while my sister is ready to throw caution to the wind. "But I do think we can stop going to holidays with them."

"Thank God," Bailey says.

I peek at her in the rearview mirror as she shuts her eyes and leans back against the headrest.

Turning my gaze to the passenger seat, I shoot Rhia a wry grin. "So, they're as bad as I thought they were?"

She gives me a sympathetic nod. "They might be worse, actually. I don't know if I've ever been in a house that felt so cold. And I'm not talking about the physical temperature."

"Right?" I ask, feeling a strange sense of excitement that someone else *gets* it. "It's like they have all the makings of a wonderful home, but the vibe is off."

"All the throw pillows in the world don't make up for a lack of real love," Rhia agrees.

I think of the house I spent so many of my formative years in, full of aesthetic decor and displays of material wealth but devoid of warmth or affection. I've always felt indebted to Jen and Tom for providing us a home with all the creature comforts we could have wanted, but maybe none of that is what we really needed. Maybe all we needed was a little love.

Bailey remains quiet for the rest of the ride, which is a bit unusual for her, but I figure she's just tired after the long day. We drop her off at her dorm, and Rhia and I arrive back at my place around seven. Neither of us is very hungry after filling up at dinner, so we curl up on the couch instead.

"Thank you for everything today," I say softly as Rhia nuzzles into my chest.

She tilts her head up to kiss my jaw. "You're welcome. I know it wasn't an easy day, and I'm glad I could be there for you." I feel her lips as they shift into a mischievous smile. "I actually have a prize for you for getting through it."

My brows jump in surprise. "A prize?"

"Mm-hmm," she hums into my neck. "I'm not sure if it's more of a prize for you or for me."

I shift my weight, trying to catch her gaze, but Rhia burrows deeper into the space between my neck and my shoulder.

"Now I'm really intrigued," I reply, wondering what has her all shy all of a sudden. I finally manage to pry her out of hiding and find that her cheeks are the loveliest shade of pink.

"I'll go get it." Rhia scurries over to where she left her purse by the door. She returns with a small, silk drawstring bag in one hand and a little plastic bottle in the other.

"What have we got here?" I ask, trying to reach for the bag, but Rhia snatches it up to her chest.

"I brought something for us to try. You seemed…intrigued when I mentioned it once, so…"

Interest piqued, I reach out and grab the bag, opening it up to find a small, t-shaped silicone item.

"Is this what I think it is?" I ask as I inspect its cone shape and flared base. There's a little plastic jewel on the flat part of the base that makes my mind spin and my cock twitch.

Rhia shoves the small bottle of lube into my hands in lieu of an answer.

My lips burst into a smile. "Best. Prize. Ever."

Rhia's cheeks have turned beet red.

"Look at me," I say, waiting for Rhia's gaze to meet mine. When it doesn't, I lift a finger to her chin to tilt her face toward mine. "I never want you to be embarrassed to ask for something in the bedroom," I tell her. "I want to give you whatever makes you feel good."

She nods silently, and I take her hand and lead her to my bedroom where we can be more comfortable. I tug off my shirt, toss it into the hamper, and turn back to Rhia.

"Now, take off this sexy little schoolgirl outfit so I can fuck you," I tell her.

Her eyes widen slightly, her pupils dilating as she dutifully begins pulling off the tease of a brown plaid mini dress over her head. The sweater she wore below comes off next, followed by the tights. I watch as she rolls them off carefully, leaving her in just a lacy black one-piece bodysuit thing that plunges low between her spectacular tits.

"Fuck," I mutter as I take in the sight of the black lace overlayed on her pale flesh. "Get on the bed." I follow, stalking Rhia as she gets comfortable on her back. She won't be in this position for long, but we can enjoy it for a bit. I give her a long kiss as I palm her breasts through the lingerie, feeling the dichotomy of the rough lace and her soft skin. Her nipple rings tease me through the fabric, but I don't give myself the pleasure of revealing them just yet.

"I love this thing," I say, running my finger along the lacy edge of the bodysuit and up over the strap keeping it up on Rhia's body. "But I'm gonna need some direction on how to get it off," I admit. Give me a regular bra and panties and I'm an expert, but this one-piece situation has me a bit puzzled.

Rhia grabs my hand. "There's a clasp," she says as she guides my hand down her stomach all the way to the apex of her thighs. "Down here."

Of fucking course there is.

"Excellent," I mutter as I find the closure and flip it open, baring her perfect little pussy to my hungry gaze. "I love having easy access to my girl."

I rub my thumb through her slit, pleased to find her dripping wet already. I slide my thumb upward over her clit, circling before sweeping it back down, collecting more moisture and dragging it lower to her other hole.

Rhia squirms as my digit brushes over the puckered skin. I'm struck by the fact that she could be so bold as to bring me a butt plug to use on her but then act all shy just by me giving her the faintest of touches in that spot. The dichotomy is so perfectly Rhia. I don't know if I'll ever fully figure her out, nor do I know that I really want to.

"You gonna take my cock in your pussy while you have a plug in your ass?" I ask.

Rhia's thighs squeeze together, trapping my hand. She swallows hard before answering, "Yes, sir."

"That's my good girl." I use my other hand to gently tease her legs back apart. I grab the bottle of lube and dispense a dollop onto my pointer finger, holding it up for Rhia to see. "Can I use my fingers to get you ready?"

She nods eagerly, her top teeth sinking into her lip.

I spread the lube over the opening I've only ever dreamt of having, getting it nice and wet for me. "Just relax," I remind her as I massage the area lightly. "If anything doesn't feel good, just tell me, and I'll stop."

Rhia nods again, letting out a small gasp as I slip just the tip of my finger inside of her. She's so tight here. I tread carefully, easing my finger in and out, going just a bit deeper with each pass.

By the time I'm knuckle deep, my cock is so hard it could cut glass. It's screaming at me to get inside of her, but it's not quite time yet.

"Flip over," I say, carefully retracting my finger.

Rhia turns over onto her stomach, and I tug at one of her thighs, urging her to bend her knees.

"Up on your hands and knees." I grab the plug and some more lube as she obeys.

Rhia makes the prettiest picture with her gorgeous ass presented to me like a feast on a fucking platter. I place my palm on her back and coax it lower until her cheek presses into the mattress and her ass is up in the air. Mine for the taking.

I can't help but palm and squeeze the pale skin stretching over the two globes of her ass. So fucking pretty. Wielding the bottle of lube, I let a few beads of it drip down right where we need it.

Rhia lets out a soft gasp when the cool gel hits her most intimate skin. I drag the tip of the plug through the moisture, teasing her asshole a few times before settling it right at the center of the target.

"Relax," I remind her, using my free hand to rub and soothe the curve of her hip as I ease the plug into her ass. "Push out," I tell her once we reach the fatter part of it. Following my command, Rhia blooms beautifully, taking the plug all the way. "That's it," I praise.

She lets out a soft, "Oh, fuck," when it's fully seated inside of her. The teasing little jewel on the base of the plug looks so goddamn cute.

"You're doing so well." I run my palm over her raised ass, admiring my work. "Does that feel okay?"

Rhia beams a shy little smile my way. "It feels *great*."

"Good," I reply, moving off the bed to shuck off my pants and boxers. "You think you can take me in here too?" I ask, running a finger through her damp folds.

Rhia wiggles her ass playfully. "Yes, sir."

I give her ass a light swat. "That's my girl."

I take her by the hips, kneading her soft flesh as I line myself up. The jewel adorning her ass teases me as I sink into her, and we release twin moans of pleasure as I bottom out.

"So. Good," I say as I pull out almost all the way and plunge back in.

Rhia's fingers are fisted in my sheets as she takes me like the perfect dirty girl she is. I can feel the bulbous shape of the plug through the thin wall separating us, and it adds a nice little bit of friction to each stroke.

"Shit!" Rhia hisses when my fingers wander to her clit, rubbing her favorite little counterclockwise circles. "It's...too... much," she huffs out.

I halt my fingers and pause all movement while I'm the

deepest I can get inside of her. "Should I stop?" I ask, a dare in my tone.

"No!" Rhia cries out, grinding her ass back onto my cock.

I lean forward to drop a kiss to the middle of her back. "That's what I thought," I say before I resume fucking her, my punishing rhythm bringing both of us to the brink in a matter of minutes.

"You like being so fucking full?" I ask as I pound into her, chasing my imminent release. "Having both of your holes stuffed?"

"Yes!" Rhia screams as she comes, her pussy squeezing the life out of my cock and setting off my own orgasm. A low groan spills from my throat as I come inside of her, swimming in a sea of pleasure as her contracting pussy milks my cock.

"Goddamn, gorgeous," I say as I pet her ass, stroking and soothing as I bring her down. I savor every twitch and flutter of her pussy before pulling out and tugging ever so gently on the plug that's still inside of Rhia. "Push out for me again."

She mumbles something incoherent but complies, allowing me to gently remove the plug and set it aside. The movement of her muscles has the added effect of pushing some of my cum out of her pussy. The sight of my release dripping out of her threatens to slash my refractory period to nothing. The sight of Rhia collapsing down onto her belly, though, reminds me that she's wrung out.

"Be right back." I head to the bathroom to wash my hands and grab a warm washcloth to clean us up. I wipe Rhia down gently as she watches me with sleepy eyes.

"That was incredible," she says around a yawn. "I don't know how I'm going to get myself out of this bed."

"Stay over tonight," I suggest, hoping she'll agree. It's late, and she seems so comfortable. The sight of her sleepy and freshly fucked has me wanting her in my bed every night for the rest of my life.

"Okay," Rhia agrees easily, giving me a lazy smile.

I make her get up and use the bathroom before tucking her into my bed. I crawl in behind her, spooning her and enjoying the brush of our bare bodies. Having Rhia here with me after a day facing my family feels so right.

I've always craved that soft spot in my life. That safe haven to come home to. I've never even gotten close to having that before, but with Rhia in my arms, it feels so close I can taste it.

It feels like everything is falling into place in my life in a way I never expected it to.

I should have known better.

CHAPTER 31
RHIA

Veronica ran her thumb over Damien's jaw, the prickly hairs there tickling her finger. "I've been waiting my entire life for this moment," she mused.

Damien's sleepy smile made her heart thump. "What moment?" he asked.

She looked deep into Damien's baby blues when she replied, "The moment I fall in love."

Waking up next to Cole Matthews is like waking up in a dream. I can feel his breath on my neck as my eyes flutter open. I stretch my legs out, pointing and flexing my toes to the light beat of the rain on the windows.

Cole stirs behind me, the arm he has draped around my waist tightening its hold. "Good morning," he says in a scratchy voice, pressing a kiss behind my ear.

"Morning," I reply dreamily, a yawn escaping with my words.

"Tired you out last night, did I?" he asks, his hand traveling down to cup my ass.

"If I recall correctly, you fell asleep first," I remind him.

He gives me a light swat, but he knows I'm right.

"What do you want for breakfast?" he asks. I've learned that feeding me is one of Cole's love languages. There's no use in telling him he doesn't have to cook.

"How about French toast?"

Cole drops a kiss on my collarbone. "Great idea." With one last squeeze of my ass, he rolls out of the bed, and I'm treated to the sight of his bare, muscular backside as he walks toward the bathroom.

I lounge in bed for a couple more minutes, marveling at how this is *actually* my life. I just woke up in bed next to a sweet, sexy man, and now he's off to cook me a delicious breakfast. This is everything I've wanted and never thought I'd have.

When I finally emerge from Cole's bedroom, wearing one of his t-shirts and a clean pair of boxers, he's busy at work in the kitchen. A laugh bursts out of me when I realize he's wearing his "kiss the chef" apron...and nothing else. The pale globes of his ass peek out from beneath where he has it tied.

"Hey, hot stuff," I greet him, and Cole touches one finger to his bare ass with a sizzling sound.

"You'd better wash your hands before you keep cooking," I say around a laugh.

He obliges, stepping over to the sink for a quick wash before flipping the French toast.

"I've been meaning to tell you," I start, slinking up behind him and pinching one butt cheek. Cole lets out a little shriek that has me doubling over with laughter again.

He turns and shakes his head at me. "You wound me."

I cock my head. "Need me to kiss it better?"

"As much as I'd enjoy that, I'm afraid I'll burn my French toast." Cole peers over at the stovetop. "What did you want to tell me?"

I step forward and wrap my arms around his neck. "Caleb invited us up to his family's New Hampshire house next weekend. He's going to propose to Hannah, and he wants me to be there to celebrate afterward. He told me to invite you too."

Cole tosses his head back, brows raised. "Seriously?"

I nod. "He's so excited about his proposal, and he thinks having me there will make Hannah happy."

"But why invite me?" Cole asks. "They don't know me that well."

"Because Caleb knows I care about you"—I brush my fingers over the short hairs at the back of his neck—"and that I'll be happier if you're there."

Cole breaks into a dazzling smile. "Then I'd love to go with you." He leans in to capture my lips in a sweet kiss that grows steamier as my hands wander down to his exposed backside. I give it a squeeze, and he snakes a hand under the oversized t-shirt I'm drowning in. I'm gasping into his mouth when the smell of burnt cinnamon tinges the air.

"Shit! The French toast!" Cole whirls toward the stove and removes the pan. He slides the slightly charred French toast onto a plate to inspect the damage. "I think it's salvageable," he announces.

"Then let's eat," I reply.

Cole runs off to throw on sweats and a hoodie before we sit down at the kitchen table to eat. The meal is perfection, despite being just slightly overcooked. I let out an orgasmic moan that earns me an honest-to-goodness blush from Cole. Wrapping my leg around his, I slide my foot up and down his calf.

I'm looking forward to serving him his next course—me—when we're interrupted by a harried knock at the door.

"Who is *that*?" Cole asks with a frown.

I unwind my leg from his, and he heads to the door, opening it up to reveal his sister, soaking wet from the rain outside. It takes me a moment to realize that her face isn't just wet from the weather but also from the tears leaking from her eyes.

"Bailey?" Cole immediately pulls her in and shuts the door behind her. "What's wrong?"

Bailey sniffles and blubbers as Cole helps strip off her soggy jacket. "I...I need your help," she manages between hiccupping sobs.

"Are you hurt?" Cole flicks his gaze over her very much intact body. "Sick?"

Bailey shakes her head, squeezing her eyes shut as a new round of tears begins to flow from them. "Not exactly," she whispers.

"Come in." Cole gently guides his sister toward the living room. "I'll grab you some towels to dry off."

"I can head out," I offer, standing awkwardly beside our abandoned breakfast dishes. This feels like a private moment, and I feel like a massive intruder. I'm wearing her brother's boxers for God's sake.

Bailey turns her tear-stained face toward me. "No. Don't leave. I...I'd like you to stay. Please."

I want to argue, but the sincerity and—is that a hint of fear? —in her eyes convinces me not to. I have no idea what type of trouble Bailey has gotten herself into, and it's a very real possibility that she just wants me to stay as a buffer between her and her brother, but something about the dread in her expression tells me she might actually need me.

Cole returns with a couple of bath towels and lays one on the couch for Bailey to sit on, handing her the other one to towel dry her face and hair. Bailey takes a couple of moments to settle herself, and Cole takes my hand with a worried expression, tugging me toward the couch. I end up sitting on the opposite end from Bailey with Cole tucked in between us.

"Bails," Cole prompts. "Please tell me what's wrong. I want to help."

Bailey wipes the remaining moisture from her eyes. Her crying seems to have died down, but her expression still reads as dread.

"I..." Bailey can't get the next words out without her tears returning in full force. "I'm pregnant." She collapses forward with her head in her hands, a heavy sob wracking her body.

Oh. *Fuck.*

Cole shoots me the most panic-stricken expression I've ever seen on his handsome face. The fear in his features turns my stomach.

A few silent seconds tick past, but they feel like an eternity. When I realize that Cole is quite literally at a loss for words, I step in, physically moving myself closer to Bailey and perching on the arm of the couch beside her.

"Okay," I say gently. "You're pregnant. Let's talk about it."

One interesting thing I've found about myself is that I panic over what may seem to most people like the most mundane things, but I'm *great* in emergency situations. One time in college, the fire alarm went off in the middle of a snowy winter night, and despite getting myself bundled in a long parka and stuffing my laptop, toothbrush, and an extra pair of panties into my backpack as a "go bag," I was still the first one out of the building.

Being hypervigilant at all times may be inconvenient, but it sure pays off when things go haywire. Basically, at any given point, my mind has already worked through the worst-case scenario, so when it actually occurs, I'm not just ready for it. I'm over-prepared.

I place a tentative hand on Bailey's back, rubbing the spot where her shoulders are pinched together. "Do you know how far along you are?" I ask quietly.

"I think..." Bailey pulls in a shaky breath. "About five weeks."

"Okay, that's good," I reply. "You're still very early on. That means you have choices. I know this is scary, Bailey. You don't have to make any decisions today, but you *do* have options."

She nods shakily, lifting the towel she's kept clutched in one hand to her face to wipe her wet eyes and nose.

"We're going to help you figure this out," I promise.

Bailey's gaze finally meets mine—the first time she's looked either of us in the eye since her confession.

"You will?" she asks, a hopeful lilt to her voice.

"Of course we will," Cole replies, finally finding his voice. "I support you no matter what, Bails."

That sentiment kicks off yet another round of fresh tears. Once those die down a bit, I get down to business.

"Like I said, Bailey, you don't have to make any decisions about the future of this pregnancy right now, but you should start following the standard pregnancy protocols. You'll need to start taking a prenatal vitamin and stop using any alcohol or drugs. You should also avoid eating sushi, deli meat, and soft cheeses. There's a whole list of foods you can't eat; I can print it out for you. You'll also need to limit your caffeine intake. And we should make you an appointment at a clinic so they can examine you and confirm the pregnancy. I can help you with that," I assure her.

Bailey swallows, her eyes slightly glazed over. Maybe that was too much information all at once, but that's the reality of the situation.

"Who's the father?" Cole asks, and I kind of want to bash him over the head. He should be more worried about his sister's well-being than who got her pregnant. But I suppose the protective older brother in him is wondering who he has to knock out for knocking up his baby sister.

Bailey's lip quivers, and she hesitates before answering. "It's Jesse's."

Cole's nostrils flare with anger before he explodes. "Are you fucking kidding me? That fucking loser? I'm gonna fucking kill him."

Three F-bombs in three sentences has to be some kind of record.

"Cole," I say calmly. "Let's not focus on the father right now." I send him my best *shut the hell up* expression. "Bailey, why don't you go take a shower and clean up? I'll run to the store for another pregnancy test and a prenatal vitamin," I offer.

She sniffles. "Okay. Coley, can I borrow some pajamas?"

Cole's features soften. "Of course. I'll grab some and leave them outside the bathroom door for you."

Bailey stands and begins gathering the wet towels from the couch. Cole stops her, gently grabbing the towels from her with one hand and pulling her into a half-hug with his free arm.

"I'm not mad at you, Bails," he adds. "I just don't like that guy, and it kills me to see you so sad and scared because of something he did."

Bailey pulls back with a wry tilt to her mouth. "I was a willing participant, you know."

Cole covers his ears. "I don't want to hear about it." He shifts his grip on the towels so he can wrap his sister in a big hug. "I love you," he says softly into her ear. "No matter what."

"Love you too," she tells him then turns toward me. "And thank you, Rhia. I just felt like...I needed a fellow woman around for this. I really appreciate you being here."

"Of course," I say. "I'm here for you." Not only is she Cole's sister, but I really like Bailey. She's a sweet kid who made a mistake, and without a mom and only a lackluster aunt, she doesn't seem to have any other females in her life to support her through this.

Bailey heads to the bathroom, and Cole sinks back onto the couch, looking wrung out and exhausted. I sit beside him, shifting gears to offer him the same level of support I just did his sister.

"How are you holding up?" I ask, placing a hand on his thigh.

Cole lets out a dark chuckle without a single trace of humor in it. "I'm...pissed at that punk. Scared for my sister. Sad at the whole situation. Thankful you're here and picked up my slack when I froze."

"It's totally understandable," I assure him. "That was big news you weren't prepared for."

He hangs his head. "This was always one of my biggest fears. My mom had me as a teenager. Look how that turned out. I never wanted either of us to repeat that pattern."

Ah. He's afraid this child will end up lost and alone in the world like he did. But with an uncle like Cole, there's no way that would ever happen.

"Bailey is *not* your mom," I remind him. "And she has something that your mom didn't. *You.*"

"And you," Cole adds. "I can't thank you enough for staying and helping me through that conversation."

I place a chaste kiss on his cheek. "I'll go pick up those things at the store. We can talk more later if Bailey's up to it."

"By the way, how do you know so much about pregnancy?" Cole asks as he walks me to the door.

I shrug. "I've written a couple of accidental pregnancy romances. I research my books *very* thoroughly."

Cole raises a brow, a hint of his usual playful self returning. "I've noticed."

I whack his arm for the obviously lascivious turn his thoughts have taken. "No innuendos right now," I tell him. "Sex is what got Bailey into this mess, so it should be the last thing on your mind right now."

"Oh, gorgeous," he says. "It's always the first thing on my mind when I'm with you."

I reward him with a quick kiss before throwing on a pair of sweatpants and a long coat and heading off to the store.

CHAPTER 32
RHIA

When I return, Bailey is curled up on the couch, swimming in a pair of Cole's pajamas. Her damp hair is pulled back into a simple ponytail, her makeup-free face puffy from crying.

"Hey," I greet her softly, placing my plastic bag of goods next to her on the couch. "I got you an extra pregnancy test in case you wanted another, as well as a prenatal vitamin and some ginger tea. I don't know if you're experiencing any nausea yet, but I know it's common in the first trimester."

"Thank you so much, Rhia." Bailey peeks into the bag and pulls the test box out. "I guess it wouldn't hurt to take another one, right? Maybe the first one was wrong, and this whole nightmare will be over."

I take a seat beside her and try to let her down easy. "I don't think false positives are very common," I say. "But it's not a bad idea to do a repeat." Cole is nowhere to be seen at the moment, so I guess I'm once again navigating this conversation solo. "When did you start to suspect you were pregnant?"

Bailey fiddles with the box, turning it over and over in her hands. "Remember that stupid comment Steve said at dinner yesterday? About how we must be on our periods because we were eating so much? It got me thinking, and I realized that my period was really overdue, and that's unusual for me. As soon as I got back to my dorm, I DoorDashed a test, and I took it right away." She drops the box into her lap and wiggles her fingers, giving me jazz hands. "Positive."

"So you've only known since last night," I realize. "It's no wonder your head is still spinning."

Bailey scratches at her eyebrow, letting out a little huff of a laugh. "It's spinning alright."

Cole appears from his bedroom, announcing that he's put clean sheets on his bed.

"Why don't you go take a nap, Bails?" he suggests.

"I'd love that," Bailey says around a well-timed yawn. "Thanks again, Rhia," she adds as she rises, taking the bag with her.

Cole plops down on the couch beside me with a heavy sigh. "She told me she didn't sleep at all last night," he says. "That can't be good for the baby, right?"

"I'm sure it's not ideal for Bailey or the baby," I reply, "but I don't think one sleepless night is going to cause either of them any harm."

Cole sags into the couch, exhausted even though we woke up less than three hours ago. "What the fuck are we going to do?" he asks.

I'm not entirely sure who the *we* is that he's referring to—whether it's him and me, him and his sister, or all three of us together—but I very much like the idea that we're a team. That we're facing this issue head on together.

"What we're already doing," I decide, infusing a level of confidence I don't really feel into the statement. "We'll take care of Bailey and make sure she's taking care of herself. We'll help her get the information and resources she needs. And we'll support her in whatever she does."

Cole plants a hand on my thigh, holding on to me like a life raft. "And if she decides to keep the baby?" he asks. "She'll be due in the summer. How is she supposed to go back to school next year with a newborn? She won't be able to live in the dorms. Where is she supposed to live? I only have the one bedroom." He points toward the closed door Bailey shut herself behind. "And what about childcare? That shit's expensive, and I'm already stretched thin."

I give his hand a reassuring squeeze. "Those are all really important questions and things we'll need to discuss with Bailey if she decides to go that route. It's a lot to figure out, but I truly do believe we *can* figure it out if that's what we need to do." I start throwing out all the options I can think of off the top of my head. "Maybe Bailey needs to drop down to part-time school and also work part-time. Maybe there are more scholarships she can apply for—maybe even ones specifically for mothers. Or maybe she needs to put school on hold until the baby goes to kindergarten."

"No. No way," Cole replies quickly, his hand flexing on my thigh. "I won't let her lose momentum with school or put her dreams on hold. Not after everything we've done to get her to where she is."

"Okay, not that last one, then." I give his hand another squeeze, trying to keep him present instead of spinning out the way I can see he's starting to. "You two have been through so much, but you've always figured out a way through it. Bailey is a smart young woman. She can handle this."

Cole scoffs. "Yeah, well, she wasn't too smart when she slept with Jesse."

I let out a sigh as I sink back into the couch, yielding to the weight of the situation as Cole already has. "True. She is still *so* young."

Cole scrubs a hand down his face. "I never wanted this for her."

I lay my head on his chest, right over his heart. "I know."

"I did everything in my power to prevent this, and it still happened."

I press a kiss over his t-shirt. "I know."

"What, do you know everything?" Cole asks, and I can hear that little hint of his usual self fighting to come out again.

"I wish," I reply, snuggling in a little closer.

Cole

Jesse, the near silent smoker, is Bailey's baby daddy. I'm going to. Fucking. *Kill*. Him.

Why couldn't it have been Mac? My sister's been making heart eyes at the guy for years, and at least I know he's a good man. I know next to nothing about Jesse, and I'm doubtful he'll even stick around after Bailey tells him her news. Truthfully, I'm not sure whether that would be a bad thing or not.

Obviously, it would be ideal for this baby to have two present, loving parents. But Bailey and I have made it through a lot just the two of us, and with Rhia on our team, I have no doubt we could do anything we set our minds to. Maybe some of her confidence in us being able to handle this situation is rubbing off on me. Plus, at this point, Jesse seems like more trouble than he's worth. But you best believe we'll be demanding child support.

As Rhia lies curled up next to me, I try to imagine what life could look like in nine months. Running my fingers through Rhia's hair, I picture Bailey rocking an infant in her arms, a little bundle of joy and hope. I wonder if the baby would have our same red hair. I hope so. I try to visualize Rhia interacting with the baby—holding them, feeding them a bottle, softly singing them a lullaby—and I like what I see a little too much.

It looks like a happy life. I just don't know if it's possible.

"Hey," Rhia says after long minutes of us sitting in silence. "I know it's terrible timing, but I just wanted to check... Do you still want to go to New Hampshire this weekend? It might actually be good to get your mind off this stuff with Bailey for a bit."

Fuck. I'd forgotten all about our plans in the midst of Bailey's crisis. It definitely is terrible timing, but it's not like I can ask Caleb to hold off his proposal because of my drama.

"Let's see how the next couple of days play out, but I'd still like to go," I reply.

Rhia relaxes against me, and I realize how tense she'd gotten when she asked that question. "Okay, great," she says. "I'll confirm with Caleb."

Bailey sleeps for almost four hours before wandering back out into the living room. I'm glad she was able to rest, but she still looks absolutely wrecked. Her hair is falling out of the bun that sits atop her head, and her eyes are red rimmed and even puffier than before, so I know she's been crying again. God, I'm worried about how to get her through the rest of college when I'm not even sure how to get her through the rest of today.

"Hi," she says, sniffling softly as she drops into a chair at the kitchen table.

"Hey," I reply. "You feeling any better?"

She shrugs silently.

Rhia left about an hour ago when it became apparent that Bailey wasn't waking up anytime soon, and I'm tempted to ask her to come right back over to help me navigate this. I have no idea what to say to Bailey. All I can come up with are empty platitudes, but how can I tell her *It'll be okay*, when I'm honestly not sure that it will be?

"Bails." I sigh, scooting my chair closer and wracking my brain for advice. I settle for, "We'll get through this," and desperately hope that it's true.

CHAPTER 33
COLE

Caleb's family's New Hampshire house is the quintessential New England lake house, complete with log siding and a covered deck dotted with wind chimes and other seemingly handmade metal decorations. It looks like it could have been decorated by Aunt Jen herself.

We pull into the driveway about twenty minutes after Cole sent Rhia the "all clear" text, letting her know that they were down at the beach, and we were good to start setting up the celebration. Rhia is practically bouncing out of the passenger seat with her excitement.

"I can't wait to hear about the proposal," she says. "He'd better get down on one knee. And use her full name. And actually say the words *Will you marry me?* Shit, and I didn't think to tell him to make sure Hannah had her nails done. Whatever. It's going to be so perfect. I just know it."

I shift the car into park and unbuckle my seat belt. "You're really into this stuff, aren't you?"

Rhia gives me a small, knowing smile. "I'm a romance author," she reminds me.

That's right. Happily ever afters are kind of her thing. The prince and the princess riding off into the sunset and all that shit.

She's clearly swept away by the concept of Caleb's sunset proposal. I'm not exactly in the same frame of mind with all that's going on right now.

We walk around to the trunk, stuffed full of balloons and decorations. I begin unloading the supplies, taking as much as I can fit in my arms in one trip. Rhia carries the "You're Getting Married (For Real This Time)" cake that she kept in her lap the whole way here.

"He left a key for us under the frog statue," Rhia says.

I peer around the garden that lines the front walkway. It's dotted with frog figurines, ranging from wearing a miniature cowboy hat and holding a rifle to one wearing a white robe with cucumber slices over its eyes.

"Which one?" I ask, a note of horror leaking into my voice.

Rhia grins widely at my uncertainty. This little setup is exactly her brand of quirky. "The one in the sun bonnet."

I squat down in front of the fat little frog in a frilly Easter bonnet like the ones Jen used to dress Bailey in. Using the hand with balloons looped around my fingers, I pry the frog loose from the soil, revealing the silver key beneath. As I'm fetching the key, a single balloon somehow manages to get loose, flying away on the wind faster than either of us can retrieve it.

"Shit!" Rhia swears when the balloon evades her reach by no more than three inches. Her face crumbles like a child's would at a lost balloon, and she watches in dismay as it floats away on the breeze. I swear, she looks like she could burst into tears, and I just can't take that right now.

"It's okay," I say. "It was just one balloon."

"It's *not* okay," she replies petulantly. "Everything has to be *perfect.*"

"I think they can live without one diamond-shaped balloon," I point out. This whole thing seems a little over the top if you ask me. Cake and balloons and dozens of other little decorations just to celebrate that they're engaged…for the *second* time. Shouldn't it be enough that they found their perfect partner? Why do we also have to have this huge hoopla about it? I'm indulging Rhia because this is clearly the shit that she lives for, but I'm not quite in the mood for all the fuss.

Rhia frowns furiously at me, her eyes suspiciously wet. "I want this to be everything Hannah's ever dreamed of. Last time around, everything surrounding her marriage was fake. She deserves to experience the joy of a real engagement."

When Rhia says it like that, this whole thing seems a little less frivolous.

"You're right," I reply. "I'm sorry." I keep a death grip on the remaining balloons as I slide the key into the lock on the front door.

Rhia blows out a breath as we enter the cabin. "It's okay. I think I'm in an extra-sensitive mood because of the Bailey stuff."

"Me too," I agree.

"Let's try to put all that out of our minds, just for this weekend," she suggests. "We deserve to have a good time too."

"You're right." I unload the bags slung over my shoulder onto a table. "I'll do my best."

By the time we're finished decorating, the cabin is unrecognizable. White streamers line the ceiling in a zigzag pattern then drape down the walls in a sea of texture. A large banner hung across the fireplace reads *You're Engaged!* alongside a small handmade sign that says *(Again)* in handwriting clearly meant to imitate the font on the banner. I have a bad feeling that joke is going to haunt every corner of this engagement and wedding.

The cake sits on the coffee table next to a bottle of champagne chilling in a plastic golden bucket, both of which are surrounded by faux white rose petals, plastic diamonds, and various other baubles. Clusters of white and gold balloons are held down by weights in a few different parts of the room, and framed photos of Hannah and Caleb are strewn about on every available flat surface.

Rhia stands at the center of it all, wringing her hands as she assesses her work. "Do you think we should have gotten fresh flowers too?" she asks, frowning at the fabric rose petals on the coffee table.

I rest my hands on her shoulders, gently massaging out the tension gathered there. "Everything is perfect. Hannah is going to love it."

Rhia turns toward me, and I gather her into my arms, placing a kiss on the crown of her head.

"You did such a great job," I tell her.

"You think?" She cuddles into my chest until rustling at the back door has her jumping back. "They're here!"

The newly engaged couple waltzes in through the back door, wearing twin adoring smiles. Hannah's eyes widen then light up when she spies Rhia, and she bounds toward her, wrapping her friend in a tight embrace.

Caleb strides over to me for a fist bump before pulling me into a side hug.

"Congrats, man," I tell him.

"Thank you," he says. "And thanks for all of this." He gestures around the room bathed in white and gold decor.

"That was all Rhia. I was just the muscle."

"Still," Caleb says. "It means a lot." He shoots a meaningful glance toward the still-embracing women. "Rhia is really special to Hannah and me. We're glad she found you."

Rhia pulls away to turn her admiring gaze toward Hannah's ring. Hannah indulges her by holding out her hand, gently twisting it to show how the stone catches the light. She's absolutely living out Rhia's dream right now. The relationship, the proposal, the happily ever after. Finding a stable, solid man to stand by her side for the rest of her life.

And that's something I just can't offer Rhia right now.

Maybe someday, many years from now, I'll have my life

together in a way that allows me to give her all of this. But right now, I'm still scraping by. I flirt for tips so I can pay my sister's college tuition, for Christ's sake. And God knows what prenatal medical bills look like, but I very likely have those headed my way too. In no world am I ready to commit to supporting yet another person in my life by marrying them. I just hope Rhia is willing to wait for me while I get there.

She finishes admiring Hannah's ring and turns her attention toward Caleb, leaping over to give him a bear hug that he returns with a soft chuckle. I give Hannah my sincerest congratulations, hoping my preoccupation with Bailey's crisis and thoughts of not being enough for Rhia don't show.

"Let's cut the cake!" Rhia suggests. "Cole, will you pour the champagne?"

I pop the bottle with a flourish, garnering "oohs" and "aahs" as I shoot the cork clear across the room. At least I can offer my bartender tricks, if nothing else. I fill four flute glasses as Rhia slices the cake, and everyone grabs one of each for themselves.

We eat and drink, and it's all very merry until Caleb announces he's going to light up the fire pit outside. Rhia shoots me a worried glance, but I reassure her, mouthing, "It's okay." I don't want to ruin the night by refusing to stand by the fire. Besides, Rhia and I have been working on my fear. I can handle a little campfire, right?

We follow Caleb outside to the round stone fire pit, gathering around it as he builds a fire at the center. I'm pleasantly surprised at how well I handle the slowly growing flames, but then again, I have Rhia's hand tucked in mine. She doubles the courage I'd have if I was alone.

The fire remains small and manageable for long enough that I feel relatively comfortable taking my eyes off of it. Rhia and I hunt around the yard for four long sticks while Hannah runs inside, returning with a bag of marshmallows, a chocolate bar, and a sleeve of graham crackers. We all agree that we're still a bit full from the cake, but no one wants to turn down the opportunity for s'mores.

Caleb stokes the fire as we open up the ingredients. By the time I have a marshmallow speared on the end of my stick, the wind has picked up, and the flames are roaring. I stare at the fire as it licks the air. These flames are so much bigger than any that we've practiced with.

Rhia brushes up against me, her own marshmallow-tipped stick in hand. "Ready?" she asks, tapping her stick against mine.

I swallow hard as I feel the heat of the flames against my skin. "As I'll ever be."

We hold our sticks out, angling the marshmallows just right above the flames as Hannah and Caleb do the same on the other side of the fire pit. My gaze remains so intensely trained on the flames that I miss my marshmallow catching on fire. By the time I lift it away from the flame, it's charred to a crisp. Too spooked to bring it any closer to myself, I stand frozen, holding the rapidly burning marshmallow at arm's length.

Rhia gently grabs the stick from me, leaning in and blowing until the flame consuming my marshmallow flickers out.

"Thanks," I say, cheeks heating with embarrassment. Hopefully, Hannah and Caleb just think that I like really crispy marshmallows and not that I'm a total scaredy cat.

Rhia sweetly removes the scorched marshmallow and replaces it with a fresh one. I give her a grateful smile as she tosses the discarded marshmallow right into the fire, incinerating the evidence.

With a subtle deep breath, I try again, holding out my stick but doing my best to watch the marshmallow this time. I spin it slowly over the flames, aiming for an even golden-brown roast. I'm so focused on *not* focusing on the fire that I don't realize the wind is picking up. A particularly strong gust hits, making the fire crackle and pop. It spits a burst of sparks toward me, and that's the last straw. I jump back from the slew of sparks, my nervous system totally shot.

"Whoops, sorry," Caleb apologizes, poking at the fire to calm it, but I've already dropped my stick to the ground. Turning on my heel, I book it to the safety of the house, shame consuming me as I sprint away from the group.

When I finally reach the house, I bend over, out of breath—and not only from my short run. Panic claws at my throat, and I grit my teeth as I force deep breaths through my nose. I tell myself over and over again that I'm safe, staving off a panic attack, until Rhia bursts into the house after me.

"Cole," she breathes as she appraises my slumped form. "I'm so sorry. That was too much. I should have known—"

I hold up a hand to cut her off. "Not your fault." I heave another breath in and out. "I just can't do this."

"I'll have Caleb put the fire out," she says, already rushing back toward the door in her haste to comfort me.

"No, Rhia," I say, halting her retreat. "I can't *do* this."

She freezes in her tracks, her brown eyes growing wide. "What?"

"I don't think I can do this anymore. It's all too much."

She shakes her head, her dark brows scrunching together. "I don't understand."

I release my breath in a frustrated sigh. "I can't do this anymore. It's over."

CHAPTER 34
RHIA

Damien slid the Jaguar into an open garage, pressing a button on a fob attached to his keyring to make the door shut behind them, sealing them in.

"Where are we?" Veronica asked, slightly panicked to be in the unfamiliar enclosed space.

"It's a safe house," Damien replied, getting out of the driver's seat and shuffling around the car to open her door. "Let's get inside."

They entered the home through a door in the garage, and Veronica felt slightly better when she saw the cushy interior of the house. A large, L-shaped leather couch faced a flat-screen television. There was art on the walls—prints of Monet and Degas. What looked to be a fully stocked kitchen sat a short distance away, beckoning her over with the promise of a snack.

"The windows are all bulletproof," Damien explained, gesturing toward the windows at the front of the house, adorned with red velvet curtains. "But keep the curtains drawn."

"Okay," Veronica replied hesitantly. "Can I make myself something to eat?"

"You can do whatever you want, baby," Damien said. "But I...I have to go away for a bit."

"What?" Veronica gasped. "You can't leave me here!"

"I don't want to," Damien said, looking pained. "But I have to take care of a few things before you can be safe to leave. I need to know you're secure here so I can do that."

"B-but, Damien," Veronica stuttered, unable to catch her breath to respond.

Damien dropped to one knee, begging for her understanding. "I will come back for you, Veronica," he promised. "I will always come back for you."

---

stare at Cole, my boyfriend and the first man I've ever trusted with my body and—more importantly—my heart, as I attempt to process what he's telling me.

"We can take a break from the fire exposures if it's too much with everything that's going on right now," I offer.

"No." Cole shakes his head in frustration. "It's not just that. I can't... I can't do any of it."

"What do you mean?" I ask slowly.

"I can't get out of my dead-end job," he says, beginning to tick off his list of failures. "I couldn't stop my little sister from getting pregnant too young just like my mom. I can't even roast a fucking marshmallow over a goddamn campfire. I can't be the man you need right now. You don't deserve to have to deal with my mess."

My hackles rise at the *it's not you, it's me* argument. "I decide what I deserve," I tell him. "Don't push me away with this *I'm not good enough for you* bullshit. I've read enough romance novels with that third-act break-up, and it's just lazy writing."

Cole scrapes a hand over his hair as he rises to his full height. "We aren't one of your silly little romance novels, Rhiannon!" he says in an angry voice that he's never used with me before. "This is real life. I know you don't have a lot of experience with relationships, but you need to grow up and realize that not everyone is going to live happily ever after. Some of us have too much trauma and bullshit in their lives for that. I'm not the hero of one of your romance novels, and I never will be."

I cross my arms over my chest, shrinking into myself as he hits all of my insecurities in one fatal blow. "So, what?" I ask. "You're breaking up with me because you don't think you'll live up to my expectations? When have I ever indicated that that might be the case?"

Cole scoffs. "I *know* I'll never live up to your expectations. How could I? I can't seem to do anything right these days."

"Cole, your issues with fire are understandable, and you're working on them. Bailey getting pregnant was *not* your fault. Stop putting all of this on yourself. You're doing fine."

"Fine isn't good enough." Cole meets my gaze, his blue eyes searing into me. "You deserve the best."

"Well, maybe you *are* the best for me," I argue. "No one is perfect, but we're good together."

He shakes his head, defeated. "I need to figure my shit out, and I can't do that if I'm also trying to be my best for you."

"Cole, please," I beg. "Don't give up on us."

"I'm not giving up," he replies. "I'm setting you free. You've had some good dating experiences now. Use them to go off and find someone better than me."

Cole pivots, reaching for his still-packed overnight bag that sits in the corner by the door.

"Cole." I try to grab his arm, but he shakes me off.

"I have to go," he says. "I need to check on Bailey. She was telling Jesse about the pregnancy today."

"I'll come," I reply, desperate not to let him leave me right now. I'm worried about Bailey too, and I want to do anything I can to help.

Cole slings the duffel bag over his shoulder. "We'll handle this on our own. You stay and celebrate with your friends."

"Yeah, because I'm in a really fucking celebratory mood right now," I spit back, anger bubbling over the fear and sadness. How could Cole do this after all we've been through? A few days ago, we were a team, and now I'm getting kicked off of it without doing anything to deserve it.

"Rhia." Cole sighs. "I'm sorry. I'm just not…good right now. I can't be safe for you right now."

His words suck all the air from my lungs. I once told him he was a safe person for me, someone I felt totally comfortable with and confident in. In this moment, I feel the opposite. My lip quivers, and I bite it to hold back the onslaught of tears threatening to fall.

Cole takes two strides toward me, bending to whisper a kiss over my forehead. "You always deserved better than me," he says softly before turning to head out the door.

He never looks back.

I don't even realize I'm crying until the tears begin to drip down my cheeks, blurring my vision of Cole's car driving off into the night. I watch until there's no trace of him left before I shut the door.

Hannah must have come in the back door, because suddenly her arms are around me, and she's asking, "What happened? Where's Cole going?"

"Home," I reply woodenly. "I think he just broke up with me."

"What?" Hannah asks, sounding as confused as I am. She ushers me to the couch, pulling me down next to her and demanding an explanation. I go through our conversation, filling her in on Cole's pyrophobia and Bailey's pregnancy and everything else. Hannah listens intently, nodding and stroking my arm comfortingly as I speak. Caleb comes to the door midway through my ramblings, quickly assessing the sight in front of him before retreating back outside with a mumbled, "I'll go put the fire out."

Hannah whistles softly when I'm finished talking. "Damn. It sounds like he has a lot going on right now, and he's probably really stressed. Maybe he just needs a little time to deal with his stuff."

"Why doesn't he want to deal with it together?" I wail, my anger spiking again. "A few days ago, we were this unbreakable team, and today he just up and decides to drop me from it. I don't get it."

Hannah squeezes my shoulder. "Honestly, I don't either, but I think the best thing you can do right now is let Cole cool down and work on his shit. A little time always puts things into perspective."

"Yeah," I reply halfheartedly, glancing out the window to where Caleb is poking at the almost dead fire. "You and Caleb should go to bed. I'll clean this up." I gesture around at the decorations littering the room.

"You don't have to do it alone. We'll help you."

"You two should go '*celebrate*,'" I say, making exaggerated air quotes.

Hannah punches me softly on the arm. "We aren't going to *celebrate* like that with you in the house."

"I'll put on some loud music," I reply with a shrug.

"Rhia!" she cries.

"Besides, I'd like to be alone for a bit."

Hannah seems more satisfied with that answer. "Okay," she relents. "But we'll be right upstairs if you need anything."

With one last hug, Hannah heads outside to grab her fiancé. I laze on the couch for another moment before heaving myself up to begin gathering the rose petals that have scattered throughout the room, blowing off the coffee table each time the door is opened to allow in the cool night breeze.

I slice up the rest of the cake and use some plastic wrap in the kitchen to seal each slice with. I'm not sure what to do with the balloons, but Hannah didn't ask me to save any of the decorations, so I take a paring knife from the kitchen and pop every last one of them. The process is oddly cathartic. It feels good to take the air out of something the way Cole took the breath right out of me.

By the time I have the living room reset, it's just past midnight. Cole is probably home by now, and I idly wonder what he's up to. Getting ready for bed? Checking up on Bailey? Or did he head to Marty's to find a quick replacement for me in his bed?

Cole wouldn't do that. Would he?

I can't help but wonder if he's as upset by this breakup as I am. He's the only guy I've ever been with. The only one I've ever really let into my life. My bed. My heart.

Cole obviously had lots of experience with women before me, and it wouldn't be all that difficult for him to find another willing companion. I, on the other hand, don't know if I'll *ever* be able to find someone else I trust enough to give them all of myself.

This whole convoluted plan may have completely backfired, because after having some of the best times of my life with Cole —and after experiencing what I can only think to describe as love—I've lost it, and I don't want to feel what I'm feeling right now ever again.

I've written plenty of breakup scenes in my career. I've done my best to get into the head of someone who has just lost the love of their life. I've imagined the sadness, the sorrow, and, sometimes, the rage people must feel when they lose a lover, but nothing my mind was able to conjure up compares to the real thing. Pure heartbreak is a hell I wouldn't wish on my worst enemy.

My third-act breakups are typically followed by a period of wallowing for both parties before one or both realizes that they were wrong to break up with the other. Then, that person plans a grand gesture to woo their partner back into their good graces and win back their love, and voila. They're reunited forever and always.

But it's like Cole said: this isn't one of my silly little romance novels.

And not everyone gets a happily ever after.

CHAPTER 35
COLE

My knees weaken as the tech wields the transvaginal ultrasound wand she's going to use to confirm Bailey's pregnancy.

"I'll wait outside," I croak as soon as I realize she intends to stick that thing inside of my sister. When Bailey asked me to come along for her first ultrasound, I pictured them waving a wand over her abdomen like I've seen in the movies. I did *not* prepare for this.

I'm so relieved Mac didn't come along like he wanted to. Since the second he found out that Bailey is pregnant, and that it is by Jesse, Mac has been overly attached to my sister, attending to her every need as if he himself is the father.

Jesse booked it back to Minnesota the second he found out, but Mac has picked up his slack and more. He assures me that Jesse will pay child support, but in the meantime, he seems determined to see Bailey through this pregnancy himself.

"Wait!" Bailey cries out, grabbing my hand in a tight grip as I try to escape the exam room. "Please stay. Just come up by my head."

"I can put up a privacy curtain," the tech offers.

I shoot her a grateful smile. "That would be great."

I give Bailey's hand a squeeze and take my place by the top of the bed. The tech sets up a little curtain obscuring Bailey's lower half from view. She explains to us that this eight-week ultrasound is meant to confirm the pregnancy, verify the baby's due date, and ensure that the baby has a healthy heartbeat. All of that is great, but I'm most excited to get a good look at the little bean.

Ever since Bailey decided to keep the baby, I've allowed myself to envision my future niece or nephew. I don't care which it is. I just can't wait to smother them with love. I won't even say that the sex doesn't matter as long as they're healthy, because I'll love them no matter what.

The tech begins the ultrasound, walking us through what she sees as she goes. The black-and-white image doesn't look like much of anything at first, but eventually it settles into a big black orb with a tiny little bean floating inside of it.

"That's the baby." The tech points to the bean. "And this"—she pushes a button on the monitor, bringing an unfamiliar sound to life—"is its heartbeat."

I listen with wonder to the whooshing sound of the baby's heart and watch as Bailey's eyes fill with happy tears. I'm instantly hit with a pang of regret that Rhia isn't here to experience this alongside me, this pure wonder and joy at the prospect of bringing a new life into the world. I hope she gets to experience this for herself some day with an amazing guy who's worlds better for her than me.

It's been just over two weeks since I decided to end things, and we haven't spoken at all. It's probably better this way. Hearing Rhia's voice or seeing her face would crush me. I hate that I hurt her, but I know it was for the best. She helped me realize that I had work to do on myself, but she doesn't deserve to be dragged through the messy process of that work or through what promises to be the stress of figuring out how to support Bailey and her baby.

I should have known better than to think that I could be what

Rhia needed in the first place. I can only hope that the good times we had together will be enough to encourage her to keep dating and looking for her person. My goal in the beginning was simply to show her that dating didn't have to be scary, and I should have kept it at that. Instead, I foolishly thought I could give her more.

I failed.

And now I miss her desperately.

The tech prints out a column of photos from the ultrasound, which Bailey proudly tucks away in her purse. I gauge her mood before asking if she'd like to go out to lunch. Bailey's hormones have had her all over the place, putting her in states ranging from euphoria over online shopping for baby items to despair that the baby may never know their father.

She seems happy after the ultrasound, and she agrees to lunch. We go to a little place I know that's near the clinic and order sandwiches with extra pickles on the side for Bailey. Turns out pregnancy cravings are very, very real.

"How are you doing?" Bailey asks before biting into a particularly crunchy pickle spear.

We haven't talked much about my breakup. For one, Bailey has enough going on herself, and I haven't wanted to burden her. But secondly, Bailey was ripshit when I told her I'd ended things with Rhia. I don't think I've ever had so many insults lobbed at me at one time as I did when I, in Bailey's words, "ruined the best thing I've ever had."

It's not that I disagree with her; I just didn't like hearing the truth come out of her mouth.

"I'm fine," I reply. "More than fine after getting to see the baby."

"That's not what I mean, and you know it," Bailey replies. "How are you *really*? Have you spoken to Rhia at all?"

"No." I take a large bite of my sandwich to avoid having to add more to my response.

Bailey watches without amusement as I chew. "I still don't get why you broke up with her."

I place my sandwich on my plate with a sigh. "I have too much shit going on that she doesn't deserve to have spilled over onto her. It wouldn't be fair."

Bailey slumps back in her seat, her eyes downcast. "Is it because of me?" she asks in a small voice. "Did you break up with her because I'm pregnant, and you're freaking out about it?"

"Oh, no," I quickly assure her. "Bails, it's not your fault. Yes, having to figure out how to get you through college with a baby is one thing that's stressing me out, but that's on top of lots of my own issues that have come to light. Trust me, it was all about me and my own problems."

"Like what?" Bailey asks, her curious tone telling me she truly has no idea how much I've been struggling since going out on my own at eighteen. And, really, how would she? I've tried to give her the best life possible, and I've probably made it look easy.

From Bailey's perspective, I have a job and an apartment and enough money to fund her schooling. What she doesn't see is the long shifts at the bar, picking up doubles whenever I can, flirting with anything that walks until it wears on me. She doesn't hear me wallow about my lost dreams of becoming a chef because I stopped talking about it as soon as I learned what culinary school entailed. I've made life so easy for Bailey that she doesn't realize how hard it's been for me.

"Well," I reply gently, figuring now is as good a time as ever to give her a dose of the reality of adulthood when you have no one supporting you, "I've been starting to feel really stuck at my job. There's not a lot of room for upward mobility there, but I also don't feel like I have the education or skills to do much else. You probably remember that I wanted to go to culinary school, but then I realized there were too many open flames involved and backed out."

"Right," Bailey says. "You always used to talk about opening your own restaurant."

I nod. "That was always the dream. Rhia tried to help me work on my issues with fire, but I might just be too fucked up to be fixed. I think all the shit with Mom and the fire really did a number on me. More than I ever realized."

"Cole," Bailey says in a gently chastising tone. "You are not *that* fucked up. Just a little fucked up." She gives me a teasing grin.

"Gee, thanks," I reply.

Her expression grows serious again. "And you don't need to be fixed. Maybe you just need the right person to talk to and help you figure things out."

"Like therapy?" I ask. "Rhia suggested that too."

"It's not a bad idea—for either of us, actually."

I take another bite of my sandwich as I mull it over. It's not a bad idea at all. Therapy seems to really help Rhia. She talks so highly of her therapist, and Jodi really helped her navigate her fears about dating. Without therapy, Rhia and I never would have met.

I promise myself I'll look into it, and I give Bailey the same answer I once gave Rhia.

"I'll think about it."

Rhia

Veronica waited for Damien to return, but it had been days...

The writer's block is back, and it's worse than ever. Reading back all the words I wrote when Cole and I were together is excruciating because I can sense my excitement and happiness in them. I even remember where we were in our relationship when I wrote certain scenes, and reviewing them crushes me. As much as it kills me, I have to face the fact that I may have to scrap this manuscript entirely. There are simply too many memories intertwined with it.

I push away my laptop with a frustrated sigh and glance at the time. I have a session with Jodi in half an hour that I have to get ready for. I've been going to see her twice a week since the emergency session I requested the day after Cole broke up with me. The haze of heartbreak caused me to have a couple of seriously scary panic attacks, one of which had me calling Hannah in the middle of the night because I genuinely thought I was going to die.

Like the incredible friend that she is, Hannah came right over and held me all night while I shivered and sobbed. She offered to have Caleb beat Cole up for me too, but I passed on that. I don't wish Cole harm. In fact, more than anything, I want him to be happy. I just wish he'd be happy with *me*.

Jodi greets me with a soft, sympathetic smile, her expression conveying no judgment on my stained sweatshirt and the leggings I've been wearing for three days straight.

"Come on in," she says.

I sink into one of her green armchairs and promptly burst into tears. What is it about being in your therapist's office that sets off the waterworks? It's like they pump something into the air here.

Jodi silently hands me a box of tissues and gets herself settled in her own chair. "Tell me about the last few days."

"Well," I begin, ticking things off on my fingers, "I rewatched an entire season of *Love is Blind* and read two mafia romances. Oh, and I considered scrapping all sixty thousand of the words I wrote when Cole and I were together because it's too painful to read them over. *But* you'll be proud of me because I did leave my apartment twice. Once to get myself ice cream, and once to go to the library."

Jodi keeps her expression neutral. "I'm very glad to hear

you're getting out of your apartment. It's important not to totally isolate yourself at times like this."

"Hannah and Caleb came over a couple times too." I don't tell her that once was because of a panic attack and the other was to bring me food because they were worried I wasn't eating.

"Good," Jodi responds. "They're very good friends to you."

"They are," I agree.

"Tell me more about why you're struggling with your manuscript," Jodi says. "Writing has typically been a helpful way for you to cope with hard times."

"Because." I groan, flopping dramatically against the back of the chair. "Every word I wrote reminds me of Cole. Not only did he break my heart, now he might have ruined my career too."

"I'm sure that's not true," Jodi replies patiently. "Perhaps you could shelve this manuscript for a bit if the feelings it's bringing up are too fresh and come back to it at a later time. I know it's hard to believe right now, but you won't feel this way forever."

I pick at my nails in an attempt to ignore her logic. I'd much rather blame Cole for the downfall of all the good things in my life right now.

"I also know this might not be what you want to hear, but you should be really proud that you put yourself out there and gave this a real shot." Jodi leans slightly forward as if she's about to expand on that thought.

I sink farther into the chair with a muffled groan. *Please* don't tell me to get back out there," I plead. "I don't know if I have it in me."

Jodi indulges me with a small grin. "I think it's healthy to take some time before trying to date again. It's how you spend that time alone that matters. It's only natural to spend some time wallowing, but you need to work on getting yourself back to baseline. Right now, I'm less worried about you dating again and more worried about getting your writing back on track."

I exhale my relief. That I can work with.

CHAPTER 36
RHIA

'm two weeks into the virtual "Back to Basics" writing workshop I found with Jodi's help when I get an unexpected text.

Bailey is the last person I expected to hear from today when I haven't heard from her brother in the past month. I've typed out and deleted numerous texts to him, each time deciding not to open the wound.

Worry steals my breath momentarily at the thought that something might be wrong. Cole was really stressed out the last time I saw him, and it occurs to me that his spiral may not have ended there.

I quickly type out my response.

Instead of another text, my phone lights up with an incoming call.

"Hello?"

"Rhia." Bailey's voice is uneven, like she's holding back tears. "Hi. I...um. I didn't know who else to call."

I push back from my desk, ready to launch into action at a moment's notice. "What's wrong?"

"I'm bleeding," Bailey replies. "I think something's wrong with the baby."

I'm out my front door with my shoes and coat on by the time she finishes her sentence.

"Are you at your dorm?" My question comes out in a breathless whisper. I'm winded from sprinting to my car, but that doesn't stop me from shoving the keys in the ignition and backing out of my space in a matter of seconds.

"Yes," Bailey answers softly.

"I'll be there in twenty," I assure her. "Why don't you stay on the line with me."

I manage to keep my voice soft and steady while driving like a maniac as Bailey recounts the past hour. Apparently, she went to the bathroom and discovered she was bleeding. It's also difficult to discern how dramatic the nineteen-year-old may be in her description of the amount of blood. Bailey is clearly terrified of what this might mean, and frankly, I am too.

I make it to Bailey's dorm in seventeen minutes flat. She trudges out to my car wrapped in a huge hoodie. She's not showing yet, and I probably wouldn't be able to tell with her oversized sweatshirt anyway, but I still find myself glancing toward her stomach. It's hard to believe there's a baby growing in there, but I suppose, in a few weeks, it will become obvious. God willing.

Bailey hangs up the phone before getting into the passenger seat. She pulls her hood off and turns to me, her face blotchy from crying. "Thank you for coming."

I give her shoulder a little squeeze. "Of course." I wait until she clicks her seatbelt into place to pull away from the curb, heading for the address of the clinic I already have plugged into my GPS.

We sit in silence for a minute or two. I'm not sure if Bailey said everything she needed to on the phone or if she's just feeling less brave being face to face, but I still have questions.

"Can I ask why you didn't call your brother?" I ask gently. Bailey made a comment in passing about not wanting to call Cole, but it had quickly turned into a monologue about why she couldn't call *Mac*, who has apparently been helping her out since his friend bailed on her.

Bailey sniffs, her gaze somewhere far away out the window. "I didn't want to worry him," she replies quietly. "Cole…he hasn't been doing well. But he's trying. He has his first therapy appointment today, and I didn't want to mess that up for him."

A spark of pride flares in my chest that Cole is starting therapy. It's quickly followed by a flash of worry. Is he as torn up about our breakup as I am? Or is he just finally getting help for his own issues?

"Bailey." I sigh. "You know Cole would do anything for you."

"Exactly." She turns her sad gaze toward me. "But I don't *want* him to. Cole needs to look out for himself right now, and he won't do that if I keep bringing him problem after problem."

Though I know she's right—Cole would drop anything and everything to help her, no matter the cost to him—it breaks my heart that Bailey feels like a burden. She's going through one of the harder parts of her life right now, and she needs all the support she can get.

"You're both going through a lot right now," I tell her. "And you'll both need to strike a balance between supporting and receiving support from one another. But I'm glad you felt comfortable calling me," I add. "I'm here for you."

"Thanks, Rhia." Bailey pulls her hood back over her head, effectively ending the conversation.

I drive us the rest of the way to the clinic, and it's not until I'm pulling into a parking spot that she speaks again.

"I'm scared," Bailey says in a near whisper.

I turn off the car. "I am too," I admit.

"What if the baby is gone?"

"Don't go there yet," I reply. "If it does come to that, we'll deal with it then. But, as my therapist would say, don't worry until there's something to worry about."

Bailey lets out a derisive little snort. "That's a dumb saying."

"But it has some truth to it." I get out of the car and walk around to open Bailey's door. "So let's not think of all the possibilities before we know what we're really working with."

Bailey exits the car rather reluctantly, shuffling alongside me into the clinic. We get her checked in and take our seats in the sterile plastic waiting room chairs. I called ahead so they would know we were coming, and we don't have to wait long.

After five minutes or so, a nurse in lavender scrubs with little rubber ducks all over them calls out Bailey's name. She rises from her chair and flashes me a panicked look.

"Do you want me to come in with you?" I ask. I don't want to overstep or be intrusive, but I also don't want her to have to potentially get bad news alone.

Bailey takes a visible deep breath. "No." She squares her shoulders. "I can do this myself."

"I'll be right here waiting for you," I promise, watching as Bailey walks away with the nurse, who fortunately seems very nice. Her kind eyes, warm smile, and bright, cheery scrubs give me good vibes. If Bailey wants to do this without one of her loved ones, I'm glad she at least has someone like that by her side.

I spend the first few minutes of my wait looking around the room at the sea of white plastic chairs, the ovular white coffee table littered with magazines, and the handful of overgrown plants hanging by the wall of windows, no doubt meant to bring some life to the space.

Despite the clinic specializing in obstetrics, there's a distinct lack of photos of babies on the walls. Considering the reason we're here today, I appreciate the clinic's sensitivity. I can't imagine the pain of seeing infants plastered all over the place only to be leaving the clinic without one.

Once there's nothing left to look at, I'm stuck twiddling my thumbs. I could scroll mindlessly on my phone, but every time I open it, I'm too tempted to text Cole. There's a big part of me that wants to tell him what's going on and beg him to get his ass down here, but I would never betray Bailey like that. She doesn't want Cole to be involved in this right now, and I have to respect that.

So I spend the next half hour doing exactly what I told Bailey not to do—worrying about things that may or may not happen. I consider every possibility my mind can come up with. What if she loses the baby? What if there's something wrong with the pregnancy and *her* life is in danger because of it? What if she needs to go on bedrest and can't attend classes? It feels like there's an endless string of potential bad outcomes.

I stand up and begin to pace. The waiting room is pretty empty—only a few others are sitting, and they seem to get people into the exam rooms rather quickly—so there's plenty of space for me to walk laps around the area. I make it around six times before stopping at the rack of brochures. I pull one out at random, hoping for some mindless reading.

The brochure is about preeclampsia, and when I flip it over, I find a list of complications it can cause for both mother and baby, including stroke, placental abruption, and fetal growth restriction. One look at the big, scary words, and I'm stuffing the brochure back onto the rack and backing away from it like it's on fire.

I drop back into my chair and try to focus on my breathing. I take some box breaths—in for four, hold for four, out for four, hold for four. The counting gives my brain something to focus on, and the deep breaths calm my nervous system slightly. I'm watching the exit to the examination area like a hawk, waiting for Bailey to emerge.

When I finally catch sight of her, her hood is down and her

eyes are red and puffy, but the wide smile on her lips tells me everything I need to know.

"The baby is fine," she tells me.

The kind nurse gives me a smile and a wave to confirm the good news.

I tuck Bailey into a gentle hug. "Thank God," I whisper into her ear, and she nods her agreement into my shoulder.

I wait until we're back out in the privacy of my car to ask, "What was causing the bleeding?"

Bailey puts on her seatbelt while she studiously avoids my gaze. "I guess the cervix gets super sensitive in early pregnancy," she explains. "Any sort of…sexual interaction can cause bleeding."

"Enough said," I reply. Bailey doesn't owe me any explanations about her sex life. I *do* quickly recognize that the baby's father dipped weeks ago, so there must be someone else in the picture, but I'm not about to dig into that. "Do you want me to take you back to your dorm? Or do you feel like grabbing some food?"

"You want to…hang out?" Bailey asks.

"We don't have to," I reply. "I just didn't know when you last ate, and I'm getting hungry, so I thought I'd offer."

"I'm hungry too," she says. "But I figured you wouldn't want to hang out since things have been off with Cole."

I pin her with an incredulous look. "What about me rushing to you immediately after you called me earlier made you think I wouldn't want to hang out with you?"

"I mean, obviously you came because you thought something might be wrong with the baby," Bailey replies. "But now that we know everything's okay…you still want to be around me?"

"Bailey." I sigh. "I know it's complicated since Cole and I aren't together, but we can still be friends. I'm here for you if you need anything, but I enjoy being with you and hanging out too."

A grin blooms on Bailey's face. "Awesome." She flops back against the passenger seat. "So, have you and Cole talked at all?"

"We have not," I reply. "And if I may, I'd like to add a stipulation to our friendship: no talking about Cole."

"Oh, sorry," Bailey says, miming zipping her lips shut. "I can do that."

"Thanks. Things are still really fresh for me, and I would just rather we stick to other topics."

"Absolutely," Bailey promises, just moments before breaking it. "Can I just say one thing?"

I give her a look, but apparently, it's not strong enough to deter her.

"I'm really sorry he broke up with you," she says. "I'm still yelling at him about it, if it's any consolation. You're the best thing that ever happened to him."

I pretend to bang my forehead against the steering wheel. "Bailey," I plead. "I can't hear these things right now."

"Sorry," she replies, but the wicked grin on her face says she's very much the opposite. "Let's go eat."

CHAPTER 37
COLE

"I can't believe you didn't call me," I tell Bailey as I sit across from her at my kitchen table. She's just finished telling me about her bleeding scare and how she called Rhiannon to bring her to the clinic. Apparently, it's not uncommon to experience some bleeding in early pregnancy, but it obviously scared Bailey. I'm not sure whether to be hurt that she didn't come to me or to respect that she's trying to handle things on her own.

Bailey shrugs. "Doctor Google told me it might not be a big deal, and I didn't want to worry you before I had to."

"I worry about you all the time," I remind her. "It's my job."

"It's not, though. It's *my* job to worry about me. You should be focusing on yourself. You're doing so much important work right now, and I didn't want to mess any of that up."

The work she's referring to *is* taking up an awful lot of my time. Therapy three times a week—two talk therapy sessions and one EMDR session—plus fire safety classes each weekend this month. The month-long intensive hosted by a local fire station includes tutorials on everything from putting out a grease fire to how to use a fire blanket. The last weekend, which is coming up in just a few days, includes firefighters coming to my apartment to do a full inspection of my fire alarms and extinguishers as well as all escape routes. I've requested that they come do the same at Marty's too.

Once I feel totally confident in my ability to put out any type of fire, I plan to ask for one shift a week in the kitchen at Marty's. I may not be able to afford culinary school while Bailey is still at Berklee, but I can still take some steps toward my dreams of becoming a chef.

"I appreciate you respecting the work I'm doing," I tell Bailey. "But I want you to feel like you can come to me anytime. I know I haven't been…quite myself lately, but just because I'm dealing with my own stuff doesn't mean I can't be there for you too."

"I know," Bailey replies with a soft smile. "And I *know* I can always come to you, Coley. You've been there for me my entire life. More than I ever realized. But I'm an adult now, and I'm going to be a mother. I can't rely on you for everything like I'm used to. The other day when I was bleeding…my first thought was that I had to call you, but then I thought about how much you've been going through, and I decided to use someone else in my support system instead. It's not fair to you to have to be my hero all the time. You deserve to put yourself first once in a while."

"I'm not used to doing that," I admit.

"I know." Bailey stretches out her legs to rest them on an empty kitchen chair and plucks a chocolate from the bowl at the center of the table. It's the week between Christmas and New Year's, and calories, like time, are just a construct right now. We spent the holiday together, just the two of us, at my apartment, with surprise guest appearances from Louisa, Mac, and Tripp throughout the day. It felt good not to have any pressure to visit Jen and Tom and their eight-foot, immaculately decorated Christmas tree. There were no falsely polite greetings or lackluster gifts exchanged. Only heartfelt presents, genuine joy and gratitude, and a Christmas classics movie marathon. It's the first Christmas I've enjoyed in many years.

"Speaking of putting yourself first…" Bailey pops the candy into her mouth and chews, making for a dramatic pause. "Rhia said you guys haven't talked—like, at all. What the hell, Cole?"

I scrub a hand down my face. My sister has never had any trouble putting me in my place.

"I don't know what to say to her," I confess. "Sorry I can't be good enough for you right now, but maybe if I keep up this grueling therapy schedule for a few months, I'll finally deserve you?"

"What is it with you and feeling like you don't deserve things?" Bailey's tone grows angry, but I sense that it's anger on my behalf and not directed toward me. "You deserve the best that life has to offer. After the way we grew up and all the ways you've been there for me over the years, you deserve nothing less than everything you want." Tears swim in her eyes, and she fans her face. "Sorry—pregnancy hormones." She quickly swipes the moisture from each eye. "You can't wait until you're magically healed to try to get Rhia back, because—newsflash, Cole—healing isn't a destination. It's a journey you'll be on forever. Sometimes you'll be deeper in the thick of it than others, but healing is never going to end, so stop waiting for some perfect time."

Damn. "That's some pretty motherly advice right there."

Bailey gives me a watery smile, running with my slight deflection. "You think so?"

"Absolutely." I grab a candy of my own and begin unwrapping the red foil. "You're going to be a great mom."

"Ugh," Bailey whines, a tear dripping down her cheek. "You can't say these things when I'm already a hormonal mess."

I present her with the unwrapped chocolate in my palm. "May I offer you this apology candy?"

Bailey snatches the treat and shoves it between her lips. "I accept," she says with her mouth full. I can hardly make out the garbled words, and we both immediately burst into laughter. Not just any laughter, but raucous, shoulder-shaking, laugh-until-you-cry laughter. It erases some of the tension of our earlier conversation and gives me the vital realization that we're both going to be okay.

I kept thinking about our conversation long after Bailey departed the other day, and I brought it up to my therapist at my next appointment. The more I thought about it, the more I realized that the concept of being "undeserving" had been a thread woven throughout the entirety of my life.

As a young child growing up in poverty, I knew I didn't have the cool things many of my peers did, and I subconsciously assumed it was because I wasn't good enough for them. Then I went to live with Jen and Tom, and suddenly, I had all of those material things, but my interests and talents weren't considered good enough.

My therapist quickly deduced that this sense of unworthiness led to Rhia's and my ultimate demise, and he gave me homework that has me doing shit I never thought I would. Journaling. Affirmations. Self-talk. Sometimes it feels silly, but I promised myself when I started therapy that I would go all in. And goddamnit—it's actually helping.

Everything I've been doing is helping. I feel more comfortable around fire than ever before. I've been lighting candles every evening and actually *enjoying* them. When Jen and Tom expressed their disappointment after I matter-of-factly told them Bailey and I wouldn't be spending the holidays with them, I didn't feel an ounce of guilt. I even tried to be the bigger person, and I invited them to my December family dinner. When they declined, I didn't feel rejected. I didn't feel like they turned me down because I didn't deserve their presence or because my apartment wasn't good enough for them. I recognized that it was because they're stuck-up pricks and *nothing* I do will ever be considered worthy in their eyes, but that has nothing to do with me and everything to do with them.

I'm not saying my self-worth is skyrocketing or anything, but I'm starting to realize how big of a role my lack of it has played in my life, and I'm feeling the effects of my burgeoning self-esteem already.

And that's why I find myself lugging two tote bags full of candles into Marty's on New Year's Day.

CHAPTER 38
RHIA

A scuffling sound at the door caught my attention. I was instantly on high alert, preparing for the possibility of an intruder. The safe house had lived up to its name so far, but there was no guarantee that would continue.

My heart pounded as I approached the door, kitchen knife in hand. The handle turned, and I sucked in a breath, ready to fight.

Relief washed over me when the door swung open, and Damien's large frame filled the doorway.

"Damien," I breathed, taking in his dirty, tattered clothing. His hair was a mess, and his beard had grown longer, as if he didn't even have time to groom himself while he was out fighting for my safety.

"Veronica," he responded, taking my face in his large hands. "I told you I'd always come back for you."

've written plenty of books at this point, but it's never felt quite this good to type *The End*. Once I muddled through everything I had written while Cole and I were a thing, my writer's block faded in gradual increments. Months ago, when I was experiencing writer's block, Cole and our budding romance had been the ticket out of it. It feels good that, this time, I pulled myself out all on my own.

Not even a minute after I type those magic words, a text from Bailey pops up on my phone.

Bailey: Can we meet up?

I haven't seen her since the day I took her to the clinic, but we've texted a bit since then.

Rhia: Sure! Where?

Bailey: Marty's? Cole's not working.

My teeth tug at my lower lip. I don't really want to go to Marty's right now. Too many memories. But what if Bailey needs me? Maybe she's already there. Cole's not working, but Mac might be, and those two have some sort of thing going on.

Rhia: Okay. When do you want to meet up?

Bailey: Whenever you're ready! I'm here now.

Rhia: I can be there in twenty.

Bailey: Perfect!

I push away from my desk and change out of my yoga pants and t-shirt into something more acceptable for going out in public. It's absolutely freezing in Boston, so jeans, a tan turtleneck sweater, and matching wool socks it is. I don't bother to put on makeup or do anything with my hair. It's not like I have anyone to impress.

The heat in my car barely has time to kick on by the time I reach the parking lot. Despite wearing my black leather driving gloves, my hands are freezing, so I wring them together as I rush toward the bar. I have my head down to try to keep the wind out of my face, so I don't see the sign until I'm right at the front door.

A handwritten note on the front door of Marty's reads: *CLOSED for New Year's Day. (Unless you're Rhia. Then come in.)*

What the hell? Marty's is closed today? Sure enough, it does look dark inside. But the note says I should come in. I have no idea what Bailey is up to, but I can't withstand the cold any longer. I try the handle, and sure enough, the door swings open.

The first thing I notice is that it's not actually pitch-black in here. A warm glow emanates from the bar, and I turn my gaze toward it to find dozens of candles in all shapes and sizes glimmering in the relative darkness. They're stationed all along the bar and in every nook and cranny possible. Their flames flicker wildly, making light dance along every surface in the place.

I stand frozen as Cole steps forward from where he's stationed at the bar. The candles illuminate his handsome face, highlighting the little smirk he's wearing. He looks well, and that sends a deluge of relief through me.

"Hi," I breathe.

Cole's grin widens. "Hey."

I make a sweeping gesture toward the multitude of candles. "What's all this?"

He crosses his arms casually. "I think it's what your romance novels would call a grand gesture."

It takes my brain a moment to calculate that this was a set-up and that Bailey isn't here at all. Her text was just a ploy to get me over here for this.

"It's also an apology," Cole goes on, "for how I ended things and for being radio silent these past few weeks."

"Bailey told me you've been pretty busy."

"I have," Cole replies. "I found a therapist to talk to, and he's been really helpful with sorting through all the trauma and shit from my childhood and the beliefs it left me with. I asked him about EMDR, and he got me set up with a therapist for that too. I know you mentioned it a long time ago, and I kind of blew you off, but you were absolutely right that it would be helpful for me."

"I'm glad," I say, unable to come up with any other words as my brain processes the enormity of what he's taken on.

"I also just finished a fire safety course," Cole adds, "and I've been incorporating fire into my everyday life to continue to desensitize myself to it. It's going well." He nods toward the candles along the bar.

"Cole, I…I don't know what to say." I shake my head as I consider the amount of healing he's packed into the last few weeks. "I'm so proud of you."

Cole nods, his smile satisfied. "I'm proud of myself too." He grabs the back of his neck with one hand, looking bashful. "I have to admit, I started doing all of this because I wanted to try to become someone who was good enough for you, but it all helped me realize that I actually want to be the best version of myself for *me*. I wanted to prove to myself that I could be the man I know I'm capable of being. I don't know if I'm there yet, but I'm on my way."

"Cole." I take a step toward the bar, longing to wrap him in my arms. "You have *always* been good enough for me, even when you didn't see it. I'm so glad you're working on the things that held you back from believing it, but I've always known that you are the *best* man I've ever met. And I know I don't have much experience with relationships, and maybe I am too much of a hopeless romantic sometimes, but we had something so good together, and I'm always going to be grateful to you for that."

Cole rushes out from behind the bar, stopping short a few feet from me. "I'm so sorry about everything I said that night. It was mean and uncalled for and just not true. I *love* that you believe so strongly in love and happily ever afters. And you may not have a lot of experience with dating, but you did the relationship thing way better than most people would, experienced or not. It was me who screwed it all up, and I'll do anything to make it up to you."

For a second, I honestly believe this man is about to fall to his knees and beg. The desperation in his voice threatens to bring me to my knees too. It's something special to have someone willing to lay themselves bare before you. To strip themselves down to their very core and present it to you on a platter.

It's brave.

And so that's what I have to be too.

I put one finger out in front of me, curling it to beckon Cole toward me. "Get over here and make it up to me, then."

His blue eyes light up, and he doesn't hesitate before hurrying into my waiting arms and crushing his lips to mine. I kiss him with the force of all the love in my heart, pouring the devotion I feel toward him into the act, showing Cole how much I want us to be together again. How much I've missed him. And thankfully, he seems to be doing the same.

We're both breathless when Cole rests his forehead against mine. "Will you give me another chance?" he asks in a whisper, taking my hand and dragging it over his pounding heart.

I press my hand to his chest as if trying to capture his rapid heartbeats. "Of course I will. I've missed you so much."

He deposits a kiss on my forehead. "God, I've missed you too."

We stand together in silence for a few moments, breathing each other in. Cole's heartbeat slows as we embrace. He keeps his forehead pressed to mine, not even opening his eyes to glance around at the abundance of burning candles.

Safe.

"So, to be clear," I say after a few long moments, "Bailey and I aren't meeting?"

Cole barks out a laugh. "No. She helped me come up with the plan to get you over here, but she's at her dorm. We can definitely call her, though, if you want to let her know that the plan worked."

"I'd like that," I reply, running a hand down his side and hooking a finger in his pocket to tug him even closer. "But I think I'd like to do something else first."

A satisfied hum rumbles out of Cole's chest. "What did you have in mind?"

My fingers dance over to his fly, unzipping it to show him *exactly* what I have in mind.

CHAPTER 39
COLE

"It's a girl," the ultrasound tech says as she glides the wand over Bailey's growing belly.

Bailey lets out a small gasp of delight. Rhia squeezes my hand and shoots me a wink. Just a few hours ago, she joked with me about being sorely outnumbered by girls if this baby turned out to be one too, but I don't mind it one bit. I can't wait to spoil the little princess rotten.

Having Rhia by my side at Bailey's twenty-week appointment feels so right. Not having her at prior appointments felt like something was missing. Today, things feel complete.

Mac is present as well. He sits at Bailey's other side, holding her hand much like I'm holding Rhia's. I'm not entirely sure what's going on between him and Bailey, but you'd better believe I had a *come to Jesus* talk with him the second I sniffed out something more than friendship.

At first, I thought Mac was just helping Bailey because he felt guilty that he brought Jesse into her life only to have him "hit it and quit it," as Mac put it. I would hear from Bailey that he brought her a milkshake when she had a craving or that he brought her Unisom in the middle of the night when she was desperate for a lick of sleep.

Eventually, though, I realized there was more going on between them. I started to notice stolen glances at family dinners, and once, I surprised Bailey at her dorm and found Mac asleep in her bed.

A couple of weeks ago, Rhia and I helped move Bailey into Mac's apartment. He insisted that she needed somewhere more comfortable than a college dormitory to finish out her pregnancy, and he happened to have a two-bedroom apartment with no one occupying the second bedroom. I'll admit that my pride took a hit that I wasn't able to provide Bailey with a room, but I'm taking a page out of her book and relying on other people in our support system for a change.

We wrap up the appointment and go our separate ways— Bailey with Mac and Rhia with me.

"Want to grab ice cream or something?" Rhia asks as we get in my car.

I clear my throat as I tug on my seatbelt. "I thought maybe you'd want to go back to my place and read for a bit."

Rhia is letting me read her manuscript while it's with the copyeditor, and I'm devouring it. I think it's her dirtiest yet. She said she never lets anyone read her books before they come out, so I feel supremely special to have the privilege.

She fans her face. "Cole Matthews, you are *such* a dreamboat. I'd love to read with you."

"Maybe we can go for ice cream tonight?" I suggest.

Rhia takes my hand over the center console. "I'd love to."

I try to take my hand back to start up the car, but she doesn't let go. I lift my gaze to hers only to find her brown doe eyes soft as they stare at me.

"I love you, Cole," Rhia says. "I think I have for a long time."

Her admission takes my breath away. I've been feeling the same for a while now, but after I got her back, I was so afraid to screw things up again, and saying those three words too soon seemed like a surefire way to do that.

These past few weeks have been a testament to the work

we've both put into ourselves and our relationship. Things have been smoother than ever for us, and we're both thriving separately and together. Rhia claims she's never written as fast as she's writing right now, and I'm loving my weekly kitchen shift at Marty's. It's not like we serve anything gourmet at the bar, but I'm learning a lot from the chefs.

I finally feel like I'm starting to live up to my potential, and that's what gives me the guts to reply, "I love you too, Rhia. So much." Leaning over the center console, I snatch her lips up in a kiss. She melts into me as much as she can with the obstacle between us, but it's clear she can't get as close as she wants to.

"Let's go back to your place and…read," she says with an exaggerated wink.

I can't help the goofy smile that stretches over my lips. "Why do I feel like we're not going to get any reading done?"

"Because we're not," Rhia replies. "But don't worry. I can tell you the ending." She leans in until her breath is tickling my neck. "They tell each other they love each other, have lots of hot sex, and live happily ever after."

I let out a little grunt of pleasure when Rhia plants her lips on my neck and sucks. I'll take any mark she wants to give me. She's already left a permanent one on my heart, after all.

Rhiannon James. Bestselling romance author, incredible friend, and the love of my life. The only person who could ever get me to believe in happily ever after.

EPILOGUE

One year later
Cole

"**P**ass the nachos, please," Mac requests over the din of the TV that's showing live coverage from Times Square. Anderson Cooper and Andy Cohen are getting increasingly hammered as the countdown to midnight approaches.

Bailey passes the plate of loaded nachos down the couch to her boyfriend. Yes, they're officially together now. Sometime between Bailey's third trimester and Stella's birth, Mac convinced Bailey to give things a real go. He's been a father to Stella in every way that counts, and I'll be thrilled if I get to call him a brother-in-law someday.

Stella is sound asleep in the other room while we celebrate the impending new year. That little lady is cute as a goddamn button, and she has me absolutely wrapped around her little finger. I get to watch her three days a week when I have late shifts at the bar, and I savor every second we spend together. It only gets me more excited to have my own kids someday, though I want to wait until Stella is well out of diapers to even consider it.

Tripp is here too, half-asleep in an armchair. He's given us strict instructions to wake him up close to midnight so he can sit beneath my kitchen table and eat twelve grapes. Apparently, it's a superstition that's supposed to get you laid or something. I don't fucking know.

We hosted Rhia's moms for Christmas, and witnessing her joy at having her parents present for a major holiday was bitter-sweet. I loved seeing her so happy, but I grieved for the little girl who didn't always have that stability. I floated the idea of making Christmas together a tradition in the hopes that if I put the bug in their ears early, they could plan their travel around the holiday.

Tonight is for our found family. The friends who have unfail-ingly showed up and supported us this year. This little gathering also serves as a housewarming party to welcome Rhia to my apartment. She officially moved into my place this past week, though she's been spending most nights here for quite some time.

We talked about finding a new place to live together, but I wanted to stay near Louisa as she ages and her health declines. She's the closest thing to a grandmother I've ever had, and I want to be there for her like a good grandson would.

Now that Rhia is paying half of the rent, I've opened up a savings account to store the half I'll no longer be paying in it. The plan is to save up for culinary school, though I wouldn't be opposed to using the money to buy Marty's when Marty finally decides to let it go instead. I'll just have to see where time takes me. I'm not as afraid of the future with Rhia by my side. I know that we can figure anything out together.

We started attending couples therapy soon after getting back together, and it's helped us avoid any major arguments or misunderstandings. We've both continued to work on ourselves in individual therapy, and couples therapy has only strength-ened our bond.

Across the room, Rhia rouses Tripp from his near slumber, handing him a bowl of grapes. Midnight is fast approaching, and he scrambles for the kitchen. She shakes her head, as baffled as I am, and joins me where I'm standing and taking in the revelry.

"Hi." She greets me with a peck on the cheek, which I swiftly turn into a proper kiss on the lips. "You're supposed to wait until midnight," Rhia adds with a giggle when I release her.

I brush a finger under her chin. "I couldn't wait. You look too beautiful tonight."

She's wearing a sleek black dress and tights, not bothering to wear shoes in the house. I know exactly which sexy lingerie set she has on beneath it because I had the pleasure of watching her put it on, like she was wrapping herself up as a present for me to tear open later. The waiting is such delicious torture.

Rhia tucks her head into my chest. "Thank you."

I rub her back in mindless strokes, the gesture achingly familiar to me now. I often find myself getting caught up in these small, soft moments. It's easy to remember what it felt like to be lost and alone in the world, but these days, it's just as easy to realize how safe I am.

My gorgeous girl never fails to tell me and show me how much she adores me, just as I do her. Everyone else in this apart-ment holds a similarly special place in my heart, from my sister, to my niece, to my best friends. They've all shown me what it's like to be part of a family. A true unit of love and support. I never would have gotten to where I am without each and every one of them, and I'm eternally grateful for them.

So, when the clock strikes midnight, I kiss the love of my life—this life and all the others. Our love spans time and space, crosses planes and universes. I know we'd find each other in every life-time, because we were meant to be. I would love Rhiannon James with my whole heart even if we were in another life.

THE END
* * *

If you enjoyed this book, I sincerely hope you'll consider leaving a review on Amazon, Bookbub, Goodreads, or another platform. This makes such a huge impact for indie authors!

Have you read about Hannah and Caleb's road to happily ever after? Check out their marriage of convenience x fake dating romance in *In Your Eyes*!

Sign up for my newsletter at www.mollymccarthybooks.com/newsletter for exclusive updates about upcoming releases, freebies & sales, and more!

Find me on Instagram, Threads, and TikTok as @mollymccarthybooks

AUTHOR'S NOTE

Anxiety is a thread woven through each and every one of my days.

I was diagnosed with clinical anxiety at age twelve when I began having seemingly random panic attacks. Many occurred during my middle school classes, but some more memorable ones were at a Jonas Brothers concert (LOL) and at the top of the Empire State Building. I began taking anxiety medication at age twelve, and it has served me well since.

In 2022, I had an intense resurgence of anxiety and panic attacks. My medication had stopped working, and I was experiencing a lot of stress at my job and in the post-pandemic world. I ended up taking a twelve-week leave of absence from work and ultimately leaving that job as well as changing medications. This was an extremely humbling time in my life and a stark reminder that my anxiety will never go away, and I will always have to continue learning how to live with it.

I sincerely hope my portrayal of anxiety in this story helps others with similar experiences feel seen. This book is also my love letter to the romance genre and romance readers everywhere. We deserve to enjoy this beautiful, nuanced genre unapologetically!

ABOUT THE AUTHOR

Molly McCarthy is an avid romance reader and writer living just outside Boston, MA. She can often be found typing away in a café, drinking a latte, and dreaming of happily ever afters. Keep up with Molly on Instagram @mollymccarthybooks.

ALSO BY MOLLY MCCARTHY

The McNally Men
Beauty In The Details
A New Beau
More Beautiful Than Before

Chronically In Love
In Your Eyes